ESCAPE

Blackstone Series, Book 2

J.L. Drake

ESCAPE

Limitless Publishing, LLC
Kailua, HI 96734
www.limitlesspublishing.com

Formatting: Limitless Publishing

ISBN-13: 978-1-68058-691-6
ISBN-10: 1-68058-691-2

DEDICATION

To my stepfather, Gordon. You are a kind, loving, giving man who came into our family with an open heart, and we love you for that. Thank you for reading my words and for your honesty and input. Your ideas helped so much, particularly with this book. We may be hundreds of miles apart, but you are here with us every day.

I love you.

CAST OF CHARACTERS

Keith: Member of Blackstone. Secretive. Savannah's "big brother."

Lexi: Ex-girlfriend.

Savannah: Held in Tijuana, Mexico for seven months. Saved by Blackstone, fell in love with Cole Logan. Now lives at Shadows.

Cole: Owner of the safe house in Montana called Shadows. Fell in love with a picture of a victim. Found, saved, and married her. Leader of the Blackstone special ops team.

Olivia: Savannah and Cole's daughter.

Mark: Best friend to Cole Logan, Blackstone member. Uses humor to escape the pain from his past.

Mia: Mark's girlfriend, nurse, and Frank's daughter.

Paul: Blackstone member.

John: Blackstone member.

Abigail: Mark's adopted mother, Cole's childhood nanny, and now house aide. Dating the house doctor.

Doctor Roberts: House doctor, kind soul, and in love with Abigail.

June: Abigail's younger sister.

Mike: Agent at Shadows. Scary-looking teddy bear, covered head to toe in tattoos.

Dell: Agent at Shadows.

Davie: Agent at Shadows.

Molly: Nurse at North Dakota Hospital. Signed NDA to work with the Blackstone men when they come in.

Scoot: Moody house cat. Has no shame.

PROLOGUE

Location: Mexico
Coordinates: Classified

Keith

Dust clawed at my eyes as I ran behind the Land Rover. Two cartel members were making away with some medical supplies from our camp. What made the chase fun was they weren't expecting this from us.

My boots barely touched the ground and my arms beat through the wind. A glance over my shoulder found Mark behind the wheel and coming up quick. Cole had climbed out of the Hummer window to sit on the ledge. Resting his gun on the roof, he reached for his radio, and I heard his voice through my earpiece.

"Move to your nine o'clock."

I did, and two bullets zipped by me, causing the driver to slow momentarily. I gained ground and made a grab for the roof rack but didn't make it.

"Damn!" My eyes were streaming with tears as I tried to focus on the Land Rover. With all my might, I leapt forward and latched onto the bar. My knees slapped the bumper and my hips took a beating on the spare tire.

Quickly, I swung my leg up and lifted myself onto the roof. My knees spread, I found my balance and gave Cole a thumbs up.

Four bullets skimmed by my left ear. I crawled forward and snatched my knife from its thigh holster. Dropping on my belly, I reached down and jammed the knife through the guy's hand and into the fabric on the door.

The driver started to panic, and the vehicle swerved back and forth as the passenger pulled and struggled to get free of the knife. A quick elbow to his temple made his head snap back and flop to the side.

Hooking my heels through the roof rack for support, my body dangled over the side. I pointed my gun through the window at the driver, who was desperately trying to control the vehicle. Sweat dripped off his face, leaving trails down his dirty cheeks. "Stop the truck!"

His hands flew up off the wheel, his eyes wild. The truck bucked from the sudden loss of power as it slowed. We both eyed the machine gun next to him.

"Don't do it," I warned, but as predicted, the guy went for it.

Pop!

The man's head shook back and forth as he eyed

the hole in the steering wheel. He was going into shock; not hard to guess he was new.

"Do it again, and the next one's between your eyes."

He spoke English. I could tell because of the way he nodded and placed both of his hands back on the wheel and kept them there after we came to a stop.

Cole came around to the driver's side window and aimed his rifle at the man's face. Then he looked up at me, his expression as calm and friendly as if he just got up from the dinner table.

"You good, Keith?"

"Couldn't be better!" I grabbed the edge of the door, released my feet, swung around, and dropped to the ground. "My guess is he's new."

"Yup, gave up pretty quick," Mike chimed in as he grabbed the driver by the shoulders and told him to sit.

"Yeah." I removed my sunglasses. "We probably weren't their target, but they figured us for an easy mark." Opening the door and letting the passed-out passenger fall to the ground, I rooted around through their crap. Christ, they were slobs. Food wrappers, Coke cans, cigarette butts, and beer bottles lined the floor. I chuckled, thinking these two were soon going to be dead of a heart attack anyway, the way they lived.

"Lopez," Cole called out. "Call it in. We have two hostages."

"Copy that."

"Colonel." I nodded toward a package in the back seat. I reached back and carefully pulled off the dirty blanket, revealing a large bomb.

"Pull back!" Cole called out, and the guys moved fast.

"Go easy, Keith," he warned.

I carefully assessed. It wasn't activated, and I gave the okay to stand down.

"Son of a bitch."

I quickly unrolled a set of blueprints over the hood of the Land Rover and scanned them, noting the circled spot. "Holy shit."

Cole finished checking out the bomb and joined me. I fought against the breeze to keep the paper flat on the hood, and pointed to where their intended target seemed to be.

My hand flexed as I approached Mike, who had the driver in zip ties. My face tight with anger and not giving a damn, I hauled back and punched him square in the face.

"You son of a bitch!" I hissed as he rolled on the ground.

"No, please!" he cried with his hands up as if to ward me off. "I have rules. I hurt no one."

"They're children, you murdering bastard! Innocent kids! You were going to kill all of them!" I glanced at Mark, who was being held back by Cole.

I knew a lot of men joined the cartels because they had nowhere else to go. They turned to the drug trade in desperation. But this type of thing, bombing a school and killing innocent children, could only be carried out by someone without a soul. It took a hell of a lot of control not to jam my gun down his throat and unload the clip.

Cole ordered Mike to secure the men in the back of the Hummer, and Mark and I removed the bomb and completely disabled it before we headed to the pickup.

"Good call on that one." Cole fist bumped me as I climbed in the back.

"Thanks."

Mark wiped his forehead with a rag. I knew he was struggling more than usual now that Mia was pregnant. It changed a man's perspective.

I ran my fingers over my forearm while I let my mind slip away for a few moments as a memory surfaced.

Her smooth hand skimmed my bare chest, bringing me out of a deep sleep. Silky hair tickled my face, and her giggle made me wiggle my hips, wanting contact.

"Morning." Her raspy voice had me standing to attention. Her big eyes held mine as she rocked back on her hips. "I'm hungry." Her pink lips opened, and I watched as she swallowed me whole.

"Holy...!" I covered my face, wondering how long I could last.

"That, right there," Mark chimed in and rudely hauled me out of my memory, leaving me with a tight knot in the groin. "What are you thinking about?"

"Nothing," I growled, annoyed.

"Always so moody."

I sighed and looked over at him. "Just thinking of home."

He nodded while he removed his hat and shook the sand out of his hair. "I only get that look when

5

I'm thinking about Mia." He smirked, then it clicked for him. "Someone special on your mind?"

Shaking my head, I looked back out of the window.

I wonder what she is doing right now.

CHAPTER ONE

*Boston
High School*

"Pass it!" Clark tapped his stick to let me know where he was. I raced down the ice, and the puck slapped against my stick. I made quick eye contact and passed it, only to get it back in two strides. This was one of our moves. I faked to my left but weaved to the right. Once in front of the net, I saw an opening and, without a thought, slammed it into the net between the goalie's legs. I grinned when the beloved sirens screamed along with the spectators.

Clark grabbed my helmet and bumped our cages together as we cheered. The ref blew the whistle as the crowd settled back in their seats. I headed to center ice, skates on either side of the line, and waited for the puck to drop.

I loved this part, where nothing could be heard but your heartbeat, wildly anticipating the moment the ref took a deep breath and then released the hard chunk of rubber.

The puck dropped, both sticks trying to claim it, then my opponent's stick came up and tried to hook my neck. I dropped my shoulder and plowed into him, pissed.

At seventeen, I weighed two hundred pounds and stood six foot three. I was a big guy, and not many would easily take me on. Needless to say, I was delighted when times like these came up.

He bounced off my incoming weight and landed on his ass. The referee immediately stopped the game and called a penalty on the other guy, who was just now peeling himself off the ice.

"Are you fucking kidding me?" he shouted, pulling off a glove. "Did you not see what he just did to me?"

"Penalty, two minutes, unsportsmanlike conduct." The ref grabbed his jersey and pulled him to the box.

I skated back around and took my place at center ice again. The puck dropped, and all that was inside my head was to focus and get it.

With the puck safe between my stick and my skate, I moved around the net and tapped it in above the goalie's ankle.

With a little smirk, I nodded to the dick in the box and fist bumped Clark at yet another win this season. We were three for three, currently holding the top spot for high school hockey.

"Party at my place!" he yelled over the roar.

***

The numbers on my lock made my head spin. I

had a hangover from the night before. All I could recall was I drank my body weight in beer, and somehow I ended up in Clark's patio chair in the morning.

Three, six, nine…

My fingers twirled the knob and finally freed my locker door. With three Advil in hand, I tossed them back and chased them with a lime Gatorade. I replaced my math textbook with my science one and carefully closed the door.

"Dude," Clark grinned at me. "Heard some fresh ones arrived today." He looked over his shoulder. "Sisters."

"And you know this, how?" I started to walk with him to my next class. Clark was a known man whore. He was bored with all the girls in our school, so when someone new came, he was the first to know.

"El and Alexi." His eyebrows wiggled as he took a seat next to me. "Heard they moved here from Canada." He rubbed his hands together in excitement. "Canadians! Can't get much better than that."

"Yeah." I opened my binder and waited for the teacher to start his class. It would be only a matter of time before Clark would have one, or maybe even both, in the locker room shower. Another one of his many accomplishments.

Class was boring, as usual. Lucky for me, I was smart, but that was a curse as well as a blessing. It reserved my seat as co-captain on the team, but it also made for a dull day due to not being challenged enough.

The rink was the place I loved the most—the sounds, the smell, everything about it. It was the place where I could just turn off and use my body weight without getting into trouble. I was made for physical contact.

I dropped my bag at my feet and sat on the bleachers next to the football field where the team went for our dry-land training. My head finally stopped torturing me, which was perfect timing, since the coach wanted us to run laps for practice. Most of our school funding went to our hockey team, as our football team was a joke. Nonetheless, they were still a team that would bring our school a trophy for third place every year.

"Let's go, ladies!" Coach Grant called through a megaphone. He had a twisted way of making us work harder when he called us that. "Can't beat St. Pat's High if you can't run your laps. Now move!"

After I tied my Adidas, stretched, and downed some Gatorade, I joined Clark as he jogged by.

Just as we made it around the fourth lap, I noticed a guy approach the coach.

"Who's that?" Clark nodded in his direction.

"Don't know."

"Oh, better yet, who is *that*?" Clark nearly tripped as his neck was bent awkwardly, looking in another direction.

"Don't know that either," I muttered and picked up the pace. It wasn't until I came back around that I saw who he was talking about.

She had dark brown hair that hit at her elbows, a small frame, and long, slim legs. I couldn't see her face, but by the way she was holding herself, I could tell she had confidence. She sat and opened a book, not even glancing at anyone.

"Ladies!" Coach waved us in and waited until we all arrived before he spoke. "We have a new player, and since Jordon got injured, we can sure use him." Clark gave me the same worried expression I was sure was on my own face. "Meet Elliot Klein. He transferred here from Toronto, which is in Canada, in case some of you ladies don't know your geography. He played left wing back home, but he'll be playing right defense for us."

I couldn't hide the smirk that broke out on my face as I eyed Clark, and he then gave me the finger. I guessed El was short for Elliot. *Awesome.*

"Hey, guys." He gave a friendly nod. "Thanks for letting me join the team. I have no interest in the football team, and I don't do baseball."

"Good to hear," Greyson, our goalie, called out from behind us.

"Okay, take ten." Coach pulled out a note pad and started to scribble something on it.

"Keith." I held out my hand to the newbie. I'd played sports my whole life and never went by my first name, Brandon.

"Elliot Klein." He returned the shake. "You play center, right?"

"Yes, I do."

"I did my homework, plus you are hard to miss. Your face is plastered all over the trophy wall by the office." He looked over his shoulder to the brunette. She still had her head down in a book.

"Friend of yours?" I tilted my water bottle and

the liquid flow down my throat. No air, no amps. It worked well for athletes.

"You could say that." He chuckled, then glanced over my shoulder at Clark as he joined us. They did a quick introduction before the coach called us to center field to do pushups.

A hundred pushups, a hundred sit-ups, a hundred squats later, and my ass was feeling the burn I always sought from a good workout. While the rest of the guys headed for the shower, Clark and I did one last easy jog around the track to help reduce the lactic acid in our muscles.

We stopped by the bleachers to grab our stuff and found Elliot speaking to the brunette. He turned when he heard us. "Hey, guys, can you point me in the direction of the cafeteria?"

"We could, but it's closed." I hooked my bag over my shoulder, still trying to sneak a peek of the girl. "We're heading to a burger joint down the road. You hungry?"

His eyes lit up and he turned back to the girl. "Hey, you in?"

She turned and flipped her hair out of her face. *Jesus*. Her perfect eyebrows rose as she took me in. She was sexy and really pretty as she studied me, but her annoyed expression wasn't lost on any of us.

"Sure." She looked out toward the field. "Why not?" She picked up her saddlebag style purse that had a long fringe dangling off the bottom and carefully made her way down in her high-heeled ankle boots. I went to offer my hand, but Clark, being Clark, beat me to it. She stopped on the last bleacher, looked at both of us, then took his offer and let him help her down. Once on the ground, I secretly took a good look at her.

Her legs appeared toned under her skin tight jeans, her black top stopped about an inch above her belt, and her skin looked as though she spent some time in the sun. Her leather jacket covered her slim shoulders, and she wore a necklace with a letter A on it.

"Hi," she said in a clipped tone, and then glanced at Elliot, who shot her a look. She closed her eyes, then turned to us. "So, burgers?"

"Christ." Elliot shook his head, clearly annoyed by her coldness. "Clark, Keith, this is my twin sister, Alexi."

"Lexi," she corrected him, then started to walk toward the parking lot.

We followed, and Clark hit me in the arm. "Fucking hot."

I rolled my eyes. He had a point, but she clearly had some issues to work out.

Clark tossed his bag in the back of my pickup and jumped up on the tailgate with ease, heading to his usual spot on the wheel well. "Lots of room, Lexi."

"I'll sit in the back." Elliot hopped up to join Clark as Lexi glanced at me.

I opened the passenger door for her and waved her in.

"Thanks." She then noticed how high my truck actually was. The floorboard was almost at her chest. I reached in front of her and pulled down the step, and her hair brushed by my face. It was so soft and smelled really nice. I lingered a little too long before I pulled away.

She took an unsteady step and hoisted herself up inside. I couldn't help but watch her body in fascination. She was incredibly proportioned.

Clark banged on the roof to let me know they were good to go. I started the *beast* and headed onto the street.

I opened the window and let the breeze cool me down. I needed a shower and hoped my deodorant would work a double shift. *Of all the days not to shower…*

I tuned into the radio and reached to turn it up, but her hand beat me to it.

"Oh." Her hand shot back a little but still hovered over mine. "I just love this song." I grinned. She bit down on her lip, and the soft pink looked pretty around her white, straight teeth. "What?"

"I'm just surprised you're a Pearl Jam fan."

She rolled her eyes. "Really?"

I only shrugged to see if it would make her keep talking. She studied me, clearly bothered.

"So, what do I look like I listen to?"

Unfortunately, I was an expert in female music, so I took a moment to enjoy her curiosity. I ran my hand along the wheel before I draped it out the window.

"Boyz II Men." I smirked when I saw her murderous expression.

"Seriously?"

I started to mouth the words playfully.

"I don't think I want to hear how you know the words to that song."

I chuckled, eyeing her from the side, then made a face at her. I liked her. She had an interesting edge to her personality. She turned to stare out the window and seemed deep in thought. She was guarded, and there was an almost angry vibe that hung around her. I wondered if it might be the fact that she didn't want to move here. I sure wouldn't want to move schools in my senior year.

I didn't attempt any conversation for the rest of the ride. Pulling forward, I checked the mirrors and backed into my regular spot and climbed out of the truck. Lexi struggled to open the door, and just as I rounded the tailgate, she hopped down, not thinking, and landed hard and off balance. I managed to reach her and catch her around the waist. Her surprisingly light frame fell into mine, and she held on to steady herself with her face buried in my shoulder.

"Wow." Her huff sent a few strands of her hair forward. "Your truck is really high." She laughed at her own words. "I'm going to try to stand now." Her hands moved to my shoulders, and she pushed herself upright.

"You all right?" I liked her delicate hands on me. Her right hand wore a purple stone that paired nicely with her mocha colored eyes, when she brushed her hair off her face.

She nodded, set her expression, and took a small step to the side, away from me.

"You good, Lexi?" Elliot's eyebrows pinched together as he checked his watch.

"Yes, just that Keith tried to kill me with his Tacoma."

I could see she was fine.

Dinner went okay. We were all so hungry no one said much. I did notice Lexi watching us eat with fascination. I got it; we did eat a lot.

Elliot had to head off to his new job, and Clark lived down the road, so he didn't need a ride back. Lexi and I started walking back toward the truck.

The night air was cool after sitting in the stuffy restaurant. Her leather jacket creaked as she crossed her arms. She struggled in her high-heeled boots on the gravel.

"Here." I held onto her arm to hold her steady.

"I'm normally not this needy." She chuckled. *Huh.* She seemed funny. Once at the truck, she sighed and twirled around with an annoyed expression.

Oh no, now what?

"At the risk of being—" she raised her hands to make air quotes, "—*that girl*, can I ask for a little help?" She pointed to the truck.

"Of course." I grinned. She *was* funny. She reached for my hand, but I grasped her hips and lifted her into the seat. I hated that step anyway.

"Jesus!" She tucked her hair behind her ear. "I was not expecting that."

"Legs in." I urged her body around and handed her the seatbelt. With the door closed, I moved around the front of the truck and eased behind the wheel. "School? Or home?"

Something seemed to dawn on her, but she quickly hid her face. "School."

She didn't say much on the way back, but I noticed her finger tapped her knee over and over.

"So, Elliot likes hockey. What's your thing?"

She kept her gaze out the window. "I don't really have a thing."

"Oh, that's too bad." I matched her tone.

She glanced over, seeming almost startled by my comment. "Why?"

"It's just something I wanted to know about you." I stared at her for a long moment before I shifted my attention back to the road.

It took her a beat before she turned back to the window. I pulled into the school parking lot, and after she pointed out her car, I parked the truck next to it.

"Where do you live?"

"Brick Street."

"Oh, my buddy lives on that street." I got out and met her at her door. I lifted my arms toward her and waited for her expression to show she was okay with it, and then took her in my hands and eased her down.

"Thanks." She stepped back and turned to leave, but she looked back.

"Keith?"

"Yeah."

Her tongue ran along her lip before she drew it back. "Never mind." She gave a wave and opened her door.

"Ah, see ya."

She left, and I followed her out. I stopped at the light next to her and noticed she was going the wrong way. *Hmmm*. I leaned over the bench and rolled down the window.

"Lexi!" She rolled her window down halfway.

"What's your address again?"

"Fifty-two-twenty Brick Street."

"You're going the wrong way. Come in my lane, and I'll lead."

She hesitated but put her window up and pulled in behind me.

There were three stoplights from the school to her place, and at every one of them I found myself watching her in the mirror.

She had interesting mannerisms. She played with her left earring, turned around a lot as if checking her back seat like someone was back there, and she closed her eyes and rubbed her forehead a few times. I wondered why she seemed so stressed and what was going through her head.

I parked and got out. She gave me a smile as I approached.

"So, here I am." She shifted her weight and looked over her shoulder at the house as if to spot her parents.

"You okay?"

"Yeah, why?"

"No reason. Well, I guess my job here is done. Goodnight, Lexi."

"Goodnight, Keith."

CHAPTER TWO

Lexi

"Lexi Klein," someone called. I pushed my textbook into my bag and turned to find three girls dressed in black and white cheerleader uniforms. The blonde with tight curls who I guessed was the head cheerleader stepped forward. "I'm Mimi, and these are my girls, Trish and Nicole." I gave a closed lip smile, not sure what was about to happen. "We heard you were in gymnastics back home. We'd be interested in seeing what you can do. We're always short girls on our cheer team, and we could really use you. Have you ever tried it?"

Oh, this is a joke, right? I'm sure Elliot is here somewhere, enjoying the show.

"Umm, I never really thought of myself as a peppy person."

"It's not about the pep, Lexi, it's about the fact that we can dance our asses off and make the team look good." She grinned back at the other girls. "Look." She took a step closer. "I get it, you're the new girl senior year, and this school is cliquey. Let us be your friends."

I hesitated, but the thought did cross my mind that this type of thing would make my mother happy. She'd been so worried about me lately, and I knew she had her hopes pinned on things being better since I started school.

Mimi's eyes sparkled when I didn't shoot her down right away. "Field, after school, tryouts?"

"Yeah, okay."

Class flew by, as I didn't really have to think about it too hard. We had done this project last year at my old school, so I pretty much knew it all. I found myself feeling uneasy about the tryout. It wasn't really something I wanted to do.

I dropped my bag on the bench, happy I had worn my sneakers today. Just as I finished my stretches, I heard the girls calling my name.

"Hey, girl!" Mimi walked ahead of the two others and blew me two air kisses rather dramatically. "Let's see your moves." She plugged in a stereo, and "Wanna Be" by the Spice Girls pumped from speakers all around me.

I jogged down to the field, then faced the girls as they watched with excitement. I sprang forward and ran as fast as I could. With my hands out straight, I twisted into a cartwheel, two front round-offs, two full flips, and at the end, I did a twist. I landed on two feet in front of them. I wasn't even breathing hard. I looked like I had just walked up to them.

"Damn, girl!" Mimi clapped, and the girls followed. She snapped her fingers, and Trish opened a bag and handed Mimi a uniform. "You are now officially a member of the West Boston Capitals!" They stood there, waiting.

I looked around, wondering if this was the right move for me. I was never one for pep rallies or yelling in unison, but there was something appealing about the idea of graduating with a few friends around me. I did notice Nicole didn't seem overly pleased. I might join just to see what her problem was.

Fine.

I held out my hand, and Mimi handed me the outfit as they all squealed enthusiastically.

"Let's get you caught up. Changing rooms are over there."

Okay...

I was starving by the time I got home. I opened the front door to find my parents reading in the living room.

"Oh my!" My mother popped out of her chair, beaming. "Oh, Rick, look at our girl!" She spun me around in my new uniform for him to see.

"It's a little short." He eyed the micro-mini skirt. "Can't you wear shorts or something?"

"Shorts are underneath, Dad." I leaned over and kissed his bald head.

"Oh, no way!" Elliot emerged out of nowhere, in his normal creepy manner. He took pride in his stealthy skills. "Kinda missing some of the shirt, there, Lex." He pointed to the plunging neckline.

"Always around, aren't you?"

I rolled my eyes and looked back at my smiling parents. If anything, this was well worth the look on their faces. They seemed happy instead of worried.

Okay, I can do this.

***

Before the sun was even up, my personal phone line rang. A loud bang had me cursing at Elliot, who always tossed his shoe at my wall when my line rang. Just like back home.

"Hello?" My voice was barely there.

"Morning, sunshine. You need to wear your uniform today. We have a game this afternoon."

This woke me up.

"Mimi, I just joined two days ago. I don't know if I'm ready."

"You are. I think you know it better than Trish and Nicole already. You'll be fine. Hair up in a ponytail, and red lipstick."

"I'll do everything but the lipstick."

"Fine, just be at the game." The line went dead.

What the hell did I get myself into?

School flew by, most likely because I was nervous about the game. I met Mimi at her car with Trish and Nicole. I was told to take the front seat, and it wasn't lost on me that Nicole wasn't pleased. I made a mental note to befriend her when we were alone. I didn't need any bad blood with anyone.

We parked a few streets away from the school, and I carried my pompoms and my new cheer bag into the freezing rink. Immediately, I felt at home with the smell of the cool air.

After we dropped our things off at a side room, we changed into our sweater tops, which were the exact same but with sleeves.

"Ready, girls?" The whole team put their hands in the middle and did some weird chant that made me want to cringe.

My stomach sank when I saw the platform that was just for us. It must have been five feet off the ground, and we were protected by the glass and extra mats. I didn't have a problem with crowds, but this was a little different because we were the display.

We walked by the hooting fans waiting excitedly for the game to start. We climbed the stairs and got into formation. At least three hundred people were there, with horns, lights, and sirens.

Just as the guys started to feed out onto the ice, we launched into our first chant while dancing in unison. I got into position and waited for my backer to hold my waist as I held on to the catcher's shoulders. Within seconds I was carefully raised into a small pyramid. With my hands on my hips, I was dropped down to my feet with three sets of hands making sure my landing was perfect.

The crowd went wild as we went into our next cheer. I couldn't lie; these girls were pretty damn good. Mimi gave me a look when she caught me lip syncing the words. I winced with a smile and tried my best to yell.

A player skated by us slowly, then hurried to another. He said something, then the two of them looked over my way. Elliot skated by, giving me a foolish fist pump. I made a face, and we both started to laugh. I loved my jackass twin.

"Lookin' good, Lexi!" I turned to find Keith by the boards. His cage was flipped up, and his blue mouth guard was hanging off to one side.

"Same to you." I grinned and thought how true that statement was. Nothing like a man in a hockey uniform. "You gonna score me a goal?" I joked and hoped my voice didn't match the excitement fluttering inside.

He gave me a wink before he hit his cage down and took his place as the buzzer went off.

"Alexi." Mimi stole my attention from Keith. "We don't talk to the players when they are on the ice. They need to focus."

I laughed. Whatever.

After second period, we were tied three-three. The music turned loud, and we started dancing with our pompoms. It actually became kind of fun as we moved about shaking our hips and jumping into splits. The music switched to techno, and songs merged into one another, every beat bringing a different dance. There were a few dance moves that were a little sexual for my liking, but the fans didn't seem to mind. So I rolled with it.

Just as we finished, the guys came back on the ice and got into position. We stood in line and shook our pompoms and waited for the whistle to be blown.

Number nineteen, Keith's number, was all I could focus on. He was massive compared to some of the other guys. I would be terrified to go up against someone like him. We all held our breath as the game went on.

Ten seconds left, and Keith had the puck. He bolted down the ice and tossed the puck with ease over the goalie's shoulder. He did a modest fist bump to Clark, then turned and skated by us. He pointed directly at me as if to say that goal was for me.

I couldn't help but grin, but it was short lived when I saw the other girls' expressions. *Yikes.*

The rest of the game, I kept my attention on the girls, not number nineteen.

For whatever reason, we didn't change out of our uniforms before we hurried into Mimi's car and off to a victory party at Clark's house.

"This is his house?" I asked as big gates swung open and we drove into a wraparound driveway.

"Yeah, crazy, hey? His father owns some plastic company over in Japan," Trish informed me. "His parents are never home, so most of our parties are here."

"Wow." I opened the door and admired the huge brick house that towered over me.

Once inside, I was surrounded by a sea of pulsing bodies. Music blared, and the smell of liquor permeated the air.

"Well, if isn't our cheer squad!" Clark yelled from the opposite side of the kitchen. Mimi took my arm and rushed me over to him.

"Have you met Lexi? She's from Canada."

"We go way back, don't we, Lexi?" He smiled as he drank beer from an old German goblet.

"We've met." I gave a small smile back, feeling uncomfortable, and wondered where the rest of the girls had disappeared to.

"Be a gentleman and get us a drink, Clark," Mimi ordered, which made me feel uncomfortable. I didn't like the way she spoke to him.

"Well, now." A guy I recognized from the team wrapped his arm around my shoulders. "Newbies need to have the house special."

"Is that so?" I challenged the quite good looking player, pulling back out of his grasp, my body stiff.

"Mmhmm." He nodded at Clark, who poured some random concoction into a plastic cup.

"Bottoms up, newbie."

I decided to brave it out and play this through, so I took the cup from him, but stopped. "Your name first."

"Steven."

"Okay." I shrugged and tipped the cup, downing the entire nasty drink. I wasn't much of a drinker, but I knew when I wanted to make a statement.

"Impressive." Steven leaned down and gave me a kiss on the cheek.

Mimi laughed, then handed me a cup full of beer.

"Dibs!" Steven yelled as he crushed me to his chest. My beer splashed over the rim, and I shook my hand dry. "This one is all mine."

"Is that so?" someone said behind us. Keith had a hint of scruff along his jaw bone and sported a tight dark blue t-shirt and jeans, and he reached around us to pour some beer.

"That's right, my friend." Steven kissed my head playfully while I cringed at the glare Keith gave him. I threw Mimi a look that pleaded for help, but she just rolled her eyes. I guessed this was normal behavior for him.

I drew in my bottom lip. I was afraid I was going to say something that might get me into trouble. I caught Keith's gaze from under his ball hat and wanted to run to him.

"Get your hands off my sister." Elliot looked less than impressed.

Steven released me quickly and sent me sailing into Keith, who caught me by the waist.

"I was just making sure she was warm." Steven laughed. "You know, skimpy uniform, ice; October in Boston is kind of cold."

"I'm okay, El." I gave his arm a little squeeze to let him know I really was all right. I would never fault my brother for looking out for me. He had every right to. After all, what happened to me back home was why we made the move down here in the first place. Elliot was just worried.

He gave a little nod as he calmed down and looked at the people around us.

"El, have you meet Mimi?"

He shook his head like he did when he needed to get it on straight. "No, sorry, I haven't." He offered a hand. "You're the head cheerleader or something, right?"

"I am. Let's go talk." She took his hand and led him outside.

"Keith." Nicole waved him over while she twirled her long red hair around her finger. "It's our song." She stretched out her hands. "Dance with me?"

I didn't miss that she was staking claim, so instead of reacting to the sting I felt inside, I took Steven's hand and played along. "Now, that sounds like fun." I led him to the living room where Montell Jordan's "This Is How We Do It" pulsed through everyone. With my hands on his shoulders,

I started to swing my hips. He followed, and in no time we had a good rhythm going. I ignored my natural instinct and the need to stay in the shadows and decided to let loose.

The song changed to Ricky Martin's "Livin' La Vida Loca." Steven grabbed my hands and did some weird hip roll with me. *Oh no, this is so not my music.* However, the playful look on his face made me give in. I wished my mother could see me now. I was relaxed and having fun for the first time in what seemed like a long time.

Steven raised his arms and rolled his hips in my direction, and right before I stepped into him, I noticed Keith was off to the side speaking to Nicole, but his eyes were on me.

"I need some air." I fanned myself and pointed to the door. "Be right back, okay?"

He took my hand and led me toward the door. I didn't mean for him to come, but okay…

I stopped at the patio, not wanting to stray too far away from the house with him.

"Pretty great spot." He sighed and leaned against the rail, looking down at me. When I only nodded, he stuck his hands in his pockets. "You have someone back home?"

I raised a brow, reluctant to answer his question. So I gave him my normal run-around comment. "Everyone wants to know the new girl's story."

"No, I just want to know if I stand a chance here or not."

The effort it took not to roll my eyes was something else. Did he even care to get to know me first? All Steven saw was a pair of legs to spread.

Suddenly, my conscience pinched me. I wasn't a hearts and flowers girl anymore, though I didn't think I ever was. Sadly, I never got the chance to get to know the real me. I could be a bit self-destructive. It gave me an outlet from the darkness that lived inside me.

Elliot, for the most part, knew what I was going through, and a part of me hated it, but the other was thankful he could see through my bullshit. My parents, on the other hand, still struggled. They constantly worried about how I was doing. I found myself trying to prove I was okay, like joining the cheerleading team. If my friends back home could see me now, they'd die. But they couldn't, and I had to build another life around false illusions.

"You want a drink or something?" I could tell my silence was bothering him. I wrapped my arms around my mid-section, suddenly feeling the cold around me. "You cold?"

I nodded just as he put his cold hand on my exposed lower back. I jumped at the uncomfortable jolt that leapt up my spine.

As we were going in, Keith was coming down the stairs. Nicole followed behind, fixing her top. She gave me a little wave with a grin.

Shit.

A lead ball hit my stomach. I needed to find Elliot and get out of here.

I raced to Clark, leaving Steven to speak with one of his friends.

"Hey, have you seen my brother?"

"Ha! Yeah, last I saw them, they were heading upstairs, and the only reason you go up there is to get—"

"Thanks!" I cut him off. I didn't need that visual. I headed outside to find Trish. I cupped the window, hoping the car was open. "Shit." *Of course not.* The road was full of people, but no sign of my new friends. *Fine.* I let my inner stubbornness show her face.

Fifteen minutes into my walk, I wondered if Clark had a permit to attend our school, because this was a lot farther than I remembered. I was thankful for my sneakers, but it was cold and my body started to shake. I was sure there must be a pay phone up ahead where I could call my parents. The number one rule in our house was if we were ever in trouble, we could call with few questions asked, but if we didn't, we'd get in real trouble. My parents were pretty frigging amazing.

Headlights flooded the world ahead of me and cast a shadow that grew as the car came closer. It slowed and the window rolled down, and there was Keith, looking mighty pissed off.

"What are you doing?"

"Hey, what's up?" I tried to act normal, but it came out forced.

"What are you doing?"

"Walking."

"Why?"

"Couldn't find Elliot, so I left."

He shook his head. "Where is your jacket?"

"Mimi's car."

He raced ahead and parked the truck. The door swung open, and he hurried toward me. He stopped when I was only a foot away.

"Do you have any idea how dangerous it is out here? Dammit, Lexi! Look what you're wearing. Any guy would pull over to check you out."

I shook off the image of Nicole's face when she figured out Keith had come after me. "I'm fine, Keith."

"Hey." He snatched my arm and pulled me to a halt. "What's wrong? Did Steven do something?" Before I could answer, he dropped down to look right into my eyes. "Did he touch you?"

"No! God, no! He didn't do a thing but be friendly."

"Come on, I'll take you home."

I squared my shoulders at his tone. *Pardon?*

He turned when I didn't follow. His eyes narrowed in on me while his fingers strummed at his sides. In two strides he was in front of me. He placed his hands on my shoulders and looked down. "Are you okay?"

"Yeah." I blinked with confusion.

"I'd really like to take you home again. I promised Elliot I would watch out for you." My stomach sank. Oh, great, I was his pet he got to babysit. My tongue pushed on the back of my teeth as my anger grew. My father was right. I was too stubborn for my own good, but I couldn't help it. It calmed me, made me feel like I was in control. Truth be told, I hated control, but I'd never felt safe enough to let my guard down.

"I'd rather walk."

Oh, the face he made was rather appealing. "Get in the damn truck, Lexi." I walked around him *and* his truck. "You're so damn lucky you're you." He

31

snickered as he went back to his truck.

I wondered what he meant, but before I could get that thought through, I tuned into the engine, the engine now rumbling away behind me with its headlights on full beam.

You've got to be kidding me. Okay, here we go.

Every once in a while, a car would drive by. I was mortified, although I'd never show it. I held my own. I had walked almost seven blocks before I felt the first raindrop. *Of course.* Second by second, they fell harder and harder.

"You about done?" he called from the window.

"No," I hissed without looking back.

A truck passed, and they slowed down and started yelling at me. "Whooooo! Damn, a wet cheerleader. My prayers have been answered!" I recognized him. He was one of the terrible football players. "Danny, pull over!"

Shit.

I stopped when they did. I heard a door shut and heavy footsteps, and Keith appeared by my side. Then he took a step forward almost as if to shield me.

"Get in the truck, Lexi," he barked over his shoulder. "Troy, shut your door before I break both your legs."

"Aw, come on, Keith, we're only playing with her."

"I've seen you play, and I know if your dad saw you now, he'd beat me to the first punch."

Keith grabbed my hand and pulled me to his side of the truck. He opened the door and lifted me in. I quickly shuffled over to the other side, becoming cooler as I relaxed.

"You are one stubborn girl." He reached behind the bench, pulled a flannel blanket free, and handed it to me.

"Thanks." I gladly took it and covered my shoulders.

He sighed heavily before his hands fell from the wheel. One rubbed his chin as he thought about something. He leaned forward and removed his slick t-shirt, tossing it behind me. I couldn't help but stare at his figure. Damn, he was seventeen but had a body of a trainer. He tugged a dry long sleeve shirt over his head and pulled it in place.

The rain beat the windshield, clearing momentarily as the wipers zipped by. The truck pumped out heat, but the thin layer of ice that ran along my skin prevented it from warming me.

"I should get you home."

We didn't speak the whole way. I wished I knew what to say, but I didn't. He pulled into my driveway and looked up at my dark house.

"Guess Elliot isn't home yet."

"Nope." I undid my seatbelt. "I was supposed to stay overnight at Mimi's house, and he was going somewhere else."

"Where are your parents?"

"They had to go back home and deal with our house closing."

He looked at me strangely as I handed him back his blanket. "Do you even have a key?"

"There's a spare in the shed."

I hated the idea of heading back there in the dark, but what other choice did I have?

I swung the door open, and the rain beat down on my shoulders. I awkwardly dropped the long way to the ground, preparing myself for the landing this time.

"Thanks for the—" I watched him jump out and start walking toward the house. "What are you doing?" I raced to catch up. My sneakers squeaked under my socks, and I lost my footing and fell on my ass. *Awesome, Lexi.* He turned around, and his expression changed into a smirk. "Really? You're enjoying this a little too much."

He offered me a hand and brought me to my feet. "Just fun when I see your wall drop for a moment."

"I don't have a wall." Water splattered from my lips.

"You're kind of cute when you lie. Come on." He pulled me behind him to the shed, and after a moment or two of searching, we found the spare set of keys.

Once inside my house, he handed me the keys. Thunder rolled above us and the rain started to really pour.

"Well, you did your duty." I kicked off my sneakers and began to wring out my soaking hair.

"Go get warm. I'll stay until you're settled."

"You don't have to."

"I know I don't." He ran a hand through his dark hair, and his eyes begged me to challenge him.

"Okay," I whispered as I took the first step upstairs.

After a hot shower, my bones finally felt warm and my lips had stopped twitching. I changed into red and black plaid pants and a tight white tank top with a black sweater that hung open in the front. Taking two steps at a time, I hurried down to the living room to find Keith watching TV. He looked over and his gaze dropped down my front.

"I'm fine, you know. You don't need to babysit me."

He shook his head as he stood. "You think that's what I'm doing?"

"It's what you said."

"Did you ever think maybe I like you?"

I folded my arms, feeling my anger rise. "How stupid do you think I am?"

"Pardon?"

"Look, I'm not someone's sloppy second."

He matched my stance. "How are you that, exactly?"

My chin lifted as I headed over to the door. "I think you should go."

"Have you always been this friendly? Or is it something I draw out of you?" He pulled his keys free from his jeans. "So glad you're home safe, Lexi." His sarcasm wasn't lost on me.

He walked straight up to me, his large body nearly touching mine. The top of my head came up to his broad shoulders, causing me to tilt my head back.

"Whatever your reason is for being so guarded, you can knock it off now."

"Excuse me?"

"You heard me."

"You're maddening!"

"So are you."

"Keith—" He grabbed my shoulders and dipped

down, pressing his lips to mine. I stayed still at first, not sure what to make of it. I was pissed, but oddly turned on. His tongue moved inside my mouth and his arm hooked around my back. My body started to take over and I wrapped my arms around his neck to deepen the kiss. He stepped forward and pressed me flat against the wall. One hand moved along my bare skin between my pants and top, and the other threaded into my hair.

Oh my God, he was a good kisser. Forceful but gentle. Perfect combination.

He pulled back and let out a heavy sigh before he lifted my leg and hooked it on his hip. His lips found mine again and consumed my mind. I ran my hands over his solid arms and shoulders; I needed more.

The phone rang and pulled us back down to reality. He didn't stop right away, and I didn't want him to. On the fourth ring, he finally pulled away.

My hands dropped away and I moved around his body toward the phone on the entryway table.

"Hello?"

"Dammit, Lexi, you scared me half to death!" Elliot shouted over the line. "Mimi has your keys and all your stuff. I thought you were going to her place tonight."

Keith was fiddling with his keys, then he looked over and found me watching him.

"I couldn't find her, but I'm fine, El. Keith drove me home and helped me find the spare keys."

"Well, tell him Nicole is on the warpath and looking for him. That girl has a scary streak." My stomach twisted. "Guess he drove you home first.

I'll let her know he's with you."

"No, don't." I closed my eyes as if that would allow me to avoid the drama. "Let him tell her."

"Okay, I'll see you tomorrow."

"Yeah." I hung up the phone with a heavy heart.

"Everything okay?" he asked in a deep voice.

Letting out a small sigh, I turned and found my voice. "You may want to head back to the party. Nicole is looking for you." His face said all I needed to know. "Thanks for the ride home, but you should go."

He had a strange expression on his face as he disappeared into the rain.

CHAPTER THREE

Keith

Lexi avoided me for two weeks after that, and even skipped one of our games. I wished I knew what was going on with her.

I caught Elliot on his way to class. "Hey, where is your sister?"

"Practice out on the field." He stopped. "Are you dating Nicole?"

What? "No, why?"

"Well, Nicole made it very clear to Lexi that you were. Lexi saw you two walking downstairs at Clark's party. When Nicole found out you drove her home, she made Mimi drop Lexi from the last game."

"Seriously?" I couldn't believe what I was hearing.

"Look, my sister has been through some rough shit, but I can tell she likes you. If you like her, then tell her, but if you're going to string her along, don't. She's had enough bad things happen in her life."

"Like what?"

He shook his head. "Not my stories to share, man."

"Yeah, I get it. Thanks." I hurried to the field to find her.

The girls were in a human pyramid. Lexi and Mimi were on top. With an effortless drop, they fell one by one into the arms of the other girls.

"Nicole!" I shouted over the music. She grinned at me and strolled over. I noticed Lexi glanced my way too.

"Hey, sexy." She went to hug me, but I stepped back.

"What are you doing telling people we're dating?"

Her face twisted as she looked back at Lexi. "Oh, come on, now, Keith. You know we'd be perfect together. We have a history."

"Right." I turned to face her crazy notions. "We are history. We dated junior year, for one week, until I found you kissing the whole damn football team. Let it go and move on."

"People make mistakes, Keith."

"Yup, but I won't be mistake number two."

I looked up to find Lexi, but she had slipped away. I cursed under my breath and started to leave when I saw Coach heading my way.

"Keith, good, I'm glad you're here. Let's talk about tonight's game."

Shit.

"Sure."

***

The ice glided beneath the blades as I skated around the rink to warm up. Clark whipped past me, showing off for the crowd. The whistle blew and we took our spots.

I used all my pent-up frustration toward Nicole to focus. Left, right, left, right, the puck flew back and forth while I planned my move. Six seconds into the game, I scored the first goal. I turned and pointed to Lexi to show her it was for her. She looked away, but I was determined to show her I didn't care about anyone else.

My second goal, I pointed my stick straight at her and headed back to the face-off. Clark shook his head, but I could hear him laughing. The other team's center didn't like that, so when the puck dropped, he charged me, ignoring the puck. I shot backward while he pounded on my chest. I grabbed his shoulder and laid him flat out.

"Really?" I skated past him as the ref blew his whistle. As predicted, the guy got two minutes for roughhousing.

Third period, we were only up one goal. I nodded at Clark so he knew we were going to race up the left side and backhand it into the corner.

We pulled the move off great. The puck went back and forth between the two of us and eased into the net, sending the crowd into a frenzy. The buzzer sounded, and the team came rushing out as we cheered.

Once I was free from the head rubs and fist bumps, I nodded at Lexi. She looked away, but I knew she got it.

***

That's how it went for about three months. Every game or practice Lexi attended, I would give her every goal. She would say hello in passing, but she mostly kept to herself. It was hard, but I stuck with it. I could tell she was softening a little, and it kept my hopes up. Nicole was a constant pain in my ass, but I kept her at arm's length. I was sure she fed Lexi lies.

"Hey, man." Clark smacked my shoulder as we walked through the hallway the student council over-decorated for Christmas. "Who are you taking to the dance?" I gave him a sideways glance, but he shook his head to stop my comment. "I heard 'Linebacker Troy' asked her out."

I stopped mid-step. "And?"

He shrugged. "You need to step up your game, my friend."

Instead of following him into math class, I raced toward her locker.

"We're ditching this afternoon to go dress shopping," Mimi whispered beside me. Her face looked kind. She must have figured out why I was there. "Troy asked, and she accepted."

"So I heard."

"She's not interested in him, Keith." She pulled her books free and wiggled them into her book bag. "And when he asked her, she said yes. After all, the dance is tomorrow night, and you never asked her." She looked at me accusingly. "She seemed to be

41

kind of sad lately. She gave her word to go with him now, so…"

"Any idea what's bothering her?"

"Lexi share something personal? You have got to be kidding me." She started to turn, but stopped. "Whatever it is, it's big, because Elliot is concerned too."

"Thanks, Mimi." I saw the principal heading toward us and made a quick dash back to my class.

After school, I pulled into my driveway and was hit with the sweet smell of dinner on the stove.

"Hey, Mom." I kissed her cheek as I made my way over to the fridge and pulled out last night's leftovers. With a hop up onto the counter, I dove into the lasagna.

"How was your day?"

"Same."

"Oh?" She glanced over her shoulder as she stirred the soup.

I gave her a shrug. "Nothing new on the Lexi front."

"Have you tried talking to her?"

"No, I thought waiting three months in constant suffering was more fun."

She smacked my leg but laughed. "Could you be any more like your father?"

"I could try."

The phone rang and I reached over to answer. "Hello?"

"Keith?"

"Yes." I knew her voice right away. "What's up, Mimi?"

"Movies, eight p.m., tickets will be at will call."

Before I could ask more, she hung up. My finger pressed down to hang up, then I called Clark.

"Wanna go to the movies?"

He cleared his voice. "Like a date?"

"Yeah," I shot back, knowing if I didn't play along, he'd give me more shit.

"You paying?"

"Yeah."

"When?"

"We leave in an hour."

"Shit, dude, that doesn't leave me much time to figure out something to wear. Well, I need to do my hair and find the right shoes…"

"Whatever. I'll be there in an hour." I hung up, shaking my head.

"Movies?" Mom gave me a suspicious grin. "When was the last time you went to the movies with Clark?"

"Never, but Lexi will be there."

"Oh?"

I slid off the counter, washed my dishes, and kissed her on the cheek. "Love you, Mom."

"Love you too, sweetheart."

"Hey," I heard from the bottom of the stairs. Nan rolled up in her chair and handed me a little blue bag. "Saw this and thought of you."

"Really? Thanks, Nan."

I pulled the tissue out and dug my hand inside to feel three little objects. Dropping the bag at my feet, I held up the keychain with a black rope holding small charms. There was a silver Army boot, a bullet, and United States flag.

"Keep you focused on your goal."

43

I kissed her cheek. "Thanks, Nan. That's pretty cool."

As sad as it was to admit, I changed my outfit two times. I decided on jeans and a long sleeve black shirt. I liked the darker colors and knew Lexi did too.

When I was tying my sneakers, I heard Two clear her throat as she flopped on my bed behind me. My sister liked to know what was up all the time.

"You look nice."

"Thanks."

"You have a date?"

"Sort of."

She moved to sit up on her elbow. "What does that mean?" She made a familiar noise when she made the connection. "Ah, you stalking Lexi again?"

I peered over my shoulder, then back to my sneakers.

"I don't think I've ever seen you chase down a girl like this. What's so special about this one?"

I stood and looked in the mirror. "Can't really explain it, Two."

I heard her grumble at her nickname. Not my fault my parents had four sisters after me. The whole nickname thing started as a joke but stuck. I knew they secretly liked it. We were all extremely close and always looked out for one another.

"Advice?" she asked as she rubbed her calf muscle. Two was addicted to ballet, but she was already having muscle problems.

"Please." I folded my arms over my chest and

waited to hear what she had to say.

"Lexi isn't romantic. I don't think you should go down that path. I think you'll need to get her alone and remind her what she's missing."

I shrugged. She was right. Lexi needed to be pushed rather than led.

"Makes sense."

"Oh, I know." She grinned as she pulled her short brown hair into a ponytail. "Now, can you do me a favor?

"Depends."

"Put in a good word for me with Clark?"

My face dropped and my hands flexed together.

"Oh, that was worth it." She laughed, pointing to my face. "You make it *so* easy."

My blood pressure dropped back down as I tossed a pillow at her.

"Dinner!" my mother called out.

I hurried down the stairs to everyone gathering around the table. I hated to miss Friday night dinners, but this was too good to pass up.

Three and Four were already digging in, and my dad was still helping One with her homework.

"Sorry, all, but I have to pass tonight."

Everyone looked up, but Three was grinning like a fool. "He's crashing a girls' night."

"How did you...?" I closed my eyes. "Stop listening to my calls, Three."

"Now, why would I do that when your life is way more interesting than mine?"

"Well, that's true." I laughed and ruffled up her short pixie cut.

"Good luck." My dad gave me my exit cue.

With a wave, I headed out to my truck and down the street to Clark's house. Within twenty minutes, we were in line at the will call office.

"Tickets for Keith," I said into the little mic.

"Here you go."

I met Clark at the food counter. I pulled the tickets free and smirked at the movie choice. *Of course.*

"Really?" Clark eyed the tickets, unimpressed.

So there I was at the movies, in line with my buddy, and handed the kid with the head gear my tickets. He couldn't help but eye us both, and of course Clark draped his arm around my shoulders, just to be the dick he was.

"Third door on your left."

I elbowed Clark, who only laughed harder as we entered the huge stadium style room. It only took a moment for me to spot Lexi three rows from the back. I made my way up, making sure she wouldn't spot me. Clark and I fought our way to the seats directly behind her.

I should have known better than to think she would be alone. I just assumed she was here with the girls. Jackson, a center from our rival hockey team, grinned when he came up the stairs. Clark and I both turned our faces so he wouldn't see us. We hated this douche bag. How in the hell did he get a date with Lexi?

"A water for my pretty." He handed her a bottle, and she gave him a little nod. "Are you cold? Hot? What?"

"I'm fine, Jackson."

"You sure?"

She sighed. "I'm sure."

Clark elbowed me to speak up, but I was second guessing if this was a smart idea. Maybe this *was* borderline stalking.

Before I could think, Clark cleared his throat. Jackson tuned in to us, but didn't turn around. Instead, he reached over and placed his hand over hers. Anyone would have to be blind not to see her body stiffen.

That was all I needed.

"I have been waiting to see this movie!" Clark blurted like he was at a ball game, making Jackson jump. "That Robin Tunney makes me excited."

I had to look away or I would laugh. Clark never stopped surprising me with his movie trivia. "She was sexy in the Mayhem episode of *Law and Order* last year," he added.

"Oh." Jackson shifted around more in his seat. "What's up, guys?"

"Jackson," Clark addressed him. "Lexi." He drew out her name.

She slowly turned, and her face lit up then quickly fell when she took me in.

"You'll need to better explain that expression." Clark pointed to Lexi.

She flipped her long brown hair out of her face. "Just a little shocked to see you guys here."

"You're not the only ones who like a good chick flick."

"Right," she muttered as she turned back around.

Jackson looked at Lexi before he spoke again. "Oh, that's right, you two had a thing or something." My fists flexed as Lexi swallowed hard. "When you were with Nicole, right?"

"Never was with Nicole," I corrected him.

Jackson's eyes lit up. "That's not how it looked the other night at the burger joint."

Oh, screw you, asshole. The psycho chick followed me there!

Lexi shook her head as the lights dimmed. Jackson smirked and settled in next to her.

Empire Records started, and all I could focus on was the fact that he kept finding some way to touch her.

It wasn't until halfway through the movie when Jackson put his arm around her shoulders that she whispered something to him. She stood with her purse in hand and hurried down the steps. Clark moved so I could follow. I saw Jackson move to get up, but Clark's hand pressed hard on his shoulder, keeping him in his seat.

"Hey!" I called out after her, but she kept her fast pace toward the front door. "Lex!" I started to jog until I was right behind her. She raised her hand to hail a cab, but I grabbed her arm and forced her to look at me. "Stop ignoring me."

"I'm not!" she shouted in my face.

My stomach rolled when I looked into those brown eyes of hers. I hadn't been this close to her since the last time we kissed. Her long lashes fluttered like she was fighting tears.

"Stop lying to me."

"I'm not."

"You are!"

She closed her eyes, and when she opened them they were red. "Keith, please."

"Please, what?" I stepped back but still close enough to grab her if she bolted again. "Leave you alone? No."

"Why not?"

Screw this. I hooked my arm around her waist and hauled her to me. The moment she was flat against my chest, I slipped my hand along her cheek. "Because I can't stop thinking about our kiss."

"That's what you missed?" Her tone confused me. Right as I was about to question it, she stepped up and slammed her mouth to mine. She ran her hands along my shoulders, up my neck, and into my hair. I sensed something was off, but at the same time, having her back in my arms was well worth it. I dove into the kiss, tasting every inch of her sweet mouth. Her tongue danced with mine, but again something was nagging at me. I slid my hand down the curve of her spine and along the top of her pants. I didn't care we were in public. I missed her too much. Suddenly, she pulled away and started to walk down the street.

What the hell?

I raced to catch up to her, stopping her dead in her tracks. "What the hell was that?"

"A kiss."

"Yeah, I know. I was there."

Her shoulders fell like she was annoyed with me. "Now you can get me out of your system. Now you can move on."

"Move on?" I turned as she edged around me. "Wait, now." I grabbed her hand. "Stop running."

"Not running."

"Yes, you are." *Ahhh,* she was driving me mad.

"Jesus Christ, Keith, what the hell do you want?" she shouted, and some people from the parking lot looked over at us. I gave a little wave to show them we were okay.

"You, Lexi! I want you. No one else, just you."

She studied me for a moment, then a tear slipped down her cheek. "No, you don't."

"Who are you to say that?" I didn't like being told how to feel.

"I'm not the kind of girl you think I am. I'm not all happy inside."

Really? "That's a nice way to think of yourself."

She leaned her head back and looked up at the sky. "It's not something I think, it's something I know."

With a step forward, I grabbed her hand and made her follow me to my truck. I opened the door, lifted her up, and slammed the door. Once inside, I turned on the heat and shifted around to look at her.

"If you think I want you for your body, you're only a quarter right." Her eyes narrowed on me, and I tucked away the smirk. "I've never lied to you, Lexi. You're beautiful. The most beautiful woman I've ever seen. But it's your personality that draws me in. Stubbornness and all. So we are going to sit here until you decide to tell me what is up your ass when it comes to letting me in."

"My ass?" She folded her arms and leaned back against the seat.

"I've got all night, sweetheart."

Raindrops started to bounce off the windshield, and a movie was just getting out, so I started the truck and headed down the road. She didn't question what I was doing, so that was a good sign. I decided to go to my favorite place. I parked at the lake and turned off the lights so only the park lamps sparkled along the edges of the shoreline.

The radio was on low, and I turned it off so only the rain could be heard.

"You know, kidnapping will land you a few years in jail." She glared at me, but she wasn't protesting that hard.

"Can't kidnap the willing, Lexi."

Her mouth dropped open, but she didn't say anything.

For over half an hour she sat silent in the corner. I fidgeted to get into a more comfortable position. She had will, that was for sure. Little did she know, silence was my strong suit. I could outlast her any day.

Her little sniff caught my attention, but instead of looking over, I glanced at her reflection in the window.

"Fine," she whispered and swiped her finger along her cheek. "But if I tell you, you have to promise not to tell a soul."

Knowing that if she was in danger nothing could talk me out of getting her help, I agreed. The look on her face told me she was about to tell me something bad. She again asked for me to keep silent.

"Okay." I looked her straight in the eyes. "I promise to stay quiet."

She held my eyes for a minute, then glanced out the window. She started to run her slim fingers through her shiny hair.

"I'm from a small area just outside Toronto…"

CHAPTER FOUR

Richmond, Canada

Lexi

El tossed a tennis ball against the wall as I pulled my gum from my mouth to see how far it would stretch before it broke.

"Kids?" Mom called out from the hallway.

"We're not here," I muttered.

"Kids?"

El groaned. "We ran away because you're making me wear this jacket."

Dad came in looking for something, and then Mom got closer, so El sank further into my closet.

"There you are." She looked stunning in a white silk blouse and black ruffled skirt. "We should have left ten minutes ago." When we didn't budge, she sighed and sat on the bed. "Look, I know these parties suck." We laughed at her comment. "It's just so important to stay visual at these things. Your father's boss is a—"

"Asshole." Dad shrugged as he emerged from behind her.

"Well, I was going to say jerk, but asshole works too." She took his hand and kissed it while we laughed harder. "Doesn't matter, though. It's important that we go." She stood and fixed her hair. "Even if we're counting the minutes to when we leave."

"Damn straight." El dodged Dad's swat to his arm as he slipped out of my room.

"Darn, you mean darn."

I rolled off the bed and grabbed my purse. "No, Dad, in this case, it's damn."

After being squashed in a tiny car, followed by meeting a million people who didn't give a crap about who I was, we were finally left alone downstairs with the rest of the employees' kids.

Two hours in, and I couldn't take the fighting over Monopoly, I needed to leave. I called my friend Darcy, and she said her mom would swing by and get me.

I weaved through the sea of big hair and smoke, determined to find my parents to let them know I was leaving.

My father's assistant appeared, and I stepped in her way.

"Have you seen my parents?"

"Oh, well, hello, sweetheart." She studied my face. "It's been a long time, hasn't it? Now, how long has it been?" Really, old biddy, you wanna do a trip down memory lane right now? I just saw you two days ago!

"Ms. Hazel, I really need to know if you know

where my parents are."

"Umm, I thought I saw your mother upstairs, or was it the garden?"

"Come on," I hissed, climbing the tall staircase. I would be nicer, but she apparently wouldn't remember this conversation in a day.

I saw an open room at the end of the hall and made my way down.

"Wow." I stepped into the room and took in the view. A solid wall was covered in different color wine bottles. It was pretty neat the way it reflected the light. The other was full of photographs, mostly black and white, but the one in the center was of a woman who looked very familiar. I walked over, letting my curiosity get the better of me.

There was Maci, my father's boss's wife, in a bright red blouse, with bright red lips that matched her nails tucked under her chin. She was staring at the cameraman, and the flash made her eyes glow. It was beautiful.

My spine prickled at the sound of footsteps behind me. I quickly looked for another door and dashed across the room. A hard tug told me it was locked. Oh no! I heard a voice, and as it grew louder, so did my heartbeat. If I was found in here, I would be in so much trouble, not to mention my father would be too.

I spotted a closet and slipped inside, in near panic before two people entered the room.

"Oh God, oh God, oh God!" I tried to close the door, but a strap of a golf bag was jammed in the middle hinge.

I had to leave the door the way it was, as I was

scared they would hear me fiddling with it.

My heart was pounding, and when I heard a voice I recognized, I wanted to cry. I really wished I hadn't realized who it was. I thought it must be God's way of punishing me and my family for not wanting to be here in the first place.

"Fine," I mouthed to the ceiling, "you win! Church once a week!"

His black suit appeared by the door, and I froze. There were wooden slats in the door, so I could see out, but they couldn't see in. Once I was sure I wouldn't be spotted easily, I leaned against the wall and watched and listened as Father Kai spoke to Maci. I shifted so I could see out the door better.

"Please, Father," she started to cry, "not here."

He moved to stand in front of her. Father Kai was tall and skinny, but he was strong in other ways. He had power over some of the townspeople. I'd heard my parents talk about it. My father wasn't overly religious, but we attended church on holidays for my mother, because she enjoyed it.

"Now, Maci, you know it's whenever the Lord feels it's the right time. I am here to serve his needs."

Her lips pressed together, but a sob managed to escape. "What if someone comes in? What if someone hears—?"

His shoulders pulled back as he cleared his throat. "Knees, now!"

My stomach sank. What the hell was going on here? My hands started to sweat, and my heartbeat thundered in my ears.

I watched in terror as she slowly lowered to the

ground and with shaky hands removed her shoes one at a time. Then, to my surprise, she carefully removed her blouse and hung it on the stool next to her.

The urge to look away was strong, but for some reason I couldn't.

Father Kai slipped his hand into his pocket and removed a long leather strap. The part that made my knees go weak was the hard little ball on the end, with what looked like spikes all over it. He dropped it at his feet and waited.

Maci let out a long breath before her pink tipped fingers swiped toward the floor, picking up the strap. She held the handle and waited.

"Say it." His voice was low and scary. The tone of it would stay with me for a long time.

"Forgive me, Father, for I have sinned."

He nodded once. "Do it."

She closed her eyes and flipped her hand up and behind her, whipping her own back with the thing.

Holy shit! I bit my lip to stop the cry that was now lodged in my throat.

"Again," he ordered.

The sound of the leather cutting through the air and the sound of the ball hitting her skin was making me lightheaded. I was way too terrified to try to stop it. I remained frozen, hidden in the closet.

None of this made sense. He was Father Kai, our church's beloved priest for many years and the one person in town who had everyone's respect. People went to him for everything.

"Again." His voice brought me back to the

horrible event that was taking place—the torture of Maci.

"I...I can't." She fell forward, and I got a good look at her skin.

I almost vomited. I couldn't take it. I started to silently sob. Her skin was beet red with tiny holes that bled down her back.

"Again," he repeated, and this time she sat straight up and continued her punishment. Father Kai rolled his neck, then leaned back. His hands moved out to the sides, palms toward the sky, almost like he was feeling God's presence.

All I could feel was the Devil's.

After three more lashings, he told her to stop. He held his hand out for her to place the weapon in it.

"Until tomorrow." He drew the cross in the air above her, then watched as she scrambled into the bathroom, still crying. Her face was all blotchy, and her mascara ran down from her eyes.

He brushed his coat with his hand as if something was on it, then fixed his hair.

Who the hell was this person?

The moment he left the room, I sprang up and was about to run out of the closet, but then froze. Did I stop to see if Maci was all right? Or should I just leave? The faucet turning off was all I needed to hear before I bolted. I burst through the outer office doors and ran smack into the house maid.

"Miss Klein, what is wrong?"

I wildly glanced down the hallway and spotted my mother downstairs. Before the maid could say anything, I was gone.

I paused my story and looked over at him. My face showed so much fear because I felt like I was right there again. His hand twitched; I could tell he wanted to touch me. I paused, and he just covered his hand with mine and kept silent. I appreciated the gesture.

"Then what happened?"

I licked my lips and continued, seeing it all again in my mind.

I ran straight into my mother's arms, and she wrapped them around me without question.

"Sweetheart, what's the matter?"

I couldn't get my head around what I just witnessed. Did I really want to say something so negative about a man who was so highly respected? What if no one believed me?

"Nothing, Mom, I just want to go home."

"Darling, you are obviously upset. Tell me what's wrong."

I knew I had to say something.

"I got in a huge fight with one of the girls over something, and I know she hates me now, and I want to go."

"Oh, dear, you know I can't just—"

I pulled away as tears burned a path down my puffy cheeks. "Tracy's mom is on her way. She said I could stay there tonight. Please, Mom."

Her soft hand brushed along my face. "All right, then. I know how much you and El hate these things. Don't be late getting home in the morning."

With a quick hug, I left.

I told them the next day that the fight was over a

59

boy. My parents left it alone, but El knew something more was up.

After that, I seemed to run into Father Kai more than I ever had before. Gas station, mall, he even showed up at my school to do a guest appearance.

"Lovely to see you, Alexi," he greeted me outside the gymnasium, looking sharp in a crisp, blue three-piece suit. My skin shivered around my bones as he peered down at me. He waited for the hall to clear before he tilted his head and gave me a smile. "Always lovely to see you." His finger curled around my side ponytail, and his touch made my skin crawl. I wanted to step back, but I couldn't. I was rooted in place. "You're turning into quite the little lady. Soon you will be dating boys and committing all sorts of sins."

"I need to go."

Sick bastard.

"Yes, you do." His eyes spoke more than his words did. "Say hello to your mother for me."

If I found out he ever touched my mother, I'd kill him and carry that sin happily straight to the Devil.

One Sunday there was a town barbeque. I didn't want to go, but my parents said Father Kai had invited us personally, so we needed to go.

I shook the whole way. El kept glancing over at me. It had been a month since I witnessed the darkness that was Father Kai, and I wasn't handling it well.

"Dad." El tapped his shoulder as we pulled into the parking lot. "Can we talk for a moment?"

"Sure, son." Both our parents turned in their seats to face us.

What was he doing?

"You two have always said it's the four of us, no matter what, and if one of us has a problem, we all do." He looked over at me. "Lex, I've never seen you like this. Please tell us what happened at that party."

I drew my bottom lip between my teeth to stop them from trembling. Here? Now? When Father Kai was fifteen feet away?

"Sweetheart, please, is there something you need to tell us?" my mother pleaded with me. My father looked concerned.

We were as close as a family could be, so maybe it would be better if I shared it with them. Then the lonely feeling I was carrying would leave.

With a deep breath, I unloaded what I had witnessed to my family. The whole time, I kept my eyes on my father's face, which hardened in shock at my words. Mom's mouth dropped open, and El just kept shaking his head.

When I was finished, I waited to see who would speak first. I was terrified. What if they didn't believe me?

"Oh, my poor, poor baby," my mother breathed.

"That sick bastard!" Dad started to move, but Mom put her hand on his arm. "We have to think about this. We can't be too hasty. He has a lot of power in this town."

"Oh my God." Mom leaned back against the window. "I wondered why Maci hasn't worn that backless swoop dress she adores." She paused, thinking. "Plus, the other day Simon Waters knocked into her, hitting her back, and she totally

overreacted with him."

*El glanced over my shoulder, then back to Dad.
"What do we do?"*

*"If he is using his power to punish people like
that, we need to report him."*

I cleared my throat as I tipped my head back to
rest on the seat. The rain was coming down harder
now, and it helped break up the tension. "He knew I
told them."

"How?"

"Turns out, the maid approached him, thinking
he had hurt me. That's when things got worse. Our
family was basically pushed out of everything after
my mother approached Maci, only to get yelled at.
She denied everything. We found out from one of
the few friends we had left that Father Kai had
something on her."

"What did he have?" he asked in a rush.

"Maci planned to kill her husband, but at the last
minute she couldn't go through with it. She went to
confession to get rid of the guilt. I guess Father Kai
took it upon himself to cleanse her of her sins. The
man is insane."

His face dropped and I could see he was
shocked.

"My father went to the police and filed a case
against him. That's when things went really dark.
Instead of the town siding with us, they turned, and
we started getting harassed. I even started getting
death threats. El wouldn't leave my side because I
got jumped on the way home from school once. We
were the black sheep of Richmond, and Father Kai

did everything in his power to make sure everyone thought we were liars. Worst of all, my father got fired from the job he loved. That's when my family decided it was time to move. It wasn't worth the fear we lived in. So here we are in Boston."

"And Father Kai?"

I rolled my heavy head to look at him. This was an emotional topic. "He's still the head of the church, still cleansing people of their sins, and I'm sure he still has his eye out for me."

His face dropped again. "You mean they never looked into it?"

"They did, but without Maci's testimony, they have nothing but some fourteen-year-old girl's accusations. He told them I was looking for attention and that he forgave me." My voice dropped while I tugged my jacket around my body. A chill settled in around me. "Right before we left, he approached me in the grocery store, told me he'd be seeing me again real soon. He terrifies me, even now."

"Do you really think he'll come and find you?"

I didn't even blink. "I watched him command a grown woman to whip her own back, during a party, no less, until she bled. He came to see me at my school. Do I think I'll see him again? No, I don't. Honestly, I think he's moved on to someone else. It doesn't make it right, but I learned I have to worry about myself first."

My eyes blurred, but I kept my tears at bay. Keith ran his hand over his mouth with a huff. I knew it was a lot to take in. He leaned over, wrapped an arm around my waist, and pulled my small body against his. Surprisingly, I let him. I even rested my head on his shoulder. Sometimes it was nice not overthinking things.

"Thank you," I whispered.

"For what?"

"For listening."

"Thank you for sharing." He waited a beat. "You want to get out of here?"

"Sure."

The lake was still, no wind to disturb the perfect mirror image of the street lamps. It was quiet and peaceful with no one around, just us. I settled into his side in the back of the truck. He had blankets to wrap ourselves in to keep warm under the starry sky.

I felt a light between us spark. Something about baring your deepest secret to someone could change how you feel, and it changed how you saw them. I shifted back to see him, his brows pinched together. He looked confused until he studied my hungry expression.

"What are you thinking?" I removed my jacket and unbuttoned my pants. "You sure?"

"I want to feel anything other than what I just told you."

He tugged me on his lap and took my hand in his, holding me so I'd look at him.

"I don't want to hurt you."

"Then don't."

He eased me down, laying me on the blanket, and made sure I was out of sight. He inched my pants off, and then did the same to his.

With his warm body against mine, his hands

trailed along my thighs under the blanket.

"I'm ready, Keith," I mumbled, but he ignored my eager pleas. His lips caught mine, slow at first, but then it turned passionate. I could tell he was fighting his own control.

We had to break contact as he slipped a condom on, my nose scrunching at the smell. *Yuck, latex.*

His lips found mine again as he straddled my hips. Fixing the blanket to make sure I didn't get cold, he lingered at my opening. *Lord, this is maddening!* My back arched and a huff of air slipped past my lips as he slowly pushed inside me. Everything he did was thought out and gentle. He paused when I flinched, and touched my cheek when I made a face. I was battling my own hurt, and he was there to help me.

"Keith," I gasped as he picked up the pace. He kept his body close to mine through each thrust. "I'm close."

"Good." He kissed me as I let go and gave myself over to him. I felt as if I shot up in the air, and then slowly floated back down to the sound of him finding his own release.

Both spent and fighting to catch our breath while staring up at the sky, his hand inched over and found mine.

The rest of the year, we were inseparable.

***

Keith

Nan wheeled into my room as I fixed my tie.

Tonight was prom. She waited until Two left and made sure the coast was clear.

"So?" I couldn't help but smirk at her through the mirror.

"Lookin' good, my boy."

I gave her a look. She was full of it. "Spill it, Nan."

"One has a date tonight." *There it is.* Nan had the entire family fooled that she was hard of hearing, but really my wheelchairin' grandmother could hear just fine and used it to her total advantage. She knew all. I was the only one who knew the truth, and, well, I was her favorite.

"Should I be worried?"

"No." She waved her hand. "It's just the young chap Edward Silver from down the street. He wouldn't know where to stick it, even if One gave him the map."

"Awesome, Nan." I rolled my eyes. "Not an image I need in my head."

I heard the zipper retract on the back of the giant brown teddy bear that stood in the corner of my room. It was originally a gift from my grandfather, but it had become Nan's secret liquor stash. She poured herself a generous shot of scotch. She sure loved her scotch.

"What about Four? She still seeing that weird guy?"

"Tuna Fish Breath?" she muttered, and it made me laugh. He did smell like a fish plant. "No, thank the Lord, that guy is history. Did you ever notice he had a wandering eye? I swear it followed me wherever I went. Like he was on to me and my abilities."

I shrugged on my suit jacket and faced her. "Well?"

"Strapping!" She beamed at me. "Lexi won't be able to keep her hands off of you."

"Mom!" my mom snapped from the hallway. "What are you doing? Are you drinking? You know you can't drink." Her voice was raised because Mom didn't know Nan could hear just fine, if not better than the rest of us.

"I'm seventy, dear. If I want a drink, I'll damn well have one." She tipped the glass back and downed the rest.

Mom looked at me. "You look lovely, dear, but if you could watch your Nan sometimes, that would be helpful."

Nan rolled her eyes. "What would be helpful, *dear*, is if you could get a mini bar upstairs. That ramp is a real bitch."

I bit back a smirk. *Such a shit disturber.*

Once Mom left, Nan's expression became more serious. "Are you going to tell Lexi tonight?"

"I haven't even told them yet." I nodded outside my door.

"Maybe start with the one it will emotionally affect the most."

I looked over, feeling uneasy. "Perhaps you're right."

I kissed her on the head and raced down the stairs. I knew this had to happen sooner than later.

***

Her head rested on my shoulder as we watched a movie at the drive-in. Clark and Elliot were out trolling for girls, and I was pleased we were alone. Prom was amazing, and now that summer had hit, it was time for us to do our summer kick-off at the lake.

"Hey." I kissed her cheek. "Can I talk to you about something?"

"Sure." She sat up and turned her chair in the bed of my truck to see me better.

My hands twisted in the blanket. I needed to do this now or never.

"So, you are off to Boston University, and me…"

Her smile hit the corners of her eyes as she waited for me continue.

"I signed up for the Army."

Her smile faded. "You did what?"

"Signed up for the Army."

Her gaze dropped to her feet and her jaw locked in place. This wasn't going to be good.

"Wait." She held up her hand, and her mood ring flashed in the light. "But that means they can send you overseas."

Shit.

"Yes, but, Lexi, they won't."

"Don't lie to me, Keith."

My eyes closed, trying to find the right words. "The odds are slim."

Her hand rubbed her stomach, then she grabbed her bag. "Slim."

"Where are you going?"

She climbed down carefully, sinking into the

grass. "I need to be away from you right now."

"Wait!" I followed after her. "Lexi, stop!"

"Why?" She swung around and pointed a finger in my face. Her eyes were glossy. "Jesus Christ, Keith! Way to make the biggest decision of our lives without me."

"I didn't mean to not include you. It's something I have been thinking about for a while, and when they came to the school, it felt right."

The way her face twisted meant this was far from over.

"Right." She threaded her bag over her slender shoulder. "Anything else?"

I shook my head, tucking my hands in my pockets. She tilted her head back and let some tears slide over her flushed face.

"How could you do this? They're going to take you away from me!"

"No, no, Lexi." I reached for her, but she stepped back. Her head bent down, and her shoulders slumped.

"I…" Her hand covered her face as she caught her cry. "Of all the things you could have done!"

"This makes sense to me."

"I thought we made sense!"

"We do! Lexi, please."

Her head shot up and her anger flared. "Please understand?" she shouted, her outburst drawing the attention of a few people nearby. "Maybe I would have if you told me your plans instead of telling me after the fact!"

"Can we talk about this somewhere else?"

"Why?" She folded her arms. "You chose to

bring it up here."

"Please, Lexi."

She let her head fall back as she let out a long sigh. Then she turned on her heel and rushed off. I wanted to run after her, but I knew better.

Lexi froze me out for six weeks. After that, I wasn't allowed to bring up anything to do with the Army. If that was what it took to show her she meant more to me and that everything would be okay, I was fine with that.

CHAPTER FIVE

Several Years Later

Keith

"You gotta do what you gotta do, son." My father sat across from me in my bedroom. "However, if it counts for anything, your mother and I are very proud of you."

My uniform hung perfectly in the closet next to my duffle bag. The airline ticket stuck out of the zipper so only my name could be read.

Though I knew this moment could come, I didn't realize how fast it would arrive when I joined the Army.

I could still remember the emotion I felt when the recruiter explained the benefits and lifestyle that came with the job. It still amazed me how right it felt, like something just clicked.

Lexi had been on a summer vacation with her family in Europe and was due to return tomorrow. She would start another year at Boston University the next week.

"I'm nervous Lexi is going to freak out."

Dad put his hand on my shoulder. "She'll be scared, but she'll come around. She loves you. Besides, some more time apart may do you two some good."

"Because only seeing her on weekends isn't long enough?"

"Oh, she'll freak out." Two shrugged from the doorway. "You know I warned you about this. Lexi will be upset because you have known you were going to be deployed now since before she left."

"I know, but I knew she wouldn't go on her trip, and I didn't want to ruin that for her."

"That shouldn't have been your choice to make."

"Not helping, Danielle," my father scolded Two.

"Truth hurts, big brother." With that, she left, leaving me with a massive knot in my stomach. She was right. I kept this from Lexi because this was a trip of a lifetime that she and her family had been planning for years. I wasn't about to take that away from her. Problem was, the opportunity came with a deadline, and I didn't have a choice.

This is going to be hard.

The next day, I waited anxiously for Lexi to be finished with her meeting with her professor. Poor girl had to dive right into preparing for her classes. Thankfully, she was wired to work with numbers, so her major in accounting came naturally. She just had to get her books bought, and some other things lined up.

I pulled into her dorm parking lot to wait for her. I knew she would head back there after getting out of class. I raced to the stairs to meet her as she appeared around the building.

"Hey, you." She leaped in my arms and kissed me like she did that very first time at her place. God, I missed her! "We need to be alone, because I have all kinds of dirty thoughts I think we should act out."

And my news can wait...

Seventy minutes later, and I felt like I couldn't move to save my life. Lexi was every man's dream, wild in bed, sexy as hell, and she had a killer smile that could make me hard just thinking of it. Which only made this conversation more difficult.

"Lexi." I pulled her from her sleep. "I need to talk to you about something."

She rolled over and started to kiss my chest. Her lips did amazing things to my body. I ran my fingers through her hair and took a moment to savor this. *Stay focused.* I tilted her head and made her look at me. "I really need to tell you something."

"Okay." She sat up when she realized I was being serious. "Whatcha got for me?"

Her dark mocha eyes searched my face. It was now or never.

"Don't freak out."

"Don't do that!" She shook her head. "Saying 'don't freak out' only makes me freak out harder. Just say it, Keith."

"I was called to do a tour in Iraq."

Her body froze, then she eased to the end of the bed. She quickly pulled my t-shirt over her head and bit her finger as she absorbed my news.

"This isn't funny."

"It's not a joke."

Her beautiful eyes met mine, and the expression in them told me I was in deep shit. Lexi and I had a unique relationship. The more we fought, the more we fell in love. I was hoping that was the case this time.

"So what does this mean, exactly?" She moved to the window as her voice dropped.

I pulled my underwear and jeans on in case her roommate returned. I closed the space between us.

"Lexi." I kissed her shoulder, but she shook me off. I hooked my arm around her waist and held her tightly to my chest. "It means I ship out to Iraq in two days."

"Two days! Are you fucking kidding me? How long have you known about this?"

I dropped my gaze to the floor. "Three months." I held my hand up to stop her. "Understand I didn't tell you because I knew how important this trip was for you—for all of you."

Her hands knotted the hem of her shirt. "For how long?"

She knew the answer, because that was always a possibility when I joined the military. I knew she just needed me to say it, because then it made it real.

"A year."

I felt her breathing hitch, but instead of our normal fight, she stayed silent. That was new.

"I know it's sudden. I know I should have told you before, but that wouldn't have changed the outcome."

She wiggled out of my hold and rubbed her head

with a sniff.

"We could have had the past two months together! We're not some summer fling. We've been together for years, and you didn't give me the chance to make my own choice whether to stay here or go on my trip. You decided that me for me *again*! Not us." Her hand covered her mouth before she flinched to stop a sob. "You always said we were a team, and that we talk about everything, especially after what happened last time. But yet—" her chin quivered, "—here we are." She turned away.

"Lexi." My stomach hurt.

Her expression was pained. "If you really loved me, you would have told me what was going on. It's not like we didn't speak when I was away."

"It wasn't something I wanted to do over the phone."

Her hands shot in the air. "So you thought waiting until two days before you left for war was a *better* option?"

"I know it looks that way, but I really thought at the time it was the right call."

A long stretch of silence passed before she finally spoke. Her eyes moved to mine. "You're breaking my heart in ways that can't be repaired, Keith."

"I'm sorry, Lexi, I am."

"Sorry for deciding not to tell me? Or sorry because you wanted to spend the summer with your boys instead of me? I died a little bit every day in Europe wanting to be back in your arms, only to come home and find out you're leaving for one of the most dangerous countries in the world!" She wiped her tears free, then stripped out of my t-shirt and chucked it at me. "Get out!"

"Le—"

"Obviously, I'm not your first priority."

"That's not fair!"

"Your *boys* are waiting."

"You're being unfair."

"I'm being real, Keith. I'm making *this* decision. Now, get out!"

Just as I closed the door, I heard her whisper...

"I knew they'd take you away from me."

***

Lexi

Seven missed calls, thirteen texts, and three attempts to see me had my stubbornness at full throttle. I hadn't left my room since I kicked Keith out two days earlier. My roommate Jaci was now standing over me with a worried face.

"Lexi, he leaves in an hour. You need to see him."

"Don't," I barely got out. The mention of him made my heart break over and over.

She sighed and picked up my phone and turned it around to show me. "He's begging for you to see him off." She sat down next to me and rubbed my back as I buried my head in my pillow. "I'm going to go *there*. What if this is the last time you ever get to see him? Would you be able to live knowing you pushed him away before you had one last chance to tell him you love him?"

I sobbed into my damp pillow. She was right, but he made a huge life decision without me. We were supposed to be a team.

"So…" She ripped the blankets off my two-day-old pajamas and smacked my butt. "Get your ass up and go tell the man you love that you'll wait for him. Because that's what you'll be doing anyway."

Fine.

A half an hour later, I jumped to avoid a puddle and raced through the automatic airport doors. My heart beat like a drum in my throat.

Where are you? Where are you?

Suddenly, I spotted army camo. "Keith!" I shouted and ran up behind him. I grabbed his arm and turned him around. *Oh!* My stomach sank as a dark-haired guy looked at me oddly. My gaze dropped to his name tag. Lopez. "I-I'm sorry."

"No problem." He grinned with a wad of pink gum between his teeth. "Hope you find who you're looking for." He shifted his bag and moved on.

My mind spun as I raced to the ticket agent. Thankfully, he was flying out of a smaller airport, so he should be easier to find.

"Excuse me, but where is flight UA765?"

She gave me a smile as she clicked away on the keyboard. "Let me see." *Click, click, click, click.* Seriously, how long did it take to look up one flight? "Flight UA765 is on the taxi about to take flight." She pointed to a blue and white airplane moving toward the runway.

No!

I raced to the window and felt my temperature

drop.

"Sweetheart." His soft tone sent me running into his arms. I loved Keith's father. It was like he was my own. Heart of warmth.

"I didn't get to say goodbye," I cried, thinking what a selfish person I was. "I was so angry, then too late." I wasn't making sense. I only knew I let him leave without knowing how much I loved him.

I felt his mother rub my back, and we all held one another as we absorbed what had happened. Keith was gone.

"It's just a year, Lexi. We can do that." His father kissed my head as Nan rubbed the back of my hand. "We have one another."

Problem is we can't predict our future. We can only try and steer it the best we can.

***

Nothing felt right after Keith left, food tasted like sawdust, my grades slipped, even my beloved job at the art gallery didn't have any appeal anymore.

Six months was a long time to not enjoy life and a long time not to speak with him. The two times he called, something came up over there, and we only had a quick hello and goodbye. It stung, but what could I do?

The phone rang and rang as I dashed to grab it next to my bed.

"Hey." His voice traveled right to my heart.

Oh, I needed to hear him.

"Hi, how are you?"

There was a long stretch of silence. "Still mad at

me?"

I looked up at the ceiling as my emotions came running to the surface.

"Lexi," his voice was low but commanding, "you may hate me for my choice, but I still love you. Always will."

Tears blurred my vision, but I managed to hold it together. "So, six more months to go?"

"Yeah." He brushed off the topic, but I heard someone speak about a bombing that happened last night. "How's school going?"

Jesus, our worlds were so different right now. It was hard for me to process that, for some reason.

"Okay," he added when I didn't answer. "I'm going to come at you from a different angle. "Let me tell you about my life right now." I swallowed hard and tried to focus. "I sleep. I have nine other bunkmates. I get up when the sun rises, run drills, then we do our run through the streets of the town. Mostly, I've seen a lot of goats." I smirked at his comment. "When we're back at the base, we play a lot of cards, baseball, and soccer to make the days go by faster. What helps the best is…" A strange sound made the phone sound funny. "This." I wished I could see him right now. "I'm holding your photo in front of me. I miss you—oh, I miss you so damn much, Lex. I hate that I didn't get to say goodbye to you, but I understand. If it counts for anything, I like it here. For whatever reason, the Army makes sense to me."

I found my walls starting to build back up. It was selfish, but I hoped he would hate it and want to come home.

"I came to the airport, Keith. I came to see you off."

"You did?"

His dad must have wanted me to tell him. I should really thank him for that. He cleared his throat.

"Keith, when you're done..." a voice said in the background, sounding close. My stomach sank. Not again!

"Yes, sir," he acknowledged before he tuned back in to my call. "Sorry."

"Wow." I felt strange. "Guess you never will be Brandon."

He let out a small chuckle, and again I could hear something was there. He liked this life. "No first names in the Army; not that Brandon ever stuck, anyway."

A weak smile spread. I wished I would stop dwelling on everything. This wouldn't help him get back home safely. I really needed to pull my shit together.

"So," his voice was low, "what were you going to say to me at the airport?"

I licked my lips and went with the truth.

"That I'm mad at you for leaving, that I've never cried so hard over someone until then." He made a noise, but I kept going. "But even though I don't understand it, if this is something you need to do, then...I'll try." I leaned back against the wall and remembered what he said to me earlier. "Because I love you, Keith, always have, always will."

"Damn." He muttered something I couldn't understand. "I have to go."

My heart dropped. "Yeah, okay."

"Lexi, I need you to hear me." It was another goodbye, just what I needed. "I love you, so no more goodbyes, just a see ya."

I rolled my head upward to try to stop the tears.

"I love you too. See ya later."

The line went quiet. He was gone. He was in the middle of nowhere surrounded by people who probably wanted to see him dead.

I took some time to deal with my feelings. Turned out I needed more time that I thought.

***

El: Hey!

El: You coming to dinner Thursday?

Thursday...

El: Hello?

Later that night...

El: I can't believe you missed dinner! I had to cover for you. Made me feel great. Thanks.

Three days later...

El: Okay, Lexi, what's up? Where are you?

El: Open your door! I will come back with my key!

Five days later…

El: You have never been this distant with me. It hurts.

That one still stung. It was true we'd never gone longer than a day without a text or a call. So now that it had been six weeks, I was considered the world's worst sister.

El: I don't want to push you away, so I'll give you your space. But we're twins, I feel what you feel. You're hurting, therefore I'm hurting. Honestly, Lex, it's lonely.

I kicked my blankets to the floor, wanting to hit something. I hated that I was avoiding him. I didn't do this.

Group Text

Lexi: Meet me at The Burrell at 7 p.m.?

Almost instantly…

El: I'll be there at 7:01.

I smirked. Such a jerk.

Mom: Yes! I'll be there.

Dad: Okay.

Mom: Yay!

With a deep breath, I let off some stress, then hurried to the bathroom to get ready. I needed to be out the door in thirty minutes.

El was already there when I arrived, and he waved at me from a booth. Once I hugged him, I couldn't let go.

"I needed this." He hugged me harder.

I kissed his cheek. "Me too."

"Oh my," Mom squealed behind me. "I've missed you, Alexi!" She nearly broke my back before my father smothered me with a hug. After a few moments, he pulled back and studied my face.

"Remember, if you ever need a teddy bear…?"

I laughed and let their warmth defrost me.

"I'll always have you, Daddy."

When he smiled, his whole face brightened, and seeing that smile made me feel like I accomplished something important.

"You always have me."

We sat around the table, and instead of asking me how I was doing, we just hung out. Picked up right where we left off seven weeks ago. Why would anyone pull away from love like this? This was a great wake-up call. It was time to move forward, and if I loved him, then roll with it, and I did. So…

***

Buzz. Buzz. Buzz.

My hand patted around my night stand. Who the

83

hell was texting at 3:00 a.m.? For once, my head didn't pound. The dinner with my family last night was just what I needed.

El: 911

El: Wake up!

El: Please, Lexi! Pick up.

El: ANSWER YOUR PHONE.

What?

I quickly answered the persistent ring.

"This better be important."

"Lexi? Fuck, finally!"

"El?" I sat straight up at his tone. "What's going on?"

There was silence, then I heard it—the page of a doctor.

"Why are you at the hospital?"

A sob ripped through the line and nearly brought my heart to a complete stop.

"Mom, Dad." His eerie cry froze my blood. "They stopped for gas on the way home from dinner, and someone…shot them."

A deep ache spread along my skin and jabbed me right in the center of the heart. Everything around me melted away. I was on my bed in the dark, with no words.

"Alexi, I need you to come to the hospital and help me."

"Where?" The words barely came out.

"Boston Memorial."

I dropped the phone and raced to get ready. My hands were numb as I clawed at the tops of my leggings.

"What's going on?" Jaci squinted at the light.

I grabbed my keys and left.

***

Keith

"Johnson! Pick up your shit!" I barked at one of my bunkmates. I was tired of tripping over his stuff.

He gave a curt nod before he started folding his clothes. When I arrived here, right off the bat, I had trouble. For some reason, Snider had a problem with me. It didn't take long to see I needed to look out for myself. So the next time he came at me to show off, I chopped his windpipe and elbowed his rib cage. Not enough to break it, just enough to bruise it. Turned out I was a quick study in hand to hand combat.

Now the men had respect for me, and that was all I ever asked for, anyway.

I rushed to the truck to start my shift.

"Keith," Green's voice cracked over the radio. "To your left."

I raised my binoculars and peered along the mountain peak. Henderson groaned as he lost his lunch into a small dugout he made. Thankfully, we had stopped for a break before he got sick. We'd been on the road for two hours, and my mouth was dry and my lips were cracked. Even my teeth felt gritty.

I knew holding still was worse. It was safer to be a moving target. We really needed to move.

With my stomach on the ground and my elbows propped up under the truck, I was covered well enough not to be seen. Using my shoulder to hit the button, I muttered, "So far, all is clear."

"Henderson, to your three o'clock," Green ordered from about twenty feet to my left. He and Henderson were hidden in some dry brush.

Henderson laughed into the radio in his dizzy state. "Ahh."

"Sorry, didn't copy that. Is there or isn't there an enemy pointing a gun at us?" Green joked.

Mic and Joe, two other men from our unit, raced to meet them and made it to cover as I watched their path. They moved to higher ground to see what was ahead.

"All clear," Mic jumped in on the radio. "Keith, we're coming to your—"

BOOM!

The bang was so loud, it blew my reality. My hands, arms, legs, feet, everything felt independent from my body. Noise felt like liquid as the shockwaves rippled over me. My eyes squeezed shut to keep out the sand. Jamming my tongue through my teeth for some padding, I waited out the horrible pain.

I wasn't sure how long it was before I started to come to. My lungs burned, and something smelled terrible.

"Yalla!"

The yelling made my body jolt and stiffen when

I heard the language. It was Arabic, and they were saying 'hurry.' That was when a pair of boots stepped down out of a Hummer and raced off toward the road. Was I still armed? My left arm moved around my leg and felt my knife. Well, that was something in case they returned.

I wasn't sure what happened, but I sure as hell wasn't about to make any sudden movements. So for the next ten minutes, I focused on making sure everything worked on my body. Other than my shoulder, I was good enough.

Scraping my forearms along the dirt, I inched out from under the truck and stood on shaking legs. My equilibrium was off, and my head beat like a drum. *What the hell just happened?* Confusion could be a tricky thing. Like, did you move? Or stay put? Were you still in danger? Or should you move and help your buddies who weren't moving? So much rode on what had happened.

"Keith!" I spun at Green's voice and saw him staggering in my direction. Holy shit, he only had half an arm. His body was covered in blood, and his exposed muscle was twitching. "Where is everyone?"

My palms slammed into his chest as he fell into me. His face was white as a sheet, and beads of sweat clung to his forehead.

Everything rushed to me at once. I sat Green on the ground, and with heavy legs, forced myself to find the others. I heard chopper blades in the distance and looked up, but the moment I did, I tripped over something.

"Shit!" I yelped and quickly shuffled backward

away from Henderson's torso. His head was a few yards away.

"Mic!" Joe took his friend's hand and rolled him onto his side. "Mic, wake up."

In my stunned state, I dropped to my knees and evaluated the two of them. Mic was gone, and Joe was missing one of his feet.

Something flashed off to my left, and I freed Mic's gun and held it up to my face.

My heartbeat evened, the cries of my men disappeared, and the pain in my head vanished. I slipped into survival mode. Moving to balance on my knee, I scanned the area and waited.

I felt the prickle start at the bottom of my spine, and it spread like milk coating the curves of my muscles. My brain was super alert and everything locked in place.

Zip! Zip!

Two bullets whipped by my ear, and I jumped over Mic to shield Joe.

"4:30!" Green shouted the direction from his slumped position.

I jerked around and saw the bastard, and without a thought, I pulled the trigger and sprayed bullets, sending him backward.

Two more men showed themselves, and I annihilated them.

"Keith!" Joe shrieked as a guy charged at me.

I turned and shot him twice in the face.

"*Ahhh*! Anyone else?" I shouted more as a release than anything else. I moved back to Joe, who was still trying to get Mic to wake.

"Lean back," I ordered. When he didn't listen, I

pulled their hands apart. "Joe, he's gone. If you don't let me pack your wound, you will be too."

He finally nodded and looked away, squeezing his eyes shut. I made quick work, keeping my mind focused on what I had on me and what resources we had to get out of there.

"Wow," Joe's face lit up, "it's so close."

I didn't want to know what he was seeing. If he muttered about a white light, I was going to have to slap him.

Dirt flew into my face, blinding me, and a moment later hands lifted me up and helped me to my feet. The *only* reason I didn't put up a fight was the American flag on his shoulder. The others were hoisted in, and we were in the air.

I watched as the truck got smaller and smaller. Joe stared at the sky, and Green was out cold. Henderson and Mic were off to the side with a blanket over them.

"How?" I mouthed to one of the men. How did they get here so quick?

"Delta Three saw the attack, called it in."

I sank in the corner and tried to understand why I was spared. I imagined if I could hold time. I pictured a bedsheet laid perfectly flat. Life going by smoothly with just a few wrinkles here and there. Then someone comes along and pulls the middle up, causing life to rush by quickly all around you. Speeding up events, attacks, loss, everything without warning. Then, just as fast as the rush came, it smooths back out and things continue on at normal speed. Only problem with that was your head was still trying to process what the hell just happened.

How was it one moment you were fighting for your life, and the next it was all over? How was that flaw not fixed when whoever it was created us? My brain was hurting.

The vibration from the chopper made Mic's face appear from behind the heavy blanket. I started at him for a bit, then closed my eyes and let my mind try to sort through everything the best it could.

After a couple of days in the hospital and some psychological tests, I was released with orders to stay at the base for the next few days. I really wasn't sure why, because as confused as my mind was it was now perfectly clear. The fog of confusion had lifted, and I felt good. I was okay.

I grabbed a case of beer and headed toward the tanks and crawled up on one of them. It was a good spot to see the stars and gave an entire panoramic view of the fenced-in base.

Green and Joe were going to be fine, but they had a long road ahead of them. Henderson and Mic were on their way home in wooden boxes.

Home.

With the side of the cap resting on the edge of the truck, I knocked it off smoothly and took my first sip of beer since I'd been here. *Oh, it was good.*

"I thought only I came here." A man I'd seen around a few times stood at the front of the wheel well. He wasn't one of us; he was a general. I sat a little straighter to show respect.

"You look like you may need it more than me." He smiled.

There was something genuine about him. I

knocked off the top of another beer and held it up as an offering.

"Thank you." He nodded before he jumped onto the tire and hiked himself up effortlessly. He took the cold beer and tapped it to mine. "General Logan."

"Private Keith."

"I know who you are, Private." He squinted as he looked up at the clear sky. "I've had my eye on you since you arrived. What happened the other day was rough, but the way you performed was impressive."

"With all due respect, General, I killed four men and let two of my own die, and the others will never serve again. Not so sure how that could be considered impressive."

He peeled at the corner of the label. He didn't remove it, just strummed his thumb as if he played a guitar.

"You were the only one who was left and able to fight, and you did. They may not be able to serve, but they get to go home to their families, and *that* was because of *you*." He looked at me, and his face changed. "I am sorry about Henderson and Mic."

I appreciated that he knew their names and nodded, taking another drink in memory of them. They were good men and good friends.

"It's hard to lose to someone. Sometimes it plays on you a lot harder when you're over here. You don't have the time to grieve, and if you do, it's not the way we're used to. If you're struggling with it, that's normal. Why not join some of us on the ridge Friday night? We have our own way of saying goodbye."

The general set his empty bottle down before he rubbed his hands together, and I felt the mood change. "Have you ever thought about special ops?"

"That's the plan someday."

"Why don't we meet up tomorrow at my base and discuss a few things? You're off this week. It won't matter if you're at this base or mine."

At least that was something to occupy my head.

"Sure."

"Chopper will be here at oh-eight-hundred."

CHAPTER SIX

I jumped down and ran away from the blades to give the pilot the polite thumbs up that he was clear to leave. It took me only a moment to feel the vibe of the base was off.

"Hey." I stepped in the way of a soldier. "What happened?"

"IED killed three more," he muttered before he rushed off.

Shit.

"Keith!" My sergeant waved me over. I jogged to where he was staring at three computer screens where newscasters were reporting today's events.

"Jesus."

"I need you out tomorrow. We're short staffed until the next round comes in." He eyed me over his shoulder. "You've proven to the men you're smart in the field. We need more of that."

With a quick nod, I waited to see if there was anything else.

"Keith," someone said from behind me. "This came for you."

93

Leaning forward, I took the scrap paper from him.

Call me ASAP—Lexi

Call home—Dad

My stomach twisted as I asked for permission to use the satellite phone. I stepped inside an adjoining room and dialed her number.

"Hello?" Her voice was quiet.

"Lexi, what's wrong?"

A strange noise brushed up against the phone before I heard her cries. "They're dead, Keith, they are both dead."

I snapped my eyes up to the ceiling. "Who? Who is dead, Lex?"

"My parents. They were shot."

A massive ball lodged in my throat as I fought to keep things down. "Oh my God, babe. I...I don't know what to say. When?"

"Two days ago."

"What in God's name happened?"

More quiet sobs found my pounding ears. I pressed my hand against my chest to try to calm my wildly beating heart. I was desperately working hard to process it all.

"Keith." There was a pause. "I need you to come home."

Fuck.

"Elliot has shut down and keeps disappearing. We have some family here we don't even know. Touching everything—it's just a mess." She hiccupped as more sobs came. "I feel as if I'm spinning faster and faster, and when it stops, I'm not sure what will be left. I really need you here, Keith."

Shit, shit, shit! I moved further away from listening ears.

"Lexi, there is nowhere else in the world I'd rather be than right there with you." I took a deep breath, knowing this was going to crush her further. "But, there's been…issues, and we're short some men. We're all pulling double shifts until the new guys arrive. I can't come home right now. I really want to, and I'll work on it, but I just can't."

"Lexi?" A familiar voice could be heard in the background, and my mind scrambled to place it. "Can we talk?"

She let out a deep sigh. "Please, Keith, try. I really need you."

I wanted to ask who was there with her, but I decided not to play the jealous boyfriend card. Lexi had never given me a reason to distrust her.

"You have my word. I love you, Lexi. See ya later."

"I love you too."

The line went dead, and I was left in shock and confusion.

I took a moment to say something nice about her parents in my form of a prayer. They were wonderful people who had loved their children unconditionally.

I made a quick call to my own parents to ask them to check in on her as much as possible. Turned out Mom was already on her way over there with a bottle of wine and takeout.

"You keep your head focused on your own safety, son." My father cleared his throat. I knew he was watching the news. "We will take care of Lexi. You just make sure you get home in one piece."

"Love ya, Dad."

"I love you too, son, and I'm very proud of you."

I pushed the guilt aside and enjoyed my father's voice. He was my rock, and I couldn't imagine him not in my life.

Oh, Lexi, I wish I could hold you.

***

Some of my buddies who were struggling from the latest attacks started to gather outside the cafeteria. It suddenly clicked that it was Friday night, so I took a bottle of water and headed out to join them.

The sergeant pulled up in a green truck, and we all hopped in the back. No one said much on the way over. Most just stared down at their feet. Spirits were low, and I wondered if this was how it was going to be for the rest of my time here.

I had no clue where we were going, but the fact that we were moving along without fear of an IED exploding made me relax a bit, and I was able to shake off some of the heaviness.

Once we made it over to the far right side of the base, we stopped at the foot of a high mountain. You could see the peak in the distance. Jumping out, I saw four men were already there with a roaring bonfire and tubs of beer.

"You came." General Logan gave me a friendly nod and joined my side.

"I did." He handed me a beer. "Thank you, sir."

"I heard you got a phone call yesterday."

How did he know?

"I did." I pushed the hurt down. "My girlfriend's parents were murdered at a gas station."

"I'm really sorry about that, son." His tone was sincere, and I knew he really did mean it. The more I got to know the general, the more I liked him. "How's she dealing with it?"

"Not that great."

"I don't imagine."

"How ironic is it that our loved ones back home are being killed senselessly? It's supposed to be here in this godforsaken place that those things are expected to happen."

"I hear you. Sometimes it makes no sense, no sense at all."

A private climbed up on the lip of the cliff and waited for us to quiet down.

"Hello." His voice was thick with an accent. "I'm from Alaska, and my name is Private Tikaani, which means wolf." He cleared his throat. "Thank you for coming tonight. I know a lot of us have lost some close friends, and even family. We don't have our loved ones with us to mourn, so I thought it would be nice to say goodbye in a different way."

I moved closer so I could hear better.

"In my family, we would gather like this around the elements of life." He gathered some dirt in his hand and let it sprinkle out the bottom. "We have earth, air, fire, and water." He pointed to his beer

97

with a smile, and a few chuckled.

"Right now, we are one with the universe. Now it's time to let hurt go and let their energy be free." He then pointed to the sky. "We have the souls of our ancestors to help guide our loved ones on to their next journey. Normally, we'd sit around and share stories, but sometimes it's not enough, sometimes we need a jolt to the system."

He smiled again right before a loud bang went off behind us. We all jumped out of our skin, only to laugh when a bright green spark of fire shot into the air and burst into a trillion sparkles.

General Logan smacked my shoulder with a laugh, then we watched as more and more fireworks were set off into the night sky.

Tikaani was right. We did need a jolt to the system to let go and move forward.

Afterward, I found myself picking his brain. I enjoyed the way Tikaani looked at life. It was refreshing and made sense. He gave me hope in an otherwise hopeless situation. I shared my situation with Lexi, and he seemed to be a great shoulder to lean on.

***

The next few months blew by. I asked many times to go home, but since Lexi wasn't my wife or immediate family, and due to the shortage of men, they wouldn't even consider it. Regardless, it was a hard thing to hear.

There were definite pros and cons to being a good soldier. You were on everyone's radar, and because of that you got pulled into multiple tasks. I barely had a moment to stop and often found myself a walking zombie. Bed was my savior.

I tried to call Lexi, but honestly, I wasn't sure what to say. I knew whenever we hung up it got harder and harder for her. So, I struggled to know what to do, thinking when I got home and she was in my arms and she knew I was safe I could explain things.

General Logan always seemed to be around. He never said much; he just watched. We'd had several discussions, and I knew he wanted to recruit me to his special ops program eventually. I knew he had some sort of private base mid-country somewhere. The details were "need to know" and only if I was interested and ready for it. I knew I wasn't ready, and I needed to do a few years in Washington first. I had a lot more to learn. Besides, joining him would mean I had to move there, and that wasn't in my plans. I wanted to ask Lexi to marry me, and I knew I would need to talk it over with her. I wasn't going to fall into that trap again.

I opened the small wooden box and placed a bright green stone Tikaani had given me in it. He had explained it meant *hope* to his people, and there was a little note inside. Flowers were carved around the curved lid, and little circles raced around the border. Locking it shut with its tiny hook, I wrapped it up in bubble wrap and put it in the envelope. I handed it off to my buddy who would add it to the outgoing mail. I may be miles away, but she'd at least know I was thinking of her.

"Keith." My sergeant stood in the door of my

corridor. "I need to speak with you."

***

Lexi

I didn't feel much anymore. I got up go to school, where I didn't retain much, and came home. I then slept and did it all over again. I barely saw Elliot. He'd been hanging out with Antonio and his crew. I guessed they helped him cope. Frankly, the *Almas Perdidas* scared the shit out of me. They were a nasty street gang with ties to the Crips in L.A. Antonio had been up for murder twice, but somehow it was always someone else who did it. Although I did like his brother, Juan. He had been around a lot, making sure I was all right, and for that I was very grateful.

My finger dug under the tab and ran across the sticky paper to free the letter. It had been sitting on my counter for three days. It was from my school, and I had pretty good idea what it was.

We regret to inform you that you have been dropped from four of your classes.
Therefore, you need to reenroll next year.

Of course, more shit to add to the pile. I rubbed my head and tried not to let the loneliness sink back in. It was a constant battle since I moved back into my parents' house. It was the right choice, as I had found a distant cousin sifting through my dad's financial records one afternoon. It didn't take me long to realize I didn't have anyone left but Elliot. The last notice to pay the mortgage haunted me, and I knew it was only a matter of time before I had to sell the house. Things were falling apart, not just on the inside, but now on the outside.

My phone vibrated and my stomach rolled as I picked it up.

Jessica: Hi sweetheart, just making sure you're doing okay since we spoke about Keith. I know it's hard, but this wasn't a choice for him. Call whenever. We love you, Lexi. Xo.

My heart twisted and the pain came on full force. I hated everything about the Army. I hated that Keith left, and the fact that he chose to put himself in constant danger festered inside me. And now he said he had to stay an extra two months!

I jumped off the counter and rested my head on the cool marble. I wanted to cry and hit something all at the same time. Life wasn't fair. Bottom line, this mess was all my doing. If I hadn't been in that office and witnessed that horrible, sadistic shit, my family would still be safe and happy in Canada.

But you wouldn't have Keith, my mind reminded me. The hell with that. I didn't have him now, anyway.

My gaze flipped up to the little wooden box I got in the mail yesterday. I couldn't bring myself to read the note yet, but the stone was gorgeous, and I hoped to make it into a necklace someday. It was thoughtful of him, and I would cherish it forever. Keith was always so considerate, I thought to myself, then a flash of anger pushed aside the good feeling and took over.

Everyone seemed to be moving forward, and I was stuck here with my memories of death and with no one who cared enough to help me. Even Elliot was always off with his new buddies and that *girl.*

None of this was fair! I kicked the buffet behind me. A drawer flew forward and fell to the floor.

I dropped to my knees and starting picking up the things that had fallen out and stopped when I found a little black baggie. Curious, I opened it and dropped three joints onto my hand. *Oh, Dad.*

With a glass of wine and a joint between my fingers, I headed out to the back porch and curled up on an overstuffed chair. The back yard looked over a small lake that we shared with three other homes. It was peaceful and exactly what I needed at the moment. Lighting the tip, I watched as the orange flame nipped away at the green bud. With a deep suck, I drew the smoke into my lungs and waited for the trip I hoped would come. Anything was better than the feeling of anger that had been building for the past month and half.

My phone vibrated, so I pulled it free from my sweater.

Ken: Getting a little worried about you, sweetheart. It's been three weeks since we've seen you.

I closed my eyes. I knew they worried; they'd

been wonderful through everything that had happened. However, the last time I was over, they were so loving and warm toward the four sisters, and so supportive of Keith, that I felt even more empty and even more like an outsider. All I brought to anyone was a dark cloud I couldn't seem to shake. No one wanted to be around someone who was angry and depressed. It just pulled the mood down in any room I was in.

Lexi: I'm all right, just need some time to think. Xo.

Ken: Our door is always open and we are always just a phone call away.

Hot tears stung my eyes while I pushed away yet another person. How did I explain the level of darkness growing inside? It almost scared me. It was starting to consume me to a point where happiness didn't even seem appealing anymore.

My phone went off again, and I almost cursed out the Keith family, but I turned it over and saw it wasn't them at all.

Juan: Be ready in ten. On my way over.

Juan was the one person who didn't want to know how I was doing. He was just bored and wanted to hang out. He was nothing like his brother Antonio.

Lexi: Back porch, ready when you are.

Here we go.

***

I should have been pissed. I should have been nervous of the outcome. I should have cared, but I didn't. The cop gave me a scolding for hanging inside the university pool after hours. Juan and I had brought a case of beer to the pool just to hang out somewhere warm. Thirty minutes later, we were sitting inside a squad car getting a lecture from an old high school friend, Clark, now Officer Clark Adams.

He removed Juan after reading him his rights and had someone take him to the station, as he had some prior convictions.

"What the hell, Lex?" Clark twisted around in his seat to talk to me, looking confused.

I shrugged. His eyes softened as he looked out the window at his partner.

Clark had always been there for me, even when my parents...I rubbed my neck, uncomfortable even thinking the words. I knew Keith told him to watch out for me, and it was nice, but I didn't want that now.

"We've spoken about this before, Lexi. Juan is not someone to be hanging around with. Nothing but bad news follows the guy. Look, I'll give you a warning, but you have to get your shit together. He and Antonio are at the top of the *Almas Perdidas*, and they are dangerous men."

Here comes the speech.

"They kill people for no reason. They just beat

up the clerk at the auto shop because he called the cops when he found evidence of blood in their trunk. He won't be able to walk again for a long-ass time." He checked the time on his phone, then thought for a moment. "Is this because of Elliot, you know, hanging out with them?"

That hurt a bit. Elliot did spend a lot of time with Antonio and their sister. I guessed there was a part of me that just wanted to see what he saw in them. Plus, I wanted my brother back.

He waited for me to respond, but I just looked away. He sighed and turned back around, then we left the campus.

The ride was quiet, and Clark kept watching me in the rearview mirror. I knew he wanted me to speak, but I had nothing to say.

"Two more months until Keith comes home. That must be exciting for you."

My eyes met his in the mirror and held them there for a moment before I went back to the window. *He should have been back now.*

We rolled into my driveway, and I waited for him to open my door since it was locked. The moment he did, I stepped out and slipped my bag over my shoulder.

"Hey." He grabbed my arm, turning me to look at him. "Lexi."

"I'm not fine, Clark." My honesty shocked me, but I went with it, with my arms in the air. "Not sure if I ever will be."

"Keith will be home soon. Things will all be okay then."

I stared him down for his comment before I gave

him a squeeze on the arm.

"Thank you for the ride home, and the free pass."

With that, I went back into my dark, empty, lifeless house.

I ended up turning off my phone as a number of texts and calls came through from Keith's parents. Clark couldn't keep his mouth shut.

***

That was how I spent the next two weeks, seeing as little of the light of day as possible.

Go away, world.

"Hey!" His muffed voice echoed through the dark living room. "Open up!"

Peeling myself off the couch, I trudged to the door, unlocking it, and found myself face to face with Juan and a bottle of vodka.

"Thought you might be up for a little fun." He stepped inside and looked around. "Umm, love what you did with the place." He kicked a pizza box before he handed me my jacket.

"I didn't know you were out of jail." My arm got caught up in the sleeve, and I pulled out a scarf, tossing it on the back of the couch.

"Never in there for long." He winked. "Now, let's go have some fun."

Sure, why not?

***

Keith

The second my feet hit the tarmac, I let out a long, heavy breath. I was home. Forty minutes later, I was debriefed, had returned my M-16, and was issued my leave pass. *Freedom!*

With a shift of my duffle bag, I headed toward my mother. She was already crying, and my father was grinning like he just won the lotto. My sisters were holding a sparkly sign that read *'Welcome Home, Big Brother!'*

I scanned the crowd but didn't see her. I pushed the disappointment down and ran into my mom's arms. I was such a momma's boy, and I didn't care.

"Oh, my boy!" She sobbed into my shoulder. "I barely recognized you."

"I missed you so much." I squeezed her hard before my dad pulled me into his hug.

"You're in one piece, and that's all I wanted to see." I knew he was proud, but he worried about what went on over there.

My sisters took their turns mauling me. I shared a moment with each until I got to Two, who gave me a worried look.

"Where is she?" I asked.

"She wanted us to have our time first."

I almost rolled my eyes at such a ridiculous notion. Like she wasn't part of the family.

"Look, she's really not herself since you left, and when her parents died, something changed." She grabbed my arm. "Seriously, I'm worried about her."

"Okay." I gave the best smile I could before I

107

kissed her cheek.

"So, son." Dad came to my side. "What would you like to do first?"

I looked around at the rest of the soldiers, some who had become like family and who were greeting their loved ones, some meeting their newborn children for the first time with such happiness. I turned back to my parents and sisters.

"I wanna go home!"

"I like that idea." He grinned and offered to take my bag. I let him because he needed to do something. I understood that.

"Wait!" Tikaani called out from behind me. "Here." He handed me a key chain with a small carved wolf in sandstone. "Something to remember the fallen and how to let go Alaskan style."

I pulled him into a hug and patted his shoulder.

"Thank you, Tikaani. Keep in touch, you hear?"

"Same to you, brother."

Once we got home, I ran up to my room and took a long shower. Wiping the mirror clear, I looked at myself and realized Iraq changed me, but in a good way. Though we had lost a lot of great men, I knew the Army was made for me.

My thumb hovered over the screen of my phone.

Keith: *I'm home, you going to come over? Or would you like me to come and get you?*

Lexi: *Happy to hear that. You need to be with your family right now.*

Seriously?

Keith: *You are my family too.*

Nothing.

I got dressed and found my mother in the kitchen. "Do you mind if I slip out real quick before the barbeque? I promise I won't be more than an hour."

Her face softened; she knew what I was doing.

"Of course not, sweetheart."

I kissed her cheek and waved at Nan, who smirked back at me. I knew she had a ton to share with me, but right now I needed to find Lexi.

Keith: *Hey, dude, any idea where Lexi might be?*

Clark: *If she's not hiding out in her house, she'd be at the Almas Perdidas clubhouse.*

What the fuck?

Keith: *Funny. Where is she?*

Clark: *You have a lot of catching up to do, my friend. AP clubhouse.*

Sure enough, she wasn't home, so I pulled into the clubhouse parking lot. I'd never had a problem with this gang, but I sure as shit wanted nothing to do with them.

It suddenly clicked whose voice was on the phone when Lexi called me about her parents. Juan Garcia was a punk who had seen the inside of a jail cell more than Clark had as a cop.

With a push, I opened the heavy door and stepped into the dark, nasty clubhouse, a pool table off to the left and a long bar top along the back.

There was Lexi in ripped jeans and a tank, holding a beer in her hand. She was just as I remembered. Beautiful. Juan had his arm around the back of her bar stool. My fists clenched by my sides as the need to stay calm rushed through me.

"Hey." My voice was low and raspy.

She turned, sending her long, shiny hair over her shoulder. Her expression was stunned when she took me in.

"Hi." A forced smile ran along her lips, and pain showed itself for a moment before she slid off the stool and wrapped her arms around my mid-section.

She flinched when I squeezed her a little too hard. She leaned back to look at me.

"You got a lot bigger."

"And you're in a bar drinking at ten in the morning. You remembered I was coming home today, right?"

"I thought you might like some time with your family first." She glanced over at Juan. He was watching us carefully.

I hated this. Something was definitely off.

My hand slipped into hers. "Can we go talk somewhere?"

She grabbed her purse and followed me out to my truck.

Our ride to the lake was quiet. I held her hand for a bit, but she pulled away and just stared out the window, her shoulders tense and her mouth in a tight line. This was not how I pictured my homecoming.

Parking the truck in our spot, I turned to look at her. Everything about her body language showed she was totally closed off.

"I can't believe how much I missed you."

Her gaze dropped to her lap with a sniff.

"Yeah," she said on an exhale.

Really, that was it? My hurt rose to the surface.

"So, you're hanging out with Juan Garcia now? The *Almas Perdidas* are insane, Lex."

Her brow rose when she looked over at me.

"He's my friend."

I couldn't help but laugh. "He's not your friend, Lexi. Those guys don't have friends. They have people they use when shit goes down."

"Well, at least *he* was there for me when my parents…left."

Ouch.

Her face flinched. I was sure she didn't mean it, but it still hurt.

"Lexi." I squeezed her hand. "You know I would have done anything to have come back here after that happened."

"But you didn't."

"I couldn't!" I snapped back.

"I don't think you understand the damage you've done here, Keith. You made two life changing decisions for me. To join the army and to not tell me you were leaving me. For more than a year, FYI." She removed her hand from mine and ran it along her head. "You chose to leave, not me. A lot has happened since then, and I don't know if I can or even want to do this anymore."

"What?" No! "Lexi, please don't cut me out because I did something for us!"

Her head shot around to me, tears threatening to fall. "Us? There was never an *us* when you chose to leave *me* with only a two day notice!"

I shook my head, not sure what to do. She was right. It was screwed up that I left so quickly, but it was something I thought would make our lives better. "So, what, you have feelings for Juan now?"

She didn't answer me, and my stomach twisted into a painful ball.

"Have you slept with him?"

"Are you kidding me?" She undid her seatbelt and hopped down to the ground.

"Lexi!" I did the same, rounding the back of the truck.

"Screw you, Keith!"

"Hey!" I raced after her, tugging on her arm and holding her in place. "Can you honestly tell me you feel nothing for me anymore?"

She closed her eyes as if to control herself.

My voice lowered as my hope floated away.

"What the hell happened to the woman I fell in love with?"

"I wish I knew." She broke into a sob. "Nothing has been right since you left. I'm lost and have no idea if I even *want* to go back!"

It was like a kick to the stomach when I realized what she was really saying.

"Are you—" I could barely say the words. For 425 days, she was what kept me going, what kept me safe, and what kept my mind sharp. Without

Lexi, what was there? "Are you breaking up with me?"

Her red, glossy eyes slowly rose to meet mine. She didn't have to say any more before I stepped back, feeling as if all the loneliness I pushed away while I was over there had come back in one whoosh to envelop me now. I *was* alone.

"Please, Lexi, don't do this."

"We are two different people now. I barely remember who I was when I was with you." She gave me an angry "whatever" kind of look and turned away.

I grabbed her face so she'd look at me, hurt burned inside me, clawing at my stomach. "Give me time to remind you."

"No, I'm not that girl anymore. I told you that!" She spat the words out as she pulled out her cell phone and made a call to a cab service.

We stood five feet apart, but it felt more like miles. Neither of us said a word, my heart was breaking…and hers was with someone else.

When the cab showed up, she looked at me for a second as if she wanted to say something but stopped herself. With that, she was gone. My whole world crumbled around me as she climbed into a cab and left me on the day I returned home from war.

I punched the side of my truck before I headed back home. *How did we get here?*

***

"Here." Clark handed me a beer as he took a seat

next to me on the porch. It had been two months since I'd come home, since Lexi broke up with me. I tried many times to get her back, but she wasn't having any of it.

"You okay, man?"

"No," I sighed into my beer. Clark was the one friend I could be honest and open with.

"Lexi still keeping you shut out?"

"Yeah."

"Give her time."

"I have, but she hates me. She doesn't want what I want anymore."

Clark sank into a chair. "She just doesn't want to be happy. She's angry with you for leaving, and she blames herself for her parents' death. It's easier to hate right now because it makes the guilt a little more tolerable."

"That's ridiculous. Her parents' death had nothing to do with her."

"Like the bombing that killed some of your men wasn't your fault," he countered. He had a point. I did struggle with my own guilt over the loss of the men in my unit, but I knew it wasn't my fault. I just didn't understand why I was spared and they weren't. But I didn't let it consume me or ruin my life.

"Is she with Juan?" I needed to know the truth.

He gave me a look I knew all too well. "I honestly don't know, but if I was to guess, I would say yes."

"Sweetheart?" My mother stood in the door way holding the cordless. "Phone call."

I knew who it was. I had to call a lot of people in

the chain of command to get to him.

Before I left, I turned around. "Clark, promise me something?

"Sure."

"If I'm not around, please watch out for her."

His eyes narrowed, but he gave me a small nod. "You know I will."

Setting my beer down, I took the call.

"Hello."

"Private Keith, this is General Logan, returning your call."

"Nice to hear from you, sir." I glanced at my father, who was reading in the room across from me. "If the offer still stands, I'll take it."

CHAPTER SEVEN

Present Day

Keith

I studied her, watched her mannerisms, tried to learn what her next move would be so I could beat her at her own game. I ducked left before she dove right. Her eyes squinted, and I thought I had her figured, but before I knew it, green fingers poked my nose.

"Oh, you got me!" I fell off my chair and rolled dramatically around on the floor. She giggled and shrieked for me to do it again. "Poisoned by something so cute. When will I learn?" Tongue clucking behind me caused me to freeze. I cocked my head to the side and waited.

"Really, Keith?" Savannah stood over me, clearly unimpressed. "More finger painting? You know she makes a huge mess, then tries to eat it."

Oliva reached out and swiped at her mother's arm, covering her sweater in green goo.

I couldn't hold back a smile at her expression. Savannah didn't get mad. She pretended to, but she didn't. Not that we'd ever tell her that. She liked to think she had an edge, when really she was just adorable. She reminded me so much of my sister, Two. Savannah grounded me, especially when I was homesick. We'd been close for a long time. I had always felt protective of her since she arrived here. I watched her relationship with Cole grow and develop into the deep bond they had now. She let me be the older brother I needed to be, and I let her be my little sister. It all worked, and this pint-sized devil covered in paint was a delightful product of all that.

"You think that's funny, Keith?" She unscrewed a bottle of blue paint and held it over my head.

"You wouldn't."

Her eyes moved to the two available escape routes. Oh, shit, she was actually considering it.

"You better run like the damn wind if you—"

The cold goo hit my neck, and in a split second she dropped the container and flew out of the kitchen and into the hallway. Of course she ran in Cole's direction for help. I grabbed Olivia and tucked her football style under my arm as I chased Savannah, her shrieks of delight adding to the pandemonium.

"Cole!" She laughed as she ran, ducking around Mark, who tried to intervene. I shoved Olivia into his arms as I raced by him. Savannah burst into Cole's office, only to find him on the phone. We both came to an abrupt halt when he gave us a strange look.

117

"Sorry, baby," she whispered and started to back up.

I bent down and code-45ed her out of the office, while she pounded uselessly at my back from her inverted position over my shoulder. Cole gave me a smirk before he went back to his call. He loved that we had fun. Our job could be serious most of the time, and Savannah was a much needed outlet for all of us here at Shadows.

"You are gonna get it now, Savi."

"Mark!" she yelped, but Mark just waved as he jammed a cookie into his mouth and pressed a tiny bit into Olivia's as well.

"We're near outta the peanut butter cookies, Savi." Crumbs sprayed as he laughed at her middle finger. "Always a lady. Don't you learn bad things from Mommy, sweetheart." He pretended to cover Liv's eyes before she wiggled to get free and raced off.

"Don't you know it," she said as she hung over my shoulder, still hitting my back for me to put her down. My phone vibrated in my pocket. I held up my hand to her as I pulled it free.

Shit.

Another tap to my shoulder brought me back momentarily.

"Seconds thoughts on the payback?"

I lowered Savannah to the floor, and when I did, my phone dropped. Before I could grab it, Savannah nabbed it and glanced at the screen.

Her eyebrows pinched together like the bold woman she was, she started scrolling through my texts.

118

"Ah, my phone, please."

She held up a finger for me to wait. I rolled my eyes and took a seat on the chair.

"So." Her mouth twisted. "All this time, all those texts you were getting, and this is who it was?"

"Sometimes, yes."

"Sometimes?"

"None of your business, thank you very much."

"Umm." She looked back to the screen. "So when do you leave?"

"Tomorrow. Flight leaves at one p.m."

She came and sat down next to me. "Who is Clark?"

I leaned forward and tried to grab my phone, but she moved it out of my reach.

"He's a friend from back home. We grew up together."

"Oh." Her eyes lit up. "Will I meet him at the wedding?"

"Maybe, if you give me back my phone."

"Will he tell me stories about you?"

"I'm sure Clark will come up with all kinds of lies for you to hear." Her face fell, and I was curious what she found now.

"Who is this?"

All the heartache that came with that picture came roaring back.

"You have a lot of her. *Damn,* Keith, she's gorgeous."

I know.

"Someone I once knew."

"Someone, like an ex?" Her eyes widened. "Holy shit, look how young you were here. Oh, you two

119

look so cute. You must like her, because you would have had to send those to your phone. They're older."

I rolled my eyes and snatched the phone away. I didn't want to talk about Lexi. No reason to rub salt on an old wound.

"She must be important for you to still keep her photos."

"Savi," Mark called out, holding Olivia like she might bite him. "Your child smells like old beans, and frankly, I can't handle it. Cole and I voted, and you won. Here." He brought the little lady over to her mommy, who scooped her up and kissed her chubby cheeks. "When will she be potty trained?"

"She's just walking, Mark. How about we don't rush my daughter through her childhood?"

He laughed. "Just give me a date, and I'll mark the calendar."

"Daddy owes Mommy big time." Savannah's face scrunched at the smell. "I know; why don't we leave your diaper in his office so he can have a little taste of what you make after he feeds you from his plate?"

"Oh, please, let me tape it." Mark smirked.

"If you play dumb when it happens, I'll let you show the world."

Mark high fived her, and then sprawled out on the couch across from me. There was a small part of me that envied Mark. He had no problem showing the world how he felt, and he got the girl of his dreams. He had a rough go as a child, at least with his family, but he sure lucked out after meeting the Logans.

"How's Mia feeling, Mark?"

He rubbed his face, but he couldn't hide the fact he was extremely excited. "Like she's having twins."

"How long until you find out the sex? A few more weeks, right?"

"Next month." He yawned. "Are you looking forward to going home?"

Warmth covered me like a blanket. "Yeah, I am."

"How long has it been?"

"Four years." Four years since I'd been home, but only a year since I'd seen my parents and my sister, Two. They came and visited with me in Florida thirteen months ago. It was a short holiday, but a much needed one. Thankfully, my friends at Shadows had become my family. I loved it here.

He whistled with a shake of his head. "Savi tells me you have a big family."

"I do. Four sisters, two parents, and a grandmother who has them all fooled."

"I like her already."

"Oh, yeah, you two would hit it off just fine."

Mark sat up and his expression changed. "How have we worked together this long and I really know nothing about you?"

I leaned back with a noncommittal shrug. He was right. I kept my private life private.

"I'm not like you, Mark. I don't express myself very well."

"You do to Savi."

"Yeah, I do. I guess it's because she reminds me of Two."

"Two?" He chuckled.

"Living with four sisters, well, names didn't happen, so we all used numbers. No, seriously, it started as a joke, but it stuck."

"So is Two the second oldest sister?"

"Yup. After all four girls were born, we started calling them by numbers. The firstborn is one then we counted up as they came. Don't ask me why, but my family is big on nicknames."

Mark laughed. I could tell he was happy I was sharing with him. I really needed to do this more.

"So, what is it about Savi that reminds you of Two?"

I took a moment to think about it. "I guess that they're both kind of like one of the guys, and they'll call you on your bullshit when it needs to be said. They're easy going but sassy at the same time. They're both full of it."

"Now I need to meet Two." Mark nodded at Cole, who was standing behind me. "Have a safe trip, man." He extended his hand. "See you at the wedding."

"Keith." Cole nodded for me to follow. "I think I found the perfect place."

"Oh, great." I followed him to the stairs, but something caught my eye. I raised an eyebrow at Abigail and Doc Roberts enjoying a kiss in the kitchen.

"Hey, Mark?" I couldn't help myself. He looked up from his phone. "Savannah made cookies."

"What?" He jumped to his feet and headed over as I pointed and waited. "The woman never told me. I'll have to—" He rounded the corner and flinched, turning his head dramatically. "Really, Abby? This is a place for food!"

"Oh, grow up, sweetheart." Abigail scowled at Mark, then beamed up at Doc Roberts, who was fixing his tie. "Did Mia get pregnant by a stork?"

"Haven't you left yet?" Mark hissed at me as he stomped toward the stairs.

"What up, Markie Mark?" Mike took two stairs at a time and slapped Mark on the shoulder. He stopped to pick up a little brown box from the table and tucked it under his arm. *What the hell did he keep ordering?* "Someone have a visit from Aunt Flo?"

"And it's time to move on." Cole shook his head and disappeared downstairs.

Just as I was about to follow, I caught Savannah heading to Cole's office with a heavy-looking diaper. "I'm going to turn up the heat." She winked and rushed off.

Oh, Christ!

Later that night, I lay in bed and wondered what Lexi was up to. I knew she wasn't with Juan, because Clark kept me in the loop from time to time. I had never been able to date anyone without comparing them to her. I willed my eyes closed and hoped morning would come sooner than later.

***

"Knock, knock." Savannah was in my doorway with a sleepy Olivia, who yawned when she saw me. "We wanted to see you off."

I reached for my little sidekick, but stopped

when she made a red face. My arms dropped, and I took a step back. "Bye."

"Really, Uncle Keith." Savannah's eyes watered as she held her out. "Give her a kiss."

In spite of the smell that wafted off the kid, I decided to go for it and leaned in and touched my nose to hers.

"Be bad and cause all kinds of trouble for your mommy while I'm gone." I winked at Savannah, and she rolled her eyes.

Mark popped his head in the door. "Have a safe—" His face scrunched, then he gagged. "Oh, pew! I think my eggs are coming back up."

"So dramatic." Savannah pushed Olivia in his arms, mumbling about how it was Cole's turn to change her.

"Speaking of which, the show should start in ten minutes. Let the mystery smell begin."

"Get the camera ready."

"On it."

Once the little stinker was gone, Savi turned back to me with a curious expression.

"Does this have anything to do with why you went home four years ago?"

I knew she saw me flinch. I wasn't aware she knew about that.

"Before you get all *Keith* on me, I overheard Sue and Cole talking. They didn't know I was there feeding Olivia. I don't know *what* happened, I just know something did."

Walking to the bed, not wanting to talk about this, I hiked my duffle bag over my shoulder. I knew Savannah wouldn't have brought this up if she wasn't worried about me. I knew I'd been off over the past year. I was just trying to come to terms with my life.

She stepped in my way and held her hands up. "Look, I know I meddle, but I'm worried about you."

She bit down on her lower lip. She was nervous of over-stepping with me.

I wrapped my arm around her shoulders, pulled her in, and gave her kiss on the top of her head and whispered, "I'll be in touch, and I'll see you at the wedding."

***

Boston

The carousel spun round and round, and its metal surface reflected light in my eyes from the sun pouring in through the airport doors. My flight had arrived fifteen minutes early, so I beat Dad to the luggage pickup.

Leaning down, I hoisted my duffle bag over my shoulder. I was happy to be home. I guessed I was more homesick than I thought.

"Keith!" Dad waved at me from his car across the street. With a hand up, I stopped a cabby from turning me into road kill and raced across the busy street.

He opened his trunk so I could toss in my bag, then gave me a huge hug.

"I swear you get bigger each time I see you, son."

"Since I joined the new unit, I've been working out more." Dad knew a lot about what I did, but I still had a contract to protect. He understood that and never pushed more than he had to.

Easing into the passenger seat, I rolled my window down and sucked in the crisp air, letting it fill my lungs.

"How was your flight?"

"Smooth." I grinned as we passed by the familiar places I used to love.

"You planning on staying a while?" I knew he was hoping it wouldn't be like last time. I only lasted four days here on that visit.

"I'm here until after the wedding."

Dad gave a small nod before a grin broke out across his face. "That's really great to hear."

One of the best parts about coming home was the smell of the familiar. Some things may have changed, but for the most part it was home the way it always was.

We pulled up behind Mom's car. She still had the **'My Son Fights For Our Freedom'** sticker on her bumper.

I chuckled at it; she was such a great supporter of anything we did.

Dad grabbed my duffle bag as we headed to the front door. It flew open and Two nearly tackled me.

"Oh my God, I've missed you!" she muttered into my shoulder.

"Hey, you!" I squeezed her tight until I heard her gasp.

"Move it!" Three yelled as she and Four both beat their way past Mom and hugged me from both sides.

"Wow, what a greeting." I patted their backs and waited for One, who was always way too cool to show her emotions as she greeted me.

Her hug was small, until I wrapped her up and kissed her cheek. "I know you missed me, One, don't deny it."

She laughed and rubbed my back. "I did."

After a very long hug with Mom, I was finally allowed to come inside. The wonderful aroma of the barbeque they had going hit my nostrils and made my mouth water. I knew it was going to be all my favorites tonight.

"There he is." Nan rolled down the ramp and over to me. "Give me some of that Army sugar." I leaned down and kissed her cheek and gave her a hug. She took my hand and squeezed it as I straightened up. "Sorry I wasn't at the airport. The car bothers my hip."

"No need to explain." Sometimes she forgot she was not twenty again.

"Why don't you hook a Nan up, hey?"

"Can I come in the door first?" I joked and thanked Two for the beer she handed me.

Nan was such a lush. Oh, it was so good to be home!

Glancing around, I quickly poured some beer into her coffee mug. I didn't think Nan ever had real coffee in that thing.

"Saw that." Dad chuckled but kept an eye out for Mom.

"You saw nothing but your sweet son helping your favorite mother-in-law in her time of need."

She snatched the mug out of my hand and took a long swig. "It's *so* good to have you back."

"Yes, I can see that." I shook my head, and Dad laughed.

"You and I have some catching up to do." She gave me a wink before she headed over for some food. I followed her out back to where my parents had the barbeque going.

Orange and green lights were strung around the high wooden fence, and the flourishing plants made me feel like I was in the country instead of a subdivision. My mother had a great eye for decorating.

"Well, as I live and breathe," Clark called out as he came out the patio doors. "Look who's back in town!"

"Hey." I shook his hand then gave a slap on the shoulder. "Looking good."

"Yeah, I clean up nice when I don't have to wear the uniform."

Two joined my side, nursing a beer. "Uniforms are hot."

I glared down at her. "You're not to find anything hot."

"I've had sex. Wanna talk about that?"

"Oh, Lord." Clark coughed and downed some more beer. Clark was like another brother to the girls, and we both always kept our eyes on them. Two was not to have sex ever...that was my rule, and she was *supposed* to stick to it.

I shoved her, but she was ready for it and returned it with force.

"Wanna know with who?"

128

"Wanna watch me jam a steak knife in my ear? No, so this conversation never happened."

"You're cute when you're mad, big brother." Her face became serious. "All kidding aside, I do need to talk to you."

I could tell by the creases between her eyes that something was bothering her, so I followed her inside to the living room. Clark came along with us.

"Okay, you have my attention."

She glanced at Clark, and he gave a slight nod. What was going on?

"I ran into Lexi the other day."

My heart jumped but I remained calm. The Army had taught me a lot; one thing was to hear all the facts before I said anything.

"She's not doing too well."

"How so?"

Two again eyed Clark, who cleared his throat. "I had a call last week that someone was drunk in the alley out by McCullan's Bar. When I got there to check it out, I found Lexi curled up in between the garbage cans, and she was covered in bruises. When she saw it was me, she let me help her up. I, ah…" He rubbed the back of his neck. "I let it slip that we have reason to believe Antonio's gang had a part in her parents' murder."

"Based on what?"

"We had a witness come forward describing the tattoo on the forearm of the shooter."

"The coiled snake?"

"Yeah." He held eye contact for a moment, silently conveying they were ninety percent certain it was them. "The look on her face said it all. She's staying at their clubhouse until she can get some real evidence."

I felt sick.

"Look, we all know she's a stubborn woman, but, Keith, she was in pretty rough shape, shaking all over and upset, but she wouldn't tell me what happened. I was going to take her to the hospital, but then Antonio showed up with some of his guys." He looked down at his beer. "Something is going on and it's bad, Keith." He looked at me, his expression worried. "Things are different since you were home last. The town is…well, the *Almas Perdidas* are becoming bolder with their killings, and honestly, we can't keep up with it."

Shit.

I couldn't bear to picture Lexi hurt that way, and fury built in my gut. I had to get a grip.

"Look, guys, we all know Lexi wants nothing to do with me. I'm not sure what I can do, but I have to do something!"

"She pushed you away because she feels unworthy," Two blurted out. Her eyes bulged when she realized what she just said.

Taking a seat on the couch, I tried to beat back my anger at someone hurting Lexi so I could think straight.

"What?" Her comment threw me. "That is based on what, exactly?"

"Based on the fact I saw her last month at the market when she was buying flowers for her parents' grave. She looked even skinnier and worn out. I asked her to come with me for coffee." Two tugged at her bracelet the way she always did when she was upset or nervous. "She asked how you were. She wanted to know why you left so quickly when you just got back last time." Her face changed. "Which, by the way, feel free to share what really happened there."

"So…Lexi?" I hoped she would leave *that* topic alone.

"She misses you, Keith. When I told her you were happy, she couldn't hide her emotions. She started to cry. Then some horrible looking guy—"

"Will Shonner," Clark added.

"Like, Will from high school?"

"Yeah, he's part of the gang now."

Shaking my head, I waited for Two to go on. I hated that guy.

"Anyway, he basically hauled her out of the chair, and her parents didn't get the flowers because he ripped them out of her hands and chucked them on the ground before he pushed her into the car."

I wanted to rip Will's throat out with my bare hands, but I had to keep my cool. I knew enough about this gang to know acting too quickly would only make things worse. I pumped my fists at my sides, trying to think.

Two sat across from me. "I think she wants out, but might be in too deep. Well, now, knowing what she does, I bet she'll stick it out for her parents. But at what cost?"

I nodded slowly, still casting about, trying to put this all together. I knew how hard it was to get out of a gang once you were in.

"Brandon." She caught my attention by using my first name. No one ever used it. "I know you love her, so go save her. That is what you do, right?"

Clark nodded. "I'll help in any way I can. I, ahh..." He paused before he looked back toward the barbeque. "We have a guy in the inside, name's Gordon. He joined them last year. He's been leaking us information."

"Let me get my head around this, okay, guys?" I caught Clark's eye when Two wasn't looking to let him know we would need to talk. "Okay, thanks, Two. I love you for caring about Lexi. Now, come on, I need a drink, and I bet you do too." I stood and headed out to the deck.

The rest of the day I tried to enjoy being home with my family, but my heart wasn't in it, and my brain was working overtime. Memories from the last time I was home haunted me.

I couldn't sleep at all that night either. I kept picturing Lexi crying and hurt in that alley. Then I would switch to her conversation with Two. Did she really miss me? And were the *Almas Perdidas* really behind her parents' death?

Finally, by 5:00, I changed into my shorts and t-shirt and headed downstairs for a run.

The pavement beat under the soles of my sneakers. The morning was cool, and there was evidence of an early rainfall from the shine on the grass. I loved morning runs. It was the perfect time to let my mind wander and get myself in check for the day ahead.

"Keith?" I heard someone yell. I turned and scanned the houses. "Wow, it's really you!"

Then I found the voice. "Mimi?"

"Don't tell me you forgot my face after all these

years?"

Laughing, I jogged over and gave her a hug. "Sorry, I was in the zone."

"Don't be sorry. I get it. I just fed my son. I think I'm full of apple sauce." She looked down at her top as she motioned for me to sit on a bench under a tree. "Have you got a sec? I know how hard it is to stop when you're out for a run. But I'm dying to know how you are and what you've been up to."

I joined her, knowing that as Lexi's friend in high school, she might have more to say.

"Still with the Army. I'm home for Three's wedding. That's about it, really. You?"

"Still with Robert. We have two kids and haven't left this town." She let out a little sigh. "Sometimes I wonder what I'm missing out there." She gave me a small smile, and I could tell this was a sore subject for her.

"It's pretty amazing, but nothing beats home."

"So..." She looked up at me, clearly wanting to change the topic. "You run into anyone yet?"

And there it was. I pretended not catch on right away.

"Just Clark, but I only got in yesterday."

"Ah, yes, Officer Clark." She chuckled. "Boston Police Department's finest. Too bad they can't do more about the *Almas Perdidas*. That gang is worse than it ever was, and growing too. Everyone is scared of them."

"Yeah, I heard they were causing trouble."

"What's crazy is we went to school with a lot of those guys. My husband says all they see is blood and money."

I nodded and stared up into the sun as it warmed the ground, drying the dew from the grass. Things in the town I grew up in weren't so happy and peaceful as they used to be. This gang was obviously a sore that needed to be addressed in more ways than one.

Mimi interrupted my thoughts. "I'm just going to come right out and say this, Keith."

Here we go.

"Nicole is going to be so excited to see you!"

Wait, what? It had been years since I heard her name.

"I swear that woman has been waiting for you to return for years. She got a boob job, an eye lift, and a neck tuck when she heard you were coming home a few years ago. Wait, are you single?"

Oh, shit.

I forced a smile. Knowing she was still friends with Nicole made this a little harder.

"I'm single, but my life isn't made for a woman."

"Are you telling me big, intense Keith swings for his own team now?"

I shook my head; Mimi had no filter.

"No!" I shook my head. This question always went there. "I mean my job takes me places I can't even talk about, and having a girlfriend fit into that is next to impossible."

"Oh, well, she'd be happy even for a quickie with you." She cupped her mouth. "Don't tell her I told you that."

"Secret is safe with me." I'd be like a damn vault if it would keep Nicole away.

"Mommy!" Mimi's husband called from the doorway. "We need you."

Mimi jumped and held up a finger. "Be sure to stop by again at least once before you head back to wherever it is you've been hiding. It was really great to see you again."

"You too."

I waved at Robert in the doorway and continued on my run. Well, so much for her friendship with Lexi.

***

After a hot shower and a fresh change of clothes, I fired up my old truck, pleased Dad kept it maintained. He used it off and on to haul plants and bags of soil for Mom's garden. I decided to head into town. I knew Mom's greenhouse took a beating after the last hurricane, and I wanted to make sure it would hold up over the coming winter.

The keychain Nan gave me knocked against my knee as the truck bumped around the old road. Tuning the radio to the local station, I leaned back and listened to "Gooey" by Glass Animals. I caught my reflection in the mirror and smiled. I looked like I was home again. White t-shirt, jeans, faded Bruins hat, and work boots.

Pulling into Home Hardware, I parked and headed inside. A half hour later, I had everything on my list.

"So, two sheets of plywood, six two by fours, a gallon of green paint, and a carton of nails?" The salesclerk held up the yellow slip, and I walked out to the guys who had loaded up my truck.

"That will be it, thanks." Someone familiar caught my eye as they crossed the street. I squinted to get a better look.

Holy shit.

I tossed the paperwork at one of the guys, thanking him. I locked my truck and raced across the street into the local market.

I grabbed a basket and weaved through the aisle until I saw her.

Her ripped jeans and heels had my stomach in a twist. Her black top and dark hair made her eyes look like deep brown pools. She wore a stack of bracelets on one wrist and long earrings that sparkled when she moved.

Holy hell, she was just as perfect as I remembered.

Right before she spotted me, I reached for a bottle of wine, pretending I didn't see her.

"Keith?" Her voice was low and raspy and hit all the right places.

With a glance to my side I granted her a big lopsided smile, which wasn't difficult, considering she made every part of my body come alive.

"Lexi?" I paused to sound more surprised. "Hey."

She looked around before she moved to close the space between us. "Wow, you look…" she gave a small smile, "…really good."

"So do you."

She stared at me for a few moments. Oh, what I wouldn't do to know what she was feeling.

She glanced at the wine bottle. "Big plans?"

"Well, if drinking with Nan when Mom isn't looking is considered big plans, then yes, I do."

She laughed lightly, and my hands twitched to reach out and touch her.

"How long are you in town for?"

I shrugged. "Honestly, I'm not sure. Three is getting married in a few weeks—"

"So I hear. High school sweethearts."

I swallowed the knot that came with those words. "Yeah, so not sure how long after that."

"Are you still in the Army?"

…And the knot grew. "Yes, special ops now."

Her eyes couldn't hide the fact she was uncomfortable with that. "Wow, sounds scary."

"It's not that bad."

She took a quick glance over her shoulder like she was watching for someone, and I caught a glimpse of some dark coloring on her shoulder as her shirt moved.

"What happened to your shoulder?"

She looked startled as she saw me pointing at it. She quickly covered up the mark. "Box dropped on it. Looks worse than it actually is."

"Right." I let my annoyance show, but she seemed too preoccupied to notice.

She placed her hand on my arm, and I immediately relaxed at her cool touch. "It was really nice to see you again."

"You too, Lex."

She started to bite her lip before she stepped back. It looked as if she wanted to say something, but she didn't.

"Lexi!" someone shouted, and her head snapped

in that direction.

"Umm." She tucked a piece of hair behind her ear. "I should go."

Antonio Garcia, the leader of the *Almas Perdidas* gang, grabbed her from behind, pulling her back into him. My hands formed into fists at my sides, and my mouth tasted like tin as my teeth drove into my cheek. I had to use every ounce of training not to react.

I've known Antonio since I was twenty-three. We hung out with the same guys for a while, until I realized they were trouble. That was when I learned Juan was his little half-brother. We met right after Lexi and I broke up, after my first tour.

"Keith?" He relaxed when he realized who it was she was speaking to. "Wow, it's been a few years."

"It has." My tone was hard to curb. My hatred for this man had my fingers twitching.

He looked from Lexi to me and back again. "Oh, yeah, you two used to date in high school, right?"

"Barely," she quickly said. I glanced at her for immediately downplaying how close we had been. I hoped it was only that she didn't want him to know, and not because she really wanted to dismiss our past so readily. I decided to play it her way.

"Yeah, we did, briefly." I stared at her. "I'm with someone else now."

The emotion that ran across her face gave me hope, hope that maybe there was still some feeling there for me. As quickly as it came, though, her face hardened and she turned toward Antonio.

"Good." He tugged her closer. "Don't need anyone filling her head with shit. Bad enough she has a mouth on her."

I loved that mouth.

Antonio looked down at Lexi's basket, which was filled with steak. "Why don't you come by the club tonight? We're having a barbeque, throw back a few beers. We're celebrating." He smiled, and his capped teeth shone under the lights. All he needed was an obnoxious clock and he'd be Flavor Flav.

"Celebrating what, exactly?"

His mouth curved. "Come on by and see for yourself. Besides, since you're in town, I want to talk to you about something."

I couldn't help but be interested. Plus, I would get to see Lexi again, and that alone was enough to make me agree to hang out at their clubhouse.

"Yeah, all right. What time?"

"Seven. You should bring your bitch."

Dismissing his comment, I shrugged. "I could use the break."

"*Pfft*, I get that." He shook Lexi, and she grimaced. "If I didn't think this one would get into trouble, I would do the same."

Pulling out my phone, I waved goodbye and headed outside.

Keith: Just got an invite to the AP clubhouse.

Clark: Meet me at the lake. We should talk.

***

The clubhouse windows were painted black, but a few areas were purposely left with a smudge so they could see out. That was different. A few years ago, they were all clear. Not exactly a subtle change.

According to my chat with Clark, Antonio always had a spotter on the roof, and at least four men were on lookout, one by every window, and two outside each door.

The Boston Police Department's informant was named Gordon, and according to Clark, I wouldn't be able to miss him.

Easing into an open spot, I parked out front and locked my doors. With my hands in my pockets, I met the ugly-ass dude at the entrance. He studied my face, and the grip on his handgun stayed tense.

"Name?"

"Keith."

"Do I know you?"

It took me a moment, but I placed him. He was one of those losers who used to sniff spray cans down by the tracks. "We went to high school together."

"Ah, you're in the Army, right?"

Gotta love small towns.

"Yes."

"You packing?"

My face scrunched. "No, they don't let you take home the M-16s." He stared at me, obviously not liking my sarcasm.

"Smart guy, aren't ya?" He stared at me. "Go on in." He flicked his head with his pierced, studded neck in the direction of the door.

Pushing the wooden door open, I stepped into the dark, smoky clubhouse. It hadn't changed much.

140

It took my eyes a moment to adjust before I spotted Antonio in the corner with a bottle of whiskey between his legs. *So much for the beer.*

Just like the dumbass at the door, Antonio was a shit, one of those loner kids in high school you might try to befriend because you felt sorry for him, but later you'd probably find him stealing from your locker. He was the type read about in the newspaper who people would remember overhearing him mutter comments about how everyone should die. His head wasn't on straight, and that was why he had been in and out of jail so much over the past ten years. His uncle used to run this gang and was more than happy to teach Antonio all he needed to know to take over. Clark told me the one thing Antonio was good at was recruiting new members. Apparently, he knew what the soulless assholes wanted, and they joined him. Once you were in, you were in, and there was no getting out easily—well, at least not alive.

"Holy shit, you came. Look who just walked in, boys!" Antonio tossed his head back and gave a horse-like laugh. "If it isn't *Private* Keith. "

"First Sergeant," I corrected him. He may not get it, but I was proud of my accomplishment.

"First Sergeant." He smirked as he rested his dirty shoe on the ledge of the table. "Hey, where's Spit?" he shouted at Will Shonna where he stood behind the bar. The other *winner* I despised.

Suddenly, Elliot appeared, looking tall and skinny. He had sleeves with black comic book characters, and of course the coiled snake wrapped his forearm. The signature tattoo of the *Almas*

Perdidas. Scales ran up his neck and curved around the ears and along the jaw bone. Not a look I would go for. My own tattoos were extremely personal.

"Jesus Christ! Keith?" He came forward and hugged me.

"Hey, man, how are you? What happened to the wrist?" I pointed to the dirty cast covering some of the snake.

His face flinched and he stepped back and glanced at Antonio, but he didn't reply.

"Spit, go get the First Sergeant a beer."

Elliot nodded and rushed to the bar.

Antonio pushed out a chair with his foot as an offering to sit.

"Spit?" I asked as I took his offer.

Antonio waited until Elliot returned with the beer.

"Thanks, El—"

Antonio spat on Elliot's shoe and laughed. "I chew tobacco, and Elliot is my cup. Better him than the floor."

Or a cup?

Elliot kept his head down in embarrassment as he took a deep breath. "Anything else?"

"Go make me something to eat."

"Okay." He hurried off toward what I assumed was the kitchen.

Antonio threw his whiskey bottle behind the counter and grabbed the beers, popping one for himself and tossing me the other. "I learned real quick that some people were made to ride with me, and others were made to be my bitch."

My hand clenched around the neck of the beer as

he talked.

"Spit back-doored his way in here. He does what he's told, but he stands up for his sister, trying to protect her and shit." He slammed his hand on the table and his face changed. "If I wanna hit a bitch, I will. All women are good for is a tight hole, anyway."

Blood pumped to my hand as my grip grew stronger around the bottle. The guy could blink and he'd be dead. Just a jab to the neck and he'd be down. *Tempting.*

"Ain't that right, Lexi?" he called over my shoulder. "Get over here."

She placed her tray down and came over, and her eyes grew wide when she saw it was me sitting across the table from Antonio. She looked incredibly sexy in her little black dress. Her hands slid over Antonio's shoulders and she kissed his cheek.

Moving her to his side, he wrapped an arm around her waist. "This one here has the tightest hole I've ever felt. I need to stick it in butter to get it in there."

Lexi gave a small smile, but I could tell she was embarrassed by how her cheeks grew pink.

I pretended not to notice when Antonio slid his hand up her skirt and she tried to move aside. The whole time he watched us carefully. I knew this was a test.

So I faked disinterest and turned to ask Will for another beer. When I turned back, he was making a show of licking his fingers. Lexi's stance told me she was mortified, but she leaned down and kissed him, drawing it out longer to prove a point of her own.

His face turned to a frown and he pushed her away, but I noticed she stayed within hearing distance.

Antonio's fingers strummed the table, and he watched me as I watched him, each wondering what the other's motives were for being here.

"I know what you did for my sister." Antonio rubbed his chin with his knuckles. He leaned back, pulled out a joint and played with it, running it back and forth through his bony fingers. "I have to ask, why?"

"You referring to Selena?"

He nodded slowly.

I blinked, remembering.

I was back hanging out at the end of the year party at Boston University with Lexi.

"It's a love-hate with beer." Clark held up his Heineken and stared through the green glass. "I love beer, but on the flip side, it makes me have to pee every seven minutes. And it's not short. You're guaranteed a minute a beer. So times that by three?" He closed one eye and laughed that he was too buzzed to do the math. "All I'm saying is I wish I could tuck an empty up my shorts and go whenever the feeling strikes."

"Oh, sure." Lexi laughed, handing me a beer before she climbed on my lap. With one arm wrapped around her waist, I balanced my bottle on her knee. "Complain about how you have to stand by a tree and pee. Whereas we, on the other

hand..."

"Yeah!" Mimi was wrapped around some guy's neck and called out at the wrong moment and made Lexi chuckle.

"Have to cop an ever so sexy squat and hope to hell we don't pee on our feet." She tipped her bottle in his direction. "At least you're working with a little distance, my friend. We have a wobbly stance working with less than an inch, and that's if we really have to go. Think of the splash factor!"

Clark shook his head, trying to keep up. "Whatever, now I need to pee."

"Lucky!" Mimi chimed in again, causing us all to laugh.

I kissed Lexi on the cheek before I stood, setting her on her feet.

"I got to go too."

"Sure, rub it in." She grinned, pretending to be pissed.

"I could get you a funnel."

She shrugged. "Not a bad idea. Maybe we could patent it. 'A woman's best friend in the woods.' Or, 'We can too." Or, 'Stick it and release it.'"

"You about done?" I was ready to burst at the seams.

"No, I have more."

Turning on my heel, I raced into the thick brush, looking for a good spot. I quivered as I passed two guys having a full blown conversation as they peed. No, thank you. Not a time for sharing. It was the one time I could just turn off and let my mind wander, alone, thank you very much.

Several more feet into the woods I saw a

clearing, I quickly crossed the tracks and found myself a spot. Undoing my fly, I let out a relaxed sigh and enjoyed the release of the last four beers from my bladder's tight grip.

I turned my head when I heard a distant puffing noise. I stepped back quickly, zipping and pulling my shirt back down. Still hidden in the brush, I heard a cry from the opposite direction.

Oh my God!

A small girl, maybe fourteen—I couldn't see in the near dark—was walking up on the tracks, sobbing into her hands. Well, shit!

The light from the train soon lit her up. She didn't move off the tracks; she just kept going. I raced toward her.

"Hey!" I cupped my mouth and forced my feet to beat harder. "Get off the tracks!" I knew it was stupid to say, but it was all that came out. "Hey!"

Maybe she couldn't hear me. The train blared a long, drawn-out horn, but she kept walking right into the light.

Almost there, I felt a jolt spring through me, and I lunged forward and tackled her, taking her with me down into the ditch below.

Arching my weight in the air, I somehow managed not to kill her and only landed on her shoulder. A moment later, the train came speeding by, again madly blowing its horn, almost like it was saying holy shit *back. Someone's heart was probably pounding on board!*

The tracks screamed as the metal on metal zoomed by us. Once I caught my breath, I looked down and was shocked to see who was below me.

"Selena?" I moved to my knees and helped her sit up.

Her wild hair, bloodshot eyes, and panting breath had me stunned.

"Why did you do that?" she whispered through a cry. Selena was only fourteen, and I knew she had just been dealt a bad blow as her parents and her baby cousin were recently killed. It was rumored it was by a rival gang that hated her brother. According to Four, who had told us all about it as she was in the same class, Selena was well past depressed and needed some serious help. "I almost got you killed!"

"Yeah, you did." I helped her to her feet, knowing not much I said at this moment would get through to her. So, I changed my approach and played the tough love card. "And in return, you're going to get some help. Okay?" I gave her a look not to push me.

"Yeah." She folded her arms around her body and shook. I knew the whole incident scared the crap out of her. I just hoped it was what she needed to jolt her back to maybe wanting to live. "Okay."

My mind jerked back to find Antonio studying my expression. "Why? I think anyone would do what I did." I shrugged.

Antonio shook his head and checked the time on his phone. "Well, she's got a family now, three kids and a husband. Wants nothing to do with the gang, never did. My sister was never like the rest of us." His face seemed to soften just a fraction, then quickly hardened over. "Whatever, it's one less person to watch over."

A guy caught my eye as he eased into a seat with a beer and opened a newspaper. Just as I was about to look away, he gave me a quick glance. That's when I noticed the scar that ran straight across his forehead. It was Gordon, the undercover informant.

"Tell me something, Keith." Antonio downed some more of his beer. "Why did you and Lexi break up?"

I saw her hand stop mid-swipe over a table. Her shoulders stiffened, and she made a loud noise when she tossed a cup on her tray.

"It was just a high school fling. We grew up. I joined the Army and moved on." I was not about to share my intimate moments with this asshole. He was clearly trying to see if he could get a rise out of me.

He smirked as he lit his joint, and the tattooed guns on the side of his neck contracted as he sucked back the smoke.

Every member of the *Almas Perdidas* had the snake coiled around their left arm, but they also wore a tightly rolled, thin, red bandana around the right wrist. His fingers idly picked at it as he sat there allowing the joint to do its work.

"Hey! Antonio!" Some meathead entered with a guy draped over his shoulder. He dumped him on the floor like a stack of fire wood.

"Brought you a present."

Sweat broke out along my shoulders when I saw the guy's head. He had a deep scar straight across his neck. He looked pretty badly beaten and was most definitely dead. I looked up to find Antonio watching me closely before he addressed the guy.

"Who did it?"

The meathead smirked. "He was running out the door, and I took a pipe to his neck. Never saw it coming."

I had seen those colors before, and that patch. It has been etched in my memory for some time now. "Is that...?" I stumbled with real fear over my words.

"Yup." Antonio blew smoke in my face.

Lexi appeared at his side, her face pale and holding her stomach.

"He just *killed* a member of the Devil's Reach?"

Antonio kicked the dead man in his badly beaten face. "I'm thinking I should stick his head out front as a symbol not to fuck with the *Almas Perdidas*."

I was still trying to control my spinning head. "Why would you want to take a chance like that? Why poke the devil from behind?"

"Trigger isn't the devil." He grabbed Lexi and slammed her down on his lap. *"I am!"* He kissed her lips, but his gaze stayed fixed on me.

"I beg to differ." Holding his disturbing gaze, I went on. "I have seen his handiwork firsthand, Antonio. I hope you know what you just did. They are the most *ruthless* motorcycle crew out there."

He pushed Lexi away and leaned back. "Gotta make my mark somehow."

"Well, you did that." I finished my beer, shaking my head.

"I can trust you to keep this between us and not tell your friend *Officer* Clark?" He glanced pointedly at Lexi when he spoke, and I wasn't stupid.

"I want nothing to do with this." I didn't. I had my own shit to deal with.

"Great, then you saw nothing."

Antonio waved the man to move the body somewhere else, then lit a cigarette.

"How long are you in town for?"

I leaned back and played with the lip of my bottle. "Few weeks."

"Any plans?"

"Not really. Just need a break to clear the head."

He stared at me a moment longer, then his eyes moved over to Lexi, who was watching us. Once they made eye contact, she slowly turned and went back to work.

"Feel free to stop by and hang out," he suddenly blurted, and Lexi's face snapped in our direction.

"I don't do gangs, Antonio."

"Not asking you to join, just saying if you're bored, you have a place to hang out. You did help my sister and all."

I wanted to say "hell fucking no" because I still was under military as well as civilian law. Plus, I wasn't stupid enough to make nice with a gang like this. However, I took a moment and thought I could use this to my advantage. I needed to keep an eye on Lexi.

Lexi was holding herself very rigid, white-knuckling the tray. I could tell she was pissed, which only made my decision to come back here to "hang out," as Antonio put it, even more appealing.

"Yeah, maybe I will."

He smiled and smacked the table, and the

undercover cop looked over.

"Perfect." He stood. "Let's go eat some meat!"

"Great, but first, where is the restroom?"

He pointed as he gathered his things. "Down the hall, second door on the left."

Once behind closed doors, I pulled my phone free.

Keith: One of Antonio's assholes just killed a DR member. Heads up, a retaliation might be on the way.

I quickly deleted the message and washed my hands, in case someone was listening. Opening the door, I heard a strange noise and looked over and saw Lexi waving me into a storage closet.

She closed the door behind me. We were in a large room piled high with boxes that looked like they had been stolen off a Best Buy truck.

Crossing her arms, I saw the fire I once loved in this woman return, and I was pleased to learn she still had it.

"Why are you even here?"

I fought the smile.

"Funny, I could ask you the same thing."

Her jaw ticked, and I could see her slipping into our old song and dance. God, I missed this—missed her.

"Do you have a death wish? Because you're guaranteed to get it hanging out here."

Reaching out, I ran my hand down her arm, but she jerked it back. "I did three tours in Iraq and one in Afghanistan. I fight cartels on a monthly basis."

Her face grew pale. "I can handle myself against Antonio Garcia."

Her eyes closed and she muttered, "Antonio is testing you to see—"

I cupped her cheek, and her skin flushed hot against my hand as her words trailed off.

"I know he is." Her gaze snapped up to mine. I stepped closer so my chest touched her, and she didn't move away.

Holding her instantly had everything clicking back into place. The moment I touched her, I felt complete, like a puzzle when you fitted in that last piece.

"Jesus, Lexi, I can't believe how good it feels to be standing here with you."

Her chin raised. "You had your chance with me, Keith, but that ship has sailed. I'm with Antonio now, and I'm happy."

"Are you?" My thumb tugged her bottom lip down, and I felt all the passion I had tucked away for so many years come rushing back.

"I am." She held her own with me.

"I missed you," I whispered but regretted it the moment the words were out of my mouth. She snapped out of my spell and stepped back, her face hardening.

"Interesting way of showing it." She turned and slammed the door in my face.

I went too far, too fast, *but*…she didn't tell me to stop.

CHAPTER EIGHT

Lexi

My hands shook as I cleared the table. The glasses clinked and rattled as I made my way back to the bar. Club members started to pour in as the party picked up and the barbeque wound down. Elliot hadn't been around all day, and I was worried about him. After what happened to him with Antonio, I was really concerned he might try to do something stupid. Poor Elliot didn't know the girl he had been hitting on was Antonio's cousin, and he had not been able to defend himself against the beating. He was obviously making sure to keep his head down for a bit.

I was completely thrown by Keith being here. Although it had been only two days since I last saw him, the whole thing was frigging with my head. A blast from the past who just happened to be the only one I ever loved. I would have thought I had enough hate inside me to push the unwanted feelings for him aside, but it was proving to be difficult, especially when he touched me.

"Hey, there." Will held onto my hips and rubbed his erection against my ass as he moved by. Of course Antonio was looking in another direction. I hated working the bar for this reason. Normally, I'd just do the bookkeeping, but since Elliot had been causing some trouble, Antonio was watching both of us more closely.

"Lexi! Beers, now!" Antonio ordered from across the room.

He could be such an ass sometimes.

I balanced six beers on a small tray and headed over. I hated the men Antonio was sitting with. They were from the mid-country somewhere and made me really uncomfortable. They loved to put their hands on me whenever Antonio looked away. I knew it kind of went with the territory when you hung with a crew like this, but up to this point Antonio had been keeping me to himself. Usually, the men took what they wanted when they wanted it. Some girls got shared and passed around. I had been pretty lucky so far. I hated it, but mainly because I never wanted to be with Antonio in the first place. I almost enjoyed myself when I was with Juan. He treated me pretty well, and we had fun. But Antonio changed all that. Things happened, and he didn't care who took the fall.

I bent and reached for the first bottle. My tray wiggled and was about to tip when someone grabbed it.

"Tha—" My heart shot right up in my throat while Elliot stared down at me. I knew he wanted to talk.

"Got it?"

"Yes," I whispered and finished handing out the drinks. Back at the bar, I pretended to drop the bottle opener and saw Elliot nod for me to join him in his room, but I felt Antonio watching me, so I looked down and shook my head so he knew right now wasn't a good time.

Later on that evening as the guys became more drunk, I decided to clean up. Picking up some empty boxes, I went out back to the trash bins. The temperature had dropped, and with bare arms, I was quickly feeling the cold. I heard footsteps and sighed inwardly.

"It's really not a smart idea—"

An arm reached around my mid-section and dipped low, grabbing my crotch.

"Stop it!" I tried to elbow whoever it was but was only slammed forward into the trash bin. *Ouch!*

"Hey, sexy." Antonio's breath reeked of booze and old smoke. I despised him when he drank; he always got so mean. "You telling me no?"

With a quick shake of my head, I gave him my normal smile. "Of course not." I chose my words carefully. "You just scared me, that's all."

He grabbed my wrists and held them down as he moved in to kiss my neck. My skin crawled and begged to be removed from my bones. The way he kissed made my stomach roll. It was more of a bite than a sensual graze over the skin. I kept my eyes on the sky and waited for it to be over.

"Antonio!" someone shouted, bringing his fumble with my pants to halt. "Dude! There's a bar fight!"

155

He cursed before he left me standing on shaky legs. *No "be right back," nothing.* Oh, right; I was only a hole with legs anyway. Why should I deserve an explanation?

I heard a strange noise and spun toward the alley. Something dark caught my eye.

"Hello?" Sometimes Elliot would wait for me in the shadows so we could talk alone. We weren't *ever* supposed to be alone.

"Elliot?" I stepped into the darkness and let it swallow me whole.

A huge hand wrapped around my wrist and tugged me sideways. Stumbling, I reached out for the chain link fence to stabilize myself.

With a twist, I was turned around and pressed with my back flat against the cold steel. A set of dark eyes towered above me, and a massive body blocked my view of the exit.

He was so close I could smell his body wash. His heat was all too comforting, and the way he looked at me made every single nerve on my body rise to attention. *Stop.*

"Tell me you love him, and I'll leave right now, and you will never see me again." His voice was low and raspy, which only made my heart pound louder.

"I love him."

"Bullshit." He stepped a little closer so we were touching. I couldn't deny the pull he had on me. It was unlike any other feeling I'd ever experienced. So I raised my hand to signal him to back off. I tried to contain the anger that rushed through me and brought my walls up fast.

156

"We've only been together for six months, Keith." I shrugged, annoyed he immediately saw through my lie. So I tried a different angle. "You can't fall in love that quickly."

"Bullshit," he snapped back as his chest pushed harder into mine. "I fell in love with you the moment I saw your stubborn ass."

"What good that did us."

His face fell, but I didn't care.

Dammit!

"Look." I tried to stay calm. "You were my first love, first everything. Dreams die, Keith. I know mine did when you left. Too much has happened since then, way too much to come back from."

"That's a cop-out."

Okay, that was more than a little annoying. *Is he trying to piss me off?*

"No, you're a cop-out, for not telling me you were leaving for a whole year!"

He stepped closer. I had no room to step back, so I leaned all my weight into the fence.

One of his hands ran along my hip and rested there while the other reached up by my head and laced itself through the fence links. His head lowered as he searched my eyes for something.

"Nice to know that after all these years I can still piss you off."

"Screw you."

His mouth tilted up on one side. "I missed your feisty side."

I rolled my eyes. He started fires inside me, but I had no time for it. I had way bigger issues to deal with right now than worrying about my old lover coming back into town.

"Antonio will be looking for me." It was lame. Antonio would just want to get some oral, and if I wasn't there, someone else would step in.

"I saw the way you looked when he was kissing your neck." He leaned down and hovered his lips above my collarbone. His warm breath made my eyes water. It was all too much. "Would you have touched him if he had let go of your wrists?"

Words failed me as I gave a little shake of the head. My mind was cloudy, and I couldn't think straight. I hated that he did this to me. It was just old feelings seeping through. It was all fake, and none of this was based on anything real.

"Then why are you touching me?"

He leaned back and looked down at my grip on his forearms. I immediately dropped them as though burned and pushed him aside.

"We have a history, Keith, but don't mistake it for anything else. This is my life now, and I suggest you leave. You must realize I am not the girl you once knew."

"Are you staying to find proof they killed your parents?"

My blood froze. How did he...? I didn't know if I wanted to laugh with relief that I had someone to share this with, or cry with the pain that filled me. I went with old faithful. Anger.

"I'm staying because this is my home, and I suggest you leave, which we both know you are good at, and go back to wherever the hell you came from."

He grabbed my arm and hauled me back to him.

His lips were so close to mine. His dark eyes flashed as he flicked them from mine to my mouth.

"Just give me an inch, Lex."

"Like you gave me? We can do this all night, but bottom line is you broke me."

I wanted to give in so badly. He was like an addiction sucking me back into a safe haven. A safe heaven that once tore a piece of me away. I was not that person anymore!

"I'm not what you need, Keith. Oil and water don't mix."

"Lexi!" Antonio barked from the doorway, making me jump. Keith let me go and stepped back. "Where the fuck did you go?" I was relieved I was still hidden from view. I noticed a girl wrap her arms around his, pulling him back into the clubhouse.

I glanced over my shoulder and Keith was gone. *Good, leave.*

Heading back inside, I went searching for Antonio, only to find I was locked out of our room. The girl's screams had to be fake. He couldn't get an erection, and his oral skills were less than good. Most women faked an orgasm, *me included,* because it wasn't about the sex, it was about who you were naked with. If you played up his oral skills and were a screamer, you'd stick around awhile. Instead, I headed for Elliot's room, but that was locked too. Damn, I really could use my brother right now.

I finally settled for the storage closet. At least that had a lock on it.

Removing some clean bar rags, I piled them up

and made myself a pillow and closed my eyes. Not that I got much sleep anyway, but Keith being here was really throwing me off my game. If I wasn't careful, he was going to screw up everything.

The next morning the place was dead. No one ever got up before one in the afternoon after these kinds of parties. I cleaned up, removing a bunch of dirty clothes from a bench and a bra from under the table. I shuddered at the thought of how much semen was probably on these surfaces. These guys were nasty in every sense of the word.

By ten I was bored, as all my chores were finished. *Hmm*, maybe I could use this to my advantage. I grabbed my keys, headed out to my car, and drove to the corner market.

"Red or yellow today?" Connie asked over the music from her TV. She loved to watch old re-runs of *Lie to Me*. I found myself hanging out watching it with her sometimes just to feel normal again.

"Red, please."

She handed me twelve long-stemmed roses.

"Thanks. See you next week."

"You know, if you just stuck with one color I could always make sure to have them in stock."

I smiled with a shrug and handed her the money. "I would, but I never know when I'll need the yellow roses."

Her eyebrows pinched together, confused by my comment.

It wasn't far off from the truth, but I learned the hard way not to share anything with anyone.

"Thanks, Connie." I held up the flowers as I walked out the door.

Parking a few yards away, I wound my way through the tombstones and stopped in front of my parents'. My flowers from last week had been removed by Elliot. I carefully placed six on Dad's and six on Mom's.

"Hey, guys," I whispered, glancing around. Talking to them helped me get through these visits. "I wouldn't say I'm closer to pinpointing exactly who did this to you, but I do have something to tell you. Gordon, one of the members, caught me listening outside Antonio's office and never reported me. I was so scared, but he never told, or I would have got it. That was really unexpected, and I'm not sure why, but he seems a little nicer than the rest."

I wiped that tears that started to overflow. "I heard where Antonio is storing the body of a guy they killed from the Devil's Reach, but I'll be keeping that quiet for a bit. It could be really useful info." I shook my head like I could hear their disapproval. "I know we're in way over our heads. I won't lose my way." I touched Mom's stone. "I just need a little more time."

With shaky hands, I pulled out a joint and lit the tip.

"Oh, Keith showed up." I blew the smoke away from us. "Crazy, right?" I smirked at my dad's voice in my head.

"Let him in."

"I can't, Dad. It's too hard. He hurt me in ways I can't begin to repair." Tears hurt as they marred my vision, forcing me to see his face. "I wish he would just go back wherever he was."

Sinking to the ground and leaning against the cool stone, I closed my eyes, wishing against all the rules of life that my parents could somehow come home.

***

Keith

Three had her arm linked with mine as we strolled through Boston Common. She was showing me where her outdoor wedding ceremony was going to be.

So…" She spread her arms out and showed me the backdrop. "Donny and I will be here, and the fathers and the guests will be here." Her excited eyes looked up at me, seeking my approval like always. Three looked at me as her second father. Perhaps it was because I was eleven years older. She and Donny had been together since the tenth grade, and no one had to tell me how much that meant, loving a person so hard for so long.

"Looks perfect." I pulled her into my side and kissed her head.

We headed for the bridge that looked like it came from a *Mary Poppins* movie set. Once in the middle, she stopped and leaned over the rail, looking back at where her ceremony would be held.

"Our main pictures will be here." She grinned and tucked her hair out of her eyes. "Look at those colors. Do you see colors like this where you live?"

I smiled at her. My family never asked much when it came to the location of the safe house. I knew they understood, but I also knew it was hard for them. Three was trying to gain some small measure of the way I lived. I knew the family all missed that I wasn't around much anymore.

"I do."

She nodded and let out a huge breath. "I wish you would come home more."

"I'll work on that."

Her rosy hands tucked in her pockets, and she turned to face me.

"Look." Her head dropped down. "I know I'm not like Two. We don't talk about stuff like this, but…"

"Say it." I encouraged her to be open with me.

"I know everyone is concerned about Lexi, and I want to tell you something."

She motioned for me to sit on a bench.

"I was visiting Poppy's grave a few months back. Nan likes me to take him his tulips since the car hurts her back now." Her hands twitched in her jacket. "Anyway, as I was leaving, I saw Lexi standing at her parents' graves with flowers. I felt so bad for her. You know, that's so hard to see." Her worried eyes looked at me. "I watched her, not wanting to interrupt something so personal. She laid flowers on each grave and seemed to have a moment with them. Then she looked off toward the road, and there was a car there. I was going to go over and see how she was, but she started walking quickly in the direction of the car."

"Okay," I said to let her know I was following.

"I followed her until I saw a man get out of the car. She was heading right for him. When they started talking, he took hold of her arm."

"Who was he?"

She shrugged but looked concerned. "Some man in a long wool coat. I've never seen him before, which wouldn't normally have worried me, but when he looked at me, he shot me a really nasty look that stopped me in my tracks. Lexi yanked her arm out of his hold, and that was what frightened me. She wasn't comfortable with him, but she got in his car, and they stayed there for a while. I didn't stick around for long. I backed off, and I couldn't see anything anyway since the windows were tinted." She rubbed the side of her head as she looked up at me. "She never saw me, but that guy gave me a really bad feeling, and whatever that feeling was hasn't left me. I'm really worried about her, Keith."

"I know," I admitted. "So am I."

"Will you pull some crazy Army strings and see if you can find out who he was?"

"Did you get the make and model of the car? Or a license plate?"

"No." She shook her head. "All I know is he drove a black four door, dressed like a sleazy used car salesman, and had an earring." She made a disgusted face. "You know how I feel about men and jewelry."

I chuckled. "I do."

"I guess I wasn't made to be a spy."

"That's actually pretty good, Three. I'll see what I can find out."

Nodding, she leaned back with a long sigh. "You still love her, don't you?"

"Yeah." I gave her a squeeze. "I really do."

"You think there's any feelings left on her end?"

I kept my gaze forward, remembering how she didn't say no about me touching her, and I went with my gut. "I do." It would just take a lot to prove to her the feelings were still there.

Three made a funny noise, and I realized she was happy.

"That would be the best wedding present, you know."

I wrapped my arm around her shoulders and pushed away the difficulties of figuring out how Lexi and I could be together with the Army keeping us apart. I had a lot to think about and a lot to consider.

For the rest of the day, Three and I mulled ideas around about her wedding, old friends, and family. I forgot how much I needed my sisters in my life. They made me feel almost whole again.

Later that evening I intended to prove to my sisters exactly how much they missed me.

***

"Bullshit!" One yelled at me from across the table, her hands in the air. "There's no frigging way you have three twos!"

I wiggled my eyebrows at my sister. She hated that I had a great poker face. Every Sunday growing up, we'd have game night. We'd start with the board game Sequence, then move on to Bullshit. Dad was the champ at Sequence, then me, then Mom. The girls hated it because you had to have a strategy to win. Bullshit was all about lying about what cards you had.

"Show me," she ordered.

Like always, I proved I was right by flipping over my three twos.

"I'm not sure why you question him, sweetheart. He doesn't lie." Dad gave me a wink.

"Only when I have to." I felt the need to add that.

She huffed, settling back in her seat. "Must be hard to sit there with a halo shoved up your—"

A squeaking made us stop as Nan rolled into the living room looking *well done* as always.

"Mom!" my mother shouted in an exaggerated voice at Nan. "Look who is playing with us tonight!" Each word was slow and loud. It took everything inside of me not to smirk at Nan. I swore she looked like she might give up her angle at any moment. She made such an exasperated face.

"I bet you could use a drink." I allowed myself to let out a grin. Her eyes lit up as she begged me to have one with her. "I bet I'm right."

"He says he bets he's right!" Mom repeated loudly after me, which only made me bite down harder on my tongue.

"Yes, I could, dear. Thank you." She eyed the bottle of scotch on the bar. I hopped up and poured her a stiff one and handed it to her.

"So good to have you back." She repeated her usual comment, which meant so much more than just the booze. I was Nan's favorite.

"Let's go, big brother. Quit stall—"

My phone rang and stopped One's comment. I grinned until I read the caller ID. With a finger in the air, I stepped away from my family.

"What's going on, Antonio?"

"You should come by the clubhouse tonight. We're going to have some fun."

This can't be good. I grabbed my keys and headed in that direction.

***

My thumb brushed over the rim of the beer as I sat at the bar across from Will, who I wanted to hurt so often that the feeling just came naturally now.

"So..." Antonio came to my side, obviously high on something. "After researching a little, I see why you can't join me this evening. Military laws and shit, so I have a different idea for you."

I took a long, deep gulp of my beer and waited for his *genius* plan.

"I have my main guys, but there's a few I don't fully trust, and I want you to keep an eye on them for me." He nodded to where Elliot was stacking boxes awkwardly with his cast.

He wanted me to do what? Babysit? *You have got to be kidding!*

"What did Elliot do, anyway?" I felt I had a right to know, if I was going to be watching them.

Antonio studied me, then motioned for Will to give him a beer.

"He's not loyal."

This piqued my interest. "How so?"

He grinned around the bottle. "That's something you should ask him. Be sure to drop his sister's name in the conversation." He hopped off the stool and went to leave, but slowly turned as if he forgot to tell me something. "If he runs, kill him. Really, his time is almost up anyway." He placed a handgun on the bar top. "Just in case."

Shit.

I let the gun sit there between us, not willing to lay my hand on one of their weapons.

"I won't need that, Antonio, and I won't kill for you, but I'll keep an eye on the place if you want."

Antonio looked at me, then shrugged and left with some of his guys, leaving the gun still lying there.

I still hadn't seen Lexi, but I didn't want it to look like I was curious, so I sat back in the corner of the clubhouse and hoped to God the Devil's Reach didn't decide to make their attack tonight.

A few times Gordon walked into the room. On the third pass through, he came over and handed me some dinner. I wasn't hungry, and the food looked like shit, but I soon realized he wasn't expecting me to eat it. He just needed a reason to come over.

"I'm here to watch you." His voice was deep as he handed me a fork. This was the first time I really studied him. He was built, and I could see he'd spent sometime in the sun by the tan lines that peeked out from under the red bandana. His blue eyes had small wrinkles from squinting, and his hair was silver. My guess would be he was mid-fifties. He played the part of an *Almas Perdidas,* but in his wry smile I could see he had a kind soul. "Antonio needs to know if you are here for him or the girl."

"Okay, thanks for that." I nodded and pushed the food around the plate. I didn't know Gordon, so I wasn't about to spill my feelings to him. "What's happening tonight?"

"It's pick-up night. He'll be back with about three hundred thousand worth of narcotics. That's when the party will start up." He made a face that led me to believe Lexi would be involved.

"Fuck."

"Yeah." He glanced over his shoulder. "Heads up; they're planning to strike the Devil's Reach clubhouse soon."

Fuck. My skin heated at that thought. Suicide. Gordon tapped his nose before he disappeared in the back. I appreciated his warning.

Kicking my feet up, I had made a show of making the conversation with Gordon look normal. I watched Will tend the bar, the doorman checking people coming in and out for weapons, and Elliot kept his head down while he finished his job.

Around eleven, music was turned on and Tragically Hip's "So Hard Done By" blasted while the lights dimmed and people poured in.

Beer wasn't cutting it, so I changed over to rum and Coke. Just as I was about to finish my last sip, I caught Elliot's obvious attempt at eye contact from across the room. He nodded down the hallway, then disappeared.

Curious, I moved to my feet and pushed through a wall of bodies and heavy smoke. I peeked my head around the corner and saw two shadows.

"Stop." The harsh whisper prompted me to push open the door to the stock room.

There was Will with his hands all over Lexi. She was telling him to stop but wasn't making any real attempt to push him away. Strange.

"Will, please, don't."

Without thinking, I grabbed him by the collar and hauled him backward. He stumbled to catch his footing but stumbled to the ground.

Lexi had a worried expression that didn't match the situation.

"Are you okay?"

She ran a shaky hand over her shoulder. "I'm fine."

"What the fuck is your problem, man?" Will rose to his feet and tilted his head to look up at me. The man was 5'6", but stocky. "We share in this house. No one is exclusive. Ain't that right, babe?"

"You know Antonio doesn't share me," she hissed, closing her eyes while her cheeks deepened to a hot pink.

I was relieved to hear that, but it was quickly replaced with pure, raw anger toward the shit in front of me.

"She likes it rough, Keith—"

"I don't care if she likes to be bent in half," I cut him off, feeling territorial. "If I hear you touched her again, I will *kill* you."

"Keith," Lexi whispered. "He didn't hurt me."

"Fucking right, I didn't, bitch!"

With a twist of my arm, I had him in a headlock and bent him backward. Everything disappeared around me—sound, color, all just gone.

Will's nails dug in as he tried to release my hold. His eyes bulged.

"You touch her or speak to her like that again, I'll rip your balls off and shove them in your fucking little mouth." I slowed my words. "Do you hear me?"

His tongue ran along his teeth, but he nodded. I stepped back and let my surroundings flood back in. Lexi had a hand over her mouth, and Will was straightening his shirt with a cough.

"Looks like the boss's girl has a bodyguard."

Stupid man.

"Too bad he won't be sticking around." He unconsciously touched his crotch as he backed away. "See you later, Lexi."

I slowly turned back to face him and he walked a little faster.

Lexi sank onto a box and let her hair fall all around her. She slumped her shoulders, looking exhausted.

Carefully, I bent down and rested my weight on my heels. I still couldn't believe I could reach out and touch the one woman who stole my heart so long ago.

My hand hovered over her knee. I didn't want to push, but I really wanted to feel her. There was something so right when we were together.

Her head snapped up when she felt me touch her. Her beautiful eyes were rimmed with tears.

"Go away, Keith. You shouldn't be here."

"If I wasn't, you'd be under Will right now."

Her neck flexed, and I saw her walls shoot up. Classic Lexi. She always channeled her emotions into anger. Thankfully, it was one of the many things I loved about this woman.

"Hey." My hand ran up her thigh. I wasn't actually trying to be sexual; I just wanted to see if my touch still grounded her like she did me. "I don't know what's going on here, but this isn't the right place for you. You don't deserve this, Lexi. You're not someone's blow-up doll or one-night stand. You're a beautiful woman who deserves to be loved in the right way."

She jumped to her feet and whirled around, and I straightened up.

"You don't get to come in here after how many years and try to tell me how I should be living my life. A lot has happened since you left me for the *second* time four years ago."

"You wanna fight, don't you?"

She does.

"What I *want* is for you to leave!" She held my gaze as the words came out.

Liar.

I folded my arms. "Fine, let's hash this out."

She shook her head and let out a long, shaky breath. "Not here. Antonio doesn't know how deep our history runs."

"Screw him. Besides, he's not even here." I stepped closer and took her hand in mine. "No one can touch our history. That's ours. What we choose to do with our future is what can be affected."

Her face broke into a sarcastic smile...I'd hit a nerve.

"Future?" Her chin tilted upward. "What future?"

"You don't have to be here."

Her laugh had a hard edge to it. "That's cute, Keith."

She tried to leave, but I grabbed her arm and

leaned down so she could see directly into my eyes.

"Toss any shit you have at me, and I'll keep coming back for more because that's what people do when they're in love with someone."

She blinked a few times before I felt her arm relax in my grip.

"You don't love me, Keith. You love Lexi from ten years ago. There's a huge difference."

Not caring, I pulled her closer so my body hovered almost completely around hers. Her gaze dropped to my mouth. We were so close...

"You don't get to come walking back into my life like you own me," she hissed. "Things are different now. I'm with Antonio."

I couldn't contain my frustration as I let out a deep laugh. "Right, because that's what you need in your life. Someone to beat on you and your brother."

"You wouldn't understand." She tried to move, but I held her in place by her hips.

"Try me." I backed her up to the wall. She wiggled and bucked, but she couldn't get out of my grip.

"You're going to screw everything up."

"What does that mean?"

"It means you shouldn't be here. There's more to this fucked up story than you know!" Her head fell. She really did look tired.

Everything inside weakened as I relaxed, my body molding to hers. I rested my forehead on top of her head, but before I got too comfortable, she pushed me away.

"So much has happened since you left the first

time." She sniffed, turning her back to me. "You were the other half to my soul, Keith, and you left me, and then when I needed you most..." She brushed away a tear. "I was running on empty until Juan came into my life and showed me I was still worthy to be loved, maybe in a different way, but still loved."

I hated that comment.

"I never meant to hurt you, Lex."

She turned to look up at me, her eyes raw with pain. "Way too much is going on to pick up where we left off, Keith. It's not only about me anymore. Just go back to wherever and leave me alone."

The way her mouth moved captivated my attention. I pushed her flat against the wall and tilted her chin. Before she could protest, I pressed my lips to hers and felt like I was seventeen again.

My thumb ran along her jaw and pulled her mouth open so my tongue could move in. She let me, and I stepped in closer so she could feel how aroused I was.

Suddenly, her hands moved to my hair and tugged roughly at the roots. I could barely contain myself. It began to seep in that her kiss was off. It reminded me of something, but I couldn't place it.

One hand moved under her shirt and up to her plump breast. I cupped and twisted just the way she loved.

She squeaked and deepened the kiss. We were wild for one another, clawing and tugging at whatever we could get our hands on.

Moving my hand from her shirt, I ran it down her thigh, and then up her leather skirt where I found her slick.

"Keith," she mumbled into my lips, wiggling to find some kind of friction.

Fuck it. My fingers dove deep inside her soft walls. Her eyes rolled back and closed as her head thumped against the wall with relief.

Her breathing picked up, her chest rose and fell, which refocused my attention on her sexy breasts. I dove down and ran my tongue between them, sucking to draw the skin inward.

"Lex!" Will barked from the hallway. "Where the fuck are you?"

She tensed, and I could see she was slapped back to reality. She fought down her desire, and I could see her pulling in.

"Stop!" She rubbed her red lips madly. "Don't screw with my head. You've done that enough for one lifetime!"

"I'm not trying to confuse you. I'm trying to remind you what we could be."

"I don't want you to!" she nearly yelled through a whisper, pushing me away so she could fix her clothes.

"Lexi!" Will was on the other side of the door…if only he knew we were still in there. "Where is that little cunt?"

The doorknob started to jiggle, and Lexi pushed me back behind some boxes.

"Keith, don't say a friggin' word."

She twisted her skirt in place before she pulled the door open.

"Where the flying fuck have you been?" Will screamed at her.

"Locked inside that room. Thanks for caring, asshole."

"Get your ass up front. Too many customers for me to handle."

"What, you can't handle a few orders?" she tossed back, leaving me spinning.

CHAPTER NINE

Once I knew they were gone, I hurried out to the hallway and acted like I was checking the rooms.

Elliot glanced at me as he tossed some dirty ice water out the back door.

"She okay?"

I nodded but kept moving back to the bar, where I came face to face with a hyped up Antonio and his men.

"How was it?" Lexi asked as she picked up an empty glass. Her cheeks still had some pink to them. She avoided all eye contact with me and acted like I wasn't there at all.

Antonio grabbed her hips and backed her into him. She leaned against him, moving her hips provocatively.

"Go get naked and wait for me in position."

She leaned back and gave him a kiss. I couldn't lie; that bothered me.

"Actually, I haven't finished helping Will. I got locked—"

"Did I ask?" His hand roughly grabbed her chin

177

so she would look at him. "I don't like to repeat myself, Lexi."

It took everything in my body not to snap his neck in two. My hands nearly shook with the need to kill.

With a snap of his fingers, a man came forward and placed three oval pills on the table and smashed them down to dust with the butt of his gun. Sprinkling them into a spare drink, he handed it to him and stepped back.

Gordon glanced at me, then back at Lexi.

"Drink," Antonio ordered, shoving the laced rum and Coke in Lexi's hand before he let her go. "Now."

She tipped the cup back, downing the entire thing. "Fun times, hey, boys?" she cheered as she slammed the empty glass down.

A flash of white caught my eye, and I saw Elliot across the room watching with a horrified expression. This was the first time I really hated her brother. He *was,* after all, the one who got her into this fucked up mess. If he had just been a man and helped his sister when she was hurting, like most siblings who lost their parents would do, they wouldn't have been here right now. Instead, he thought only about himself and acted like an idiot. Then chased some pussy right into the *Almas Perdidas'* cesspool, taking Lexi with him.

"Move." Antonio shoved her forward, using her elbow. "Go, before that shit kicks in."

"I'm going." She kissed him before she left again, avoiding all eye contact with me.

The minute I could, I quickly fired off a text to

Clark.

Ten painful minutes later, I got the distraction I hoped for. Two heavily made up hookers came strolling in, looking to make a few bucks. This caught Antonio's attention. I waited for him to disappear into a random bedroom before I made my move. I couldn't help but feel happy for them. They sure as hell weren't going to get sex tonight.

I found Lexi in her room, wearing only her thong and a t-shirt. Pulling her skirt back on, I grabbed a blanket and wrapped it around her, then gathered her in my arms. Just as I was about to leave, I caught sight of the little wooden box I sent her from my first tour. It may not have meant much to anyone else, but it gave me a glimmer of hope knowing she kept it all these years. I hurried out the door and down to the last bedroom near the exit door.

I found Elliot listening to his headphones on the bed. "Get out." He jumped up at my clipped tone and made room for his sister. "I need you to make sure Antonio doesn't come looking for her tonight."

"Antonio sure as hell won't listen to me. I'm on his radar."

"Why?" I asked. I wanted some god damn answers. I carefully fixed the covers around her limp body. "Why, Elliot?"

"I broke a rule."

Rules. I could understand that. One of the main things I loved about living at Shadows were the rules. They were set in place for a reason and were meant to be followed. They were for our safely— for the protection of everyone and everything.

179

Keeping the location of the safe house a secret depended on everyone following those rules. Cole was extremely strict that we followed them, or there were immediate consequences. The worst punishment was the peak. Duty at the peak wouldn't harm you, but it was hellishly cold and miserable.

"Which was?"

His hands went to the top of his head as he squeezed his eyes shut. I could actually hear him grinding his teeth.

"I…" He tried to go on, and I could see the battle he was fighting. Saliva pooled in the corners of his mouth as his hands trembled under the pressure. "It was bad." His haunted eyes found mine. "These guys make the Devil's Reach gang look like pussies."

I wanted to correct him—there was nothing worse than the DR, but I wasn't about to interrupt.

He stood, jerked open a drawer, and removed a bottle of vodka.

"Want some?

"No." I waited.

Pouring a triple, he held it between his tattooed fingers and stared at the mix of colored numbers on each one as if seeing them for the first time.

Once he seemed to regain control, he rubbed his thigh and nodded to himself as if to make amends with his fears. I respected that. It meant he still had some rational thinking going on inside. They hadn't completely broken him yet.

"I slept with Antonio's cousin. I didn't know, and she sure as hell didn't tell me who she was.

Later, she wanted more from me and I said no. So, she told him. Told him a completely different version, that is."

"Yeah, that would piss him off."

"That, and Lexi tried to side with me." His eyes flinched. "Despite what you think…" He cleared his throat and his voice became stronger. "I never wanted her here, you know. I was lost and out of control. She begged me to come home, but I didn't feel home was home anymore. I didn't really fit anywhere. I didn't realize how far gone she was either. I mean, I knew she was hurting too, but what the hell could I do? I was a mess."

I had to grit my teeth not to punch him in the face. I needed to let him talk it out.

"Then when she got involved with Juan, things were different." He paused to look at his sister's pale face. Her chest barely moved from the heavy dose of Vicodin.

"He was nice to her at first, but then he started beating on her. Only a little, but…must be a family trait. I tried to jump in the first time, but they only beat me worse. I tried to talk her out of hanging out at the clubhouse so much. We still had our parents' house then. Wasn't till two years ago we had to sell it. She was real sad when we let it go. She looked at a couple of apartments, and I thought she had decided on one, but she just started staying with Juan. Now, with Antonio, she's here full time and things are worse." He rubbed his sweaty lip. "Juan never told Antonio that you and her dated for so long. Those two are always butting heads, and he didn't want Antonio to make jabs at him about it."

181

He took a drink, and downed about half of it. "Although Antonio knew anyway, he seems to know everything. It's a small town." He made a wry face. "Place like this is the shits for anyone, but she stayed. Her decision, right?"

So Lexi hadn't told him about the possibility that the gang was behind their parents' murder. That was interesting.

"Man, that girl can flip from the old Lexi to someone completely different. I hardly know her anymore." As he leaned forward, he said, "They've threatened to kill me if she doesn't do what she's told. They've got us both with a noose around our necks, and since she's moved in full time, it just gets tighter. They mean it, too, Keith. Once you're in, you're in."

Jesus Christ, what a fucking coward!

"What happened to Juan?" I wanted as much information as possible so I knew what I was dealing with.

Elliot leaned back and kicked his feet up on the table, taking a moment. "Antonio wanted Lexi, and the only way he could make his move on her was if his brother was gone. So, about nine months ago, he planted some evidence and even testified against him on a murder charge. Juan got fifteen to life. The next day, Lexi was moved into Antonio's room, and now she belongs to him. Minus the sharing. Antonio, for whatever reason, won't share her. That just makes her more of a target to some guys."

"Will?"

"Yeah, that asshole!" He jerked his hand and sloshed some vodka onto his pants.

I cleared my throat, not wanting to think about Will and Lexi.

"Go on."

"She, umm…" He paused and shifted like he was suddenly uncomfortable. "She had this plan one time. Antonio was away, and she called him told him she was real sick and complained of bad stomach pains, and Antonio told her I could take her to the doctor. We're not really supposed to leave together, but like I said, things are different now, but because he was away, he gave her permission. That's when she got an IUD put in."

I nodded, knowing what that meant. When Three got hers, I had to hear all about it. The *joys* of living with five women. Birth control wasn't a taboo subject in my house.

"Antonio doesn't know. Not that he would care, but Lexi did. She actually considered getting her tubes tied just so, you know, it couldn't happen. The doctor talked her out of it, saying it was risky if she ever wanted kids later on." He looked at me with red eyes. "I helped convince her not to. I didn't want my sister to lose the chance if she ever changed her mind. Obviously, she wasn't worried about Antonio, but he normally does share, so…" He held my stare, trying to convince me he had actually done something to help her. His eyes shifted from one of mine to the other, searching for something I wasn't going to give him.

"Good luck getting through to her, Keith. Part of her died years ago after you left. No joke, she wouldn't let any of us speak your name in the house after that. She was so damaged by what you did, she just turned that part of herself off. The old Lexi is gone, mostly, and she isn't going to listen to either of us."

I knew he was trying to deflect his lack of effort to help Lexi onto me, and as much as it hurt to hear, I didn't want to go there right now.

"Elliot, I have to ask you something." I needed to keep him talking. There was still something I wasn't getting here.

He nodded and made an attempt to cover his sister a little better with the blanket.

"Antonio mentioned you did something to lead him to believe you aren't trustworthy. What was that?"

His jaw ticked. He hesitated, then turned and shrugged. "Besides the mix-up with his cousin, he just doesn't like me defending my sister. I think he's jealous of our relationship. Other than that, I don't know."

The thing about Elliot was he was pretty easy to read. I was sure he was lying to me, and he was definitely hiding something.

We sat together in silence, me absorbing what I heard, and Elliot enjoying his shoulder to lean on. There was a time Elliot and I had been close. There was something about him, though, that I never liked. But he was Lexi's brother, and she adored him, so I made the effort. He'd always had a bit of a reckless side. This time it had gotten him into the kind of trouble that was only going to get more dangerous as time moved on, and he was taking Lexi right along with him.

Elliot started to talk again.

"When Antonio realized Lexi was great with numbers, he started letting her work on the books. She's proved she's trustworthy and she can be useful to him. He doesn't like me, well, because, I ahh…stepped over the line by sleeping with his cousin. Lexi tried to defend me, and he didn't like that at all. Now he's questioning her loyalty. He's pissed at her, and that's why he's making her work the bar with Will." He closed his eyes for a second. "Now the only time she's allowed to leave on her own is every Thursday, when she goes to visit our parents' grave, or when she's sent out on errands. At first they'd follow her to make sure she wasn't lying about where she went, but she wasn't. Lexi is too scared to run off."

"How did you get into the gang, Elliot?"

His face flinched, again indicating he was about to lie. "I fell into this place through Antonio's cousin. She really is pretty. Later I became close with his uncle when I got four months at the county jail for taking the heat for a marijuana charge. They found it in his car. It was a tradeoff, and anything was better than having to do their initiation." He put a hand over his heart. "I wouldn't have been able to murder someone for no reason." He paused like he wanted to say something, but stopped himself. Much like his sister did.

What was really going on here?

"Where have you been, Keith? What have you been up to?"

I didn't plan to answer that. He didn't have the right to ask, and it came with too many unanswerable questions. Thankfully, I didn't have

185

to reply. The door slowly opened, and a girl with green hair popped her head inside the room.

"Is she out?"

Feeling like I was missing something, I looked over at Elliot. He shook his head at her.

"Not tonight, Renny."

Dismissing his comment, she moved into the room, closing the door behind her. I couldn't believe it when she started to remove her top.

"What the hell is this?" My expression was murderous. Elliot jumped to his feet, then oddly enough, he hesitated.

I couldn't believe what I was seeing as this green-headed chick whipped off her skirt, jumped on the bed, and started to kiss Lexi's limp lips.

Elliot stood like a statue, watching with a weird expression on his face like he was *enjoying* it. "What the fuck?" I started for the bed, stopping myself from flinging her against a wall when Elliot shouted.

"Renny, get out!" Elliot jolted out of his trance. "Get the fuck off of her!"

She looked confused as she peeled herself off Lexi.

"What the shit, Elliot? Never bothered you bef—"

"Get out!" he interrupted her, but not before the sickening comment was heard.

I wanted to punch something as my stomach rolled in a violent twist.

"If Antonio finds out—"

"She's my goddamn twin, you crack whore. I'm protecting her."

Renny gave him a dirty but confused look before she grabbed her clothes and headed for the door. Oh my God, this had happened before.

"Hey!" She pointed her chin at me. "You wanna BJ or somethin'?"

I stared at her, my head completely thrown by this whole cluster fuck. I started to pick Lexi up, wrapping the pathetically small blanket around her.

"I'm taking her to my parents." I stood holding her in my arms as Elliot stepped in front of me. "Get out of my way, Elliot."

"If you take her, they'll kill her when she comes back. Trust me." He shifted gears. "She'll be just as angry at you for taking her out of here as they will." His face grew pale. "Everything here comes with a consequence. Don't risk her life with this. It's nothing new. Trust me."

Fuck! Fuck! Fuck!

He might be right. Shit, I needed to think. I stepped back and tried to shake off my frustration. I slowly put her back on the bed, brushing the hair from her pale face. *Oh, Lexi, what am I going to do with you?* Taking the cleaner looking corner, I dropped my ass to the floor and closed my tired eyes.

It was going to be a long night, and I wasn't going anywhere.

* * *

Lexi

The clouds rolled by at a lazy pace, and my

sleepy eyes created shapes and faces. A warm breeze moved over my skin while the ocean pawed at the shoreline. A soft cream colored cotton dress fluttered around my legs. I enjoyed the feeling of it as it flirted with my thighs.

A perfect day. My skin, sun-kissed under the hot rays, reminded me I wasn't in Boston anymore. A smile crept along my lips when I spotted him wading in the water. His broad shoulders and lean stomach gleamed with water. He was wearing a ball hat, and I almost laughed out loud at the happiness that bubbled up from inside. I lay in my hammock and enjoyed watching him.

"More margarita, miss?" Eddie, my favorite Bajan bartender, leaned down and offered me another.

"Thanks, Eddie." I always tipped him well. He was the best. I happily sucked on a piece of pineapple, letting the juices mingle with my taste buds.

Keith and I had been planning to go on a trip for some time now, so when we turned twenty-one, we pooled our money, and there we were on a beach down by the Gap in Barbados. We absolutely loved this island. The people were warm and friendly and the food fantastic. We both loved the flying fish, a specialty here.

We had booked a catamaran with our new friends, Clint and Laura. They owned a company that delivered boats around the world. Clint entertained us with many stories of his escapades on the sea. An expert sailor, he also raced boats, and one of his favorites was the Clipper Round the

World race. They were locals and took us under their wing right from the start and showed us nothing but a great time. We were extremely fortunate to have met them.

I rolled over to enjoy watching Keith again, but he had disappeared from view. Damn. I leaned back and closed my eyes.

"I think you should lose the dress," he said from somewhere behind me.

"You should lose the shorts."

He stopped my hammock and carefully crawled in next to me.

"Yikes!" I jumped and nearly spilled both of us into the sand. He had been swimming, "You're freezing!"

He rolled into me more. "Warm me, then." He started to kiss my chest and his hand roamed my leg. "God, you taste amazing."

"Keith," I laughed. "We're going to tip!"

He swung his leg over mine and flipped us so I landed on his chest with a thud. All I could do was laugh harder until he flipped me again and he was on top. He grabbed my arms and held them above my head as he rubbed his wet hair over my stomach. I squealed and begged for mercy.

Pulling back, he leaned his weight on his forearm. Brushing my hair out of my face, his liquid dark eyes stared into mine. I swore I could see our future in there, all mapped out with a neat little bow. Keith was my first and my last love. I didn't care what anyone said; falling in love young didn't always have to be a bad thing. It could just mean we were lucky enough to crash headlong into our one

189

and only soulmate and would live as one from then on.

"How can something so beautiful be real?" He always made me feel like I was the only one for him. Like no one else mattered. Dipping down, he caught my lips and gave me a soft peck. It was all I could do not to rip his shorts off.

Keith might ravish me when were alone, but he was respectful when others were around us.

"Come." He stood and brought me to my feet. "I need you alone now."

Practically dragging me behind him, we headed down a path through thick palm trees. Once we were halfway through, he stopped and pulled me into a tiny clearing that could only be seen from the water.

"What are you doing?" I looked over my shoulder but saw we were completely alone.

"I found this place the other day, when we were kayaking." He yanked off his shorts, giving me a grin right before he dove in the crystal clear water. His head popped up, and he shook the water from his eyes. "Come, Lexi, lose the dress."

How could I say no to that? Ditching my clothes, I dove naked into the warm water. When I surfaced, Keith pulled me into his arms and gathered me tightly.

"Mmm, your body feels so smooth against mine," he muttered into my lips.

I squeezed my legs around his waist and gave a little wiggle. He granted me a sexy smile before he stood straight up and walked me out of the water and laid me on top of my dress.

Dripping wet, we made love right there on that tiny beach. At that moment, we were the only two who mattered in the whole, wide world.

I knew I was awake. I just had to will my eyes open. I wondered how many pills he put in my drink this time. Oh! This was one of the times I was glad we didn't have windows. No light to hurt the achy eyes.

It took me a moment to realize I was in Elliot's room. He was slumped over in his chair with his black work boots still on. He always was ready to run. I couldn't blame him. You never knew when you might have to look for a quick escape.

I did a brief assessment of my body, and nothing seemed to hurt. The relief that spread through me was quickly replaced with fear.

Where was Antonio?

Suddenly, there was a sound of heavy footsteps, loud bangs along the hall wall, and then an eerie silence that had me scrambling to my feet.

My world tilted; my hands went to my head.

Oh Lord, my head!

I saw movement from the corner of the room. *Oh no!* It was Keith. He had jumped to his feet at the sound as well. I quickly froze as he held up his hand and put a finger to his lips.

Shit!

"Don't," I pleaded in a whisper. Oh my God, we were all going to be killed! Think fast! "If you feel anything for me, please go in the closet and don't come out!" It was a dirty thing to use to stop him, I knew, but I couldn't risk him getting killed over me

191

and my screwed up life.

He started to argue, but my face must have convinced him otherwise. Right before he closed the door, Elliot opened the bedroom door to Antonio's furious face.

His flew into the room, and he yanked me into him hard, his grip hurting my arm.

"Where the fuck have you been?"

"She was with me." Elliot moved to show him his bed. "I went to the bathroom and your door was open." His voice started to shake while I fought to breathe. "I knew it was our pick-up night and she looked really still. I was worried. I...I was just looking out for her...and for you. I went to look, but I couldn't find you. I'm sorry if I stepped over a line, but she is family."

Antonio's chest heaved, but I felt his grip loosen a little.

"Alone the whole night?"

"No." He shook his head, and I glared at him. He wouldn't...

"Renny came by, tried to play a bit. She's been pissing me off lately, and I didn't want to see her face."

Antonio let me go, and I staggered back. I prayed Keith wouldn't open the door, knowing he was watching and that it wouldn't take much.

"Get showered and meet me back in my room," he ordered before he left. He slammed the door hard behind him.

Crying with relief, all thoughts of the sleepiness that had consumed me now gone, my hands shook as I ran them along my arm. Small black spots were already appearing where his fingers had held me.

"Hey." A pair of strong hands wrapped around my waist. "Let me look." Keith stood in front of me, his dark, angry gaze slowly moving from my eyes, to my lips, then my sore arm.

"I'm fine." I batted him away and stumbled around his massive frame. "Thank you for listening to me," I said, beyond grateful.

"It won't happen again, so there better not be a next time. I'm not a guy to cower in closets, Lexi."

Elliot began patting my back, checking to see if I was all right. I knew I only had a short amount of time before I was expected to be clean and naked in Antonio's room.

Stumbling on weak knees, I held the desk for support as I tried to clear my head. I hated when my mind was like this, but knew it was the damn drugs he liked to feed me when he needed me out of his way. They left me feeling like a swimmer underwater at night, unable to find a way out in an endless, murky sea.

In a quick moment, he was in front of me again and bent down to get a good look at my face. I knew he was fighting for control. He did that when he was worried, and it was why I let him talk to me that way. Keith carried a lot of love.

"I'm going to kill him, you know. It's only a matter of when."

"Don't. Please." A fresh tear slipped down my cheek. "I've got this."

"I can't let him hurt you anymore, Lexi. It goes against anything I believe in, everything I *am*."

"I know." I sniffed, closing my eyes. "I know

how much you care, but I need this, Keith. I need to do this."

"I want so much to interfere. I want to kill Antonio. I want to watch the life go out of him while I choke him with my bare hands. But I understand, Lexi. You see how hard this is for me? But I do understand."

I nodded and my gaze flickered to Elliot, who was trying to follow our conversation. Keith gave me a nod in return. He knew I didn't want my brother to know yet. He might try to do something on his own, and I needed him to stay out of trouble. He was in over his head as it was.

"Okay…" he grunted as he examined my bruised arm for another beat. "I think we should…"

My stomach sank as old emotions came dancing back. I let my gaze drop to his chest, and up popped my wall.

"Excuse me? You think? We?" I let my icy layer return. This was where I felt safe; this was my mask. "I don't think so. Back off, Keith!"

His hands rose in the air and he stepped backward, then he did a pivot and left.

Stop! I yelled at my emotions. *Just don't.*

"He still cares about you, Lexi." Elliot sank onto the bed. "He wouldn't have spent the night here ready to kill anyone who came near you if there weren't feelings there."

I grabbed my clothes and headed for the bathroom, but I stopped at the door. Keeping my eyes locked on his round mirror, I spoke to my reflection.

"It's just guilt, El. Don't let him trick you into

doing something stupid."

***

I suspected Keith somehow had a hand in making Antonio leave on an unexpected road trip for a few days, but either way, I was more than thankful. Only thing was it gave Will the green light to move in.

My stomach twisted as I waited for the phone line to connect. My palms were sweaty, and my head hurt.

"What?" His tone was always the same, annoyed.

"Hey, so, since you're away, I thought I might be able to go visit my parents' grave and maybe get some food and stuff? I won't be gone long, and you know I'll be here when you get back."

"No."

My eyes stung with disappointment. I needed to get out of here so badly. So, I tried a different angle.

"Um, it's just that Will is being a bit aggressive. He makes me uneasy, Antonio."

"Just give him what he wants, and he'll move on to the next whore."

I had to ease onto a bar stool and pour myself a double whiskey to hold back my tongue. When he made comments like that, I wanted to chop off his penis. I imagined tossing the nasty, useless little thing into a blender, then making him drink it.

"Lovely way to look at your girlfriend." My lips formed into a hard line. "I thought you didn't share me."

"I don't, but there are always exceptions to the rule."

"Hmm, good to know."

"Don't make this into something, Lexi."

"*Or* I could just go visit my parents?"

A long measure of silence followed. I really wasn't sure what was about to happen.

"Did you just question me?"

My mouth went dry.

"The answer is no. Get your fuckin' ass behind that bar and do what you're told."

I hate you.

"Got it." I didn't mean to sound sarcastic, but my bitchy side was clawing at the surface.

"I think I need to remind you who is in charge here."

"I guess between the drugs and booze, it must have slipped my mind." My eyes shut as my mouth kept going. This would for sure earn me the beating of a lifetime. "When you treat someone like a blow up doll, all you get is hot air."

"Who the fuck do you think you're talking to, bitch?"

"Someone who once told me he cared for me, that I was special and worthy of something better. Interesting way of showing it. All I wanted, Antonio, was to go visit my parents, and because I am really sick and tired of being chased around by Will's dick. Sorry for not wanting to sleep with the boys while you were gone. What an asshole I must be."

Before I knew what I was doing, I hung up and headed for our room.

Breathe, breathe, breathe. I pushed the panic aside and tried to focus.

My phone rang, and each ring felt like a punch to the gut. Quickly packing my bag, I hurried out the back into the blinding sun to my car. I stopped dead in my tracks when I saw Will sitting on the hood.

"Yeah, man, she's right here, bags packed, keys in hand." Dammit! Antonio! "Whatever you say, boss." He grinned as he tucked his phone away.

"Move," I hissed, terrified at what might happen.

"Sorry, doll, boss wants you to stay put." He looked over my head with a delighted smile. "He left me in charge." He stepped forward, and I stepped back. My heart pounded in my chest as Will approached.

"Don't touch me."

"Or what?" He yanked on the strap, my bag fell to the ground, and I stumbled. He took that moment to grab me around the waist. One moment I was in his grasp, and the next I was in someone else's.

The tenderness of his hold told me who it was, and relief rushed through me.

Keith turned his body to shield me as he yelled at Will.

"I thought I had made myself clear. If I ever see you touch her, I will kill you and your brother."

Brother? Oh, that's right. He was much younger than Will and was still in college. Yikes, it was scary that Keith even went there.

"I don't belong to your crew, Will, which means I don't have to play by your rules. I warned you once, and I'm not in the habit of repeating myself. Get in your car, Lexi, and go."

Will flinched, but when his eyes found mine, he grinned.

"You better enjoy yourself, Lexi. I can guarantee you'll regret this."

That I was sure of.

I reached for my keys, scooped up my bag, and headed for my car while Keith acted like my shield.

Once inside the safety of my car, I turned over the engine and roared down the alleyway toward the open road.

I fumbled with my phone as I sent a quick voice text to Elliot explaining what was going on. Tossing it aside, I let my mind slip back to a different time.

"You okay?" Elliot sat on the edge of my bed as I stared out at the falling snow. I loved the winters in Toronto. You could almost guarantee there wouldn't be school the next day. I was really banking on that this time around.

"Did he hurt you?"

I pulled back my sleeve and showed him the bruise. Amazing that at fifteen I actually had a boyfriend who hurt me physically. Needless to say, I nipped that real quick.

"I'll kill him!"

"Don't worry about it, Elliot. I punched him in the nose."

He couldn't help but smirk, which made me do the same.

"Man, did I ever get a kick-ass twin." He laughed harder.

"I'm not someone's punching bag."

"Damn straight, you're not. You're perfect. You

have to be...you're half of me." His eyes lit up as a big grin spread across his face, and he pulled me into a hug. "I love you, Lexi. Anyone hurts you, they hurt me, and I don't want to be hurting. You're so much better than that! You remember that, okay?"

I wiped a tear and tucked that memory away. There was more to it this time—much more.

Smoke swirled around my fingers. It dipped and dived between my knuckles along with the breeze from the vent. With my nail, I flicked the end and let the ash tumble down over the steering wheel. Pot calmed my nerves, but nothing could remove the fear from my chest. I knew better than to think this would all work out.

Checking my blind spot, I exited on Lake Drive and mindlessly drove down the surface streets.

My phone lit up, and I glanced over to see who it was this time.

Calling: Yellow

My stomach sank as I flipped it over. *Not now.*

I turned my brain off and tried to remember better times.

The sun was starting to set, and I had nowhere to go. That was part of my problem. I had no friends, no family, and no home. We had to sell the house because we couldn't afford to keep it. That was almost as painful as the funeral. Just one more tear in the thin fabric holding what was left of me together.

I found myself pulling into my favorite spot at

the lake. It was the one place that brought me any kind of comfort. Reaching behind me, I pulled my blanket and a bottle of wine free and headed down to the dock.

Warmth spread through me at the sound of my combat boots on the red cedar planks. Sounds had a big part in my memory, and this was one of them.

The dock lamp was low and only lit up a small area, but it was enough to feel safe. Removing my shoe, I hit the bottom of the wine bottle, and after some good, hard smacks the cork was free. Sadly, I mastered this technique years ago when life was good.

I wrapped my blanket over my shoulders and sat with my legs around a big, round post high enough it came up to my chest. In earlier times, I loved to lean forward and dangle my legs and arms above the water, pretending I was flying. The calm water skimmed the pillars as it cruised by at a lazy pace.

My tongue pushed back in the top of my mouth. Cold red wine was not a favorite of mine. Why didn't I grab a white?

Chugging more, I soon felt the effects I had been waiting for. Warmth lapped around my belly like a small fire on a stormy night. I got up and hopped from post to post like a child at a playground. Yes, it was incredibly unsafe, but it was fun and made my heart beat faster when I almost lost my balance.

My feet wiggled, trying to curve to the shape of the rounded post. It wasn't easy in my boots. Everything suddenly tilted, and I fell sideways. The cold water felt like a punch to the stomach as I landed. My jacket clung to me like a dead weight attached to the bottom of a buoy. It was almost like my brain was stuck a few seconds behind in time. Then it hit me. *Move!* I kicked toward the surface as hard as I could while the cold water tried its best to pull me back down. My lungs burned until my head broke the surface and I sucked in a deep, wonderful breath. My muscles stung as I clawed at the ladder with numb hands. It took every ounce of strength to haul myself up onto the edge of the dock, then to climb over and onto the top. I gasped and let out a high pitched yelp before I caught my breath. *What the hell was I thinking?* I knew I needed to get dry fast.

I struggled to my feet and grabbed my blanket and started up the small hill toward my car. My feet felt so heavy, like frozen blocks of ice water. It made my socks squeak uncomfortably. My fingers were so cold, they seemed to be locked around the soft fabric of my blanket. *Damn painful.*

Headlights blinded me, then a truck stopped a moment later, and out jumped Keith.

Christ! Does he have a tracker on my damn car or something?

"What the hell happened to you?" He seemed pissed off, which put my back up.

"Went for a swim."

His fist hit down on the hood, making me jump. I could see he was past his normal tolerance. So I went with the truth.

"I slipped."

"Slipped?" His lips pressed into a hard line. Oh, that look made my blood thaw a little, but not in a good way.

"Yup, it's when you miss your footing and your body falls." I tucked a cold piece of hair behind my ear, avoiding his murderous stare. It took everything I had not to fall to the ground in a shivering mess.

"Get in."

"I'm fine. I have clothes in my car. I was just going—"

He tilted his head back and looked toward the sky, holding his arms out to the sides.

"Give me strength! Between you and Savannah, I'm going to have a stroke at forty."

Who was Savannah?

He moved around to open the passenger side door.

"Please, get in."

I waited a few beats to calm my anger *and* to fuel his.

With a heavy sigh that I didn't try to hide, I moved around to the front of his truck and placed a hand on the door and the seat.

He suddenly grabbed my hips and hoisted me inside.

"Jesus, I should've expected that."

He ignored my comment and pulled off my boot to dump out the water. He did the same to the other.

"Keys?" He held out his hand with an annoyed look. Biting my tongue, I removed them from my jacket, thankful they didn't fall out when I took my unexpected swim. I handed them to him, and he slammed the door shut.

He returned a moment later with my bag and tossed it at my feet. Once he was inside, he turned the vent to point directly at my face and blasted the heat.

I was freezing but didn't want to act like I was. I felt seventeen all over again. Only now my stubbornness was way worse.

Finally, I tugged off my jacket. Everything was starting to fuse to my skin. Yuck, my socks felt like wet plastic bags plastered to my skin as I peeled them free. My hands shook as I attempted to yank off my jeans, but they wouldn't budge. *For the love of God! Come on!*

"Here." Keith motioned for me to turn toward him. I nearly told him off. I was so pissed at the entire situation. If it wasn't for the fact I was about to lose my shit with my damn pants, I would have left. *I should have just jumped in my car and left.*

But no, I twisted my body, and his fingers wrapped around the top of the jeans and slowly pulled them down. His eyes dragged with exaggerated slowness southward over my chilly skin, and the whole time I stayed quiet. It was exquisitely intimate, and I felt my heart rate pick up. If someone were to tell me I would be okay half naked alone with Keith in his truck at this point, I would say they were insane. Yet, here we were, and now I wasn't sure what to do or how to feel about it. Should I scream and kick or try to be civil? Funny, I couldn't decide.

Once I was free of my pants, I pulled myself to a sitting position, not sure what to make of the moment.

"This is all too familiar." I jammed my leg through my tights awkwardly.

He grinned, then went back to looking out the

windshield. "Ahh, yes, the good old days, where everything made sense and I had you to myself."

"Who's fault was that?" I snapped. *Really?* I hated I just made that jab, but it was what I did. Anger before any other feeling. It was my shield.

His jaw locked then twitched like the hand on a clock. "It was never my intent to have you cut me out of your life." He then closed his eyes and settled into the corner of the door.

"No," I huffed quietly. "It was just your intent to break my heart."

"You broke mine too."

I held back my pity comment. After all, we weren't children. We were two grown adults with so much baggage we could spin in circles all night. Plain and simple, we weren't anything anymore, only a distant memory.

"Are you staying here tonight?" I needed some space before I said anything I regretted.

"If you are going to do it, Lexi, then do it." His raspy voice seemed to come from deep in his chest. "I fought your battles all day, and could use some sleep."

"Battles?" *Oh, there's my temper.* "I never asked you to fight shit for me!"

I swore I saw a smirk.

"Okay."

I sat up a little straighter. "Okay? That's it?"

"Yup."

"Are you trying to piss me off?"

"Yup."

My head snapped back. What the hell? I twisted on the bench seat. "Why?"

I blinked, and he slid around to face me, his hands in his lap, but I could tell he wanted to touch me. *Not in this life!*

"Because you only know how to fight, and if that's the only damn way to get you talking, then let's do this."

I hated that he knew me so well.

"I wanted a better life for us. It's why I left in the first place."

"Don't." I held up a hand. I couldn't go that far back right now. "I can't...don't go there."

I struggled to get my shoes on, opened the door, and then I hopped down and caught myself on the door. I was freezing, and it gave me a huge reality check that I only had tights on.

"Don't go where?" Keith slammed his door shut. "To the root of our problems?" He followed me. Lord, it was cold. "Fine, let's change directions. Then let's talk about how your boyfriend drugs you and treats you like crap. Yeah, let's start there."

"Screw you." It was a low-handed, dirty comment which made me want to get as far away as possible. "At least Juan was there for me—" I stopped myself.

"For when?" he shouted, his shoulders rising along with his anger.

Don't, I told myself.

"For when, Lexi?" He hands went up. "For when you turned eighteen and broke your ankle, and I stayed by your side for twelve hours in the ER? For when your best friend moved away, and you two missed your chick flick marathon, and I was your stand-in date? Or when you passed your very first test in university, and we went out and celebrated?" He shook his head. "I never forgave myself for not getting home when your parents died. I wanted to, I really did, but I just couldn't, but dammit, Lexi, I have been there for you for so much more."

A drop of water traveled down my hair and landed on my chest. My arms wrapped around my middle. I tried to lighten my voice. His words were chipping at my armor.

"Let it go, Keith. It's the past."

"No," his tone was eerie, "I waited for you all these years, only to find out my girl has reduced herself to less than a—"

I lunged forward and slapped him across the face. The moment I did it, my hands covered my mouth. Never had I ever hit anyone I loved before, and tears filled my eyes. I wanted to sob.

"Do it again," he whispered.

I shook my head.

"Do it now." His teeth clenched, and a vein in his neck popped.

Weakly, I shoved his arm, and his eyes held mine. He looked so different.

"I left you."

Hey, that comment hurt. I shoved him harder.

"With only a two-day notice."

This time I punched him in the arm, but he didn't even flinch. My anger started to burn inside my skin, leaving wounds at every prick. I wanted him to hurt like I had been hurt.

"I should've called more, but I didn't, because I didn't know what to say."

My eyes felt sore, and I blinked to moisten them

as I shoved him even harder.

"I didn't come home when your parents were killed."

My fists beat his chest, and he took it. Every emotion I'd ever felt came roaring out. Tears raced down my face, one after the other. I could easily break if I wasn't careful.

His tone turned strange, but he fought the emotion back. "And when I returned four years ago, I didn't stick around."

"No, you didn't!" A sob ripped through me, rattling my composure. "You keep screwing with my emotions walking in and out of my life."

"Say it!" he ordered over my cries.

"I hate you!" flew out of my mouth. I didn't care because it felt so good to finally say—no, scream—the words. "I hate you!" My hair was all over the place as I took the last how many years of pain out on him. "I hate you, I hate you so much!"

"I know," he whispered.

Oh, hell no! He doesn't get me to lose it, bare my feelings, then say he knows. You don't know shit! So you know what, that you destroyed my heart? So you know how many nights I cried with no end in sight just to gain the tiniest relief? You don't know. You have no fucking idea!

"Do something!" My anger boiled over. I despised that he just took my punishment. This wasn't enough! "Christ, Keith, do something!" I was barely making sense in my head. I wanted those feelings I had spent so long fighting to bury themselves back down again.

Suddenly, he snatched my flailing wrists and

slammed me to the door of the truck. His lips were on mine before I could catch up. His tongue swirled around and demanded me to follow.

Fine! He wanted my body, then take it!

I pushed my morals to the wind. *You want closure, here I am.*

I met him with the same force. I gripped the brim of his hat and turned it around. His hips pressed into my belly, and I felt how aroused he was.

I huffed when he lifted me in the air, opened the door, and sat me down. He reached next to me and lowered the back of the seat. It unfolded into a big cushion. He climbed in over top of me and closed the door. Oh, the heat felt good.

His hands twisted in the fabric of my shirt, and he hauled it over my head. Doing the same to his, I could only reach so high before he did the rest, chucking it to the dashboard.

With some quick work, he pulled my tights down and inched them off until I was in my bra and panties.

He pushed my knees apart and shifted inward so he loomed over me. Heat followed his fingertips as they dragged down my stomach and along my pelvic bone.

Turning off all emotion, I let myself feel how good it was to be touched by someone other than Antonio.

He leaned over and hit the screen on his stereo. "The Hills" by The Weekend started to play, and it only made the ache worse.

His lightly tanned skin tugged and stretched over his muscles, and the sight of it made me clench around his sides. His dark brown eyes flashed as he blinked at my eagerness. *Yes, I'm horny! Aren't you?*

I reached down and eased the pulse between my legs myself. Once my finger found the spot, I couldn't stop. Keith watched with passion mixed with amusement, his gaze darkening with each moan that leapt from my lips. I couldn't help but use his body to build me up, as every part of me strained for release. My breasts felt heavy and hard. I gripped my nipple and tugged. His eyes moved, and he licked his lips at my show. My skin had a thin layer of sweat, and my breathing was shallow. I was enjoying the hold I had on him. I had to admit I had dreamed of this many times.

His palm flexed on my stomach, sending a hard jolt to the center of my building climax.

His mouth tugged upward, and I arched my back and shot forward toward the sea of colors where my orgasm took me down its crazy path of pleasure.

His hand pressed harder on my stomach as I shook underneath him. He picked up the hand that I used and slipped my two fingers into his warm mouth and sucked gently. Slowly, his eyes closed and his tongue pressed to the pads of my fingers.

It was such an intimate moment that instead of enjoying the high, I let my world sneak back in. I pressed up into his chest and pushed him away.

"That shouldn't have happened." I flipped over onto my stomach to get up, but he grabbed me from behind and sat me back on his lap.

"Bullshit," he hissed in my ear. "Don't act like you don't want me, Lexi. I can see it. Right when you're at the peak, you have a dance in your eye. It's your tell." He ran his nails up my thighs, and I nearly moaned. "I know you better than you know yourself." He brushed my hair off my shoulder and started to kiss the back of my neck. It felt good— no, amazing. My head flopped back as his fingers started to massage my sensitive parts.

Spreading my knees wide, he whispered. "Let me remind you how you like it."

Yeah, you do that, I snickered to myself.

He lined up and gently pushed inside me at a steady rate. I shot forward, but he grabbed my hips to hold me in place. Once he was fully in, he slowed the pace and started to rub my thighs.

"Mmm," I moaned, forgetting everything. I just followed the climax train.

Circling my hips the way I knew he liked, I was granted a little groan of his own.

His lips grazed my shoulder before he moved me forward so he could get into a better position. My hands pressed against the glass as he bucked me from behind. His teeth dragged down my spine, then moved to bite softly but deeper at my side. He pinched and twisted my nipple, and I gave in. It had been too long since I had an orgasm like that. One that made me scream without a care, made my toes curl, and made me feel every single inch of my burning skin before I burst outward into a swirl of cotton candy.

Da-mn!

I fell onto my side, hair covering my face, my breathing off the charts.

Wow.

Keith flopped down next to me, panting in opposite time. I thought you were supposed to come down from an orgasm, but I just kept floating.

I didn't care as he tucked me into his side, and I fell into the best sleep I've had in years. I didn't care because all the pent-up aggression was gone for the moment, and I wanted to enjoy it.

Mmm, bliss…

***

Buzz! Buzz! Buzz! What the hell was that sound? I willed my eyes to open and saw my phone was lit up like a Times Square between the seats. I tried to move but couldn't. *What the hell?* It took me a moment before I remembered last night.

Oh shit…

He had covered us with his jacket, and we were tangled around one another.

Carefully, I slid his arm away from my center, grabbed my phone and clothes, and hopped outside. Thankfully, the parking lot was empty so no one saw my bare ass as I stumbled to get my tights back on.

Lord, I was classy.

"Shit." Sixteen missed calls from Antonio and eight from Elliot. Nervously I pressed play on the first voice message.

My eyes squeezed shut as his words lashed hard and deep. Then he pulled his dirty card, and I knew what I had to do. Taking a breather, I fought the urge to run to Keith and tell him everything, let him save me like he wanted to, but…this was my mess I needed to fix. Besides, how did I know he wouldn't make me fall in love with him and ditch me again? My wounds might have been old, but they were still raw, and I had spent too long clinging to the pain to help me move forward. To run back backward now would be weak. I was not weak. I had this.

Jamming my arms through my shirt, I finger combed my hair and saw my stressed out reflection in the window. Though I still looked youthful, my soul felt old and worn out. *Not much longer, Lexi.*

Thank God Keith didn't know how I left things with Antonio.

Trying to be quiet, I opened the door and started searching for my keys.

"Sneaking out?" I jumped at the unexpected sound of his voice.

"Sneaking out would imply I belonged here."

"You do."

Ignoring him, I tossed everything out of his center console. "Where are my keys? I need to leave."

"Back to Antonio?" He propped himself up on one elbow and rubbed his sleepy eyes.

"Yeah."

"No."

My gaze snapped over to his. *Pardon?*

"No way! He's insane!"

I felt my switch click, and I was back to my normal self again.

"Yeah." I laughed a little. "He is." My hand moved under the seat and around the carpet. "I'm not worried."

"I am!" His voice nearly shook the windows.

I closed my eyes, begging my feisty side to settle down.

"I know you're worried—"

"Right now I'm flippin' pissed!"

I shook my head, ignoring him, and went back to my search.

"Tell me something, Lexi." His voice had a warning to it. "Did you feel anything between us last night?"

"What I felt was my needs being taken care of."

"Don't lie to me, Lexi. I can tell when you do."

I licked my lips, which made his gaze drop to them. The truck felt warm and small as he stared at me, tempting me to lie.

"Things are—"

He quickly shifted and pulled me onto the seat. "Fucked up?" he growled before he grabbed my face and kissed me breathless. He tasted like mint, and I couldn't help but lose myself, but only for a few minutes. I hated that he felt like home, the kind of comfort only he could remind me of.

I heard Antonio in the back of my mind and I snapped out of it…and pulled quickly away.

"Stop." I could barely form a thought.

"Lexi, what is going on with you?" One of his hands cupped my face. "Tell me you feel something."

"I did," I whispered before I realized what I said. I could lie well.

I saw the hurt but ignored it. Like he ignored me when I begged him to stay.

"Why are you running back to him?"

"Because I love him."

"No, you're scared, and you let him order you around—"

My back straightened as I shuffled back.

"I do not!" My head was foggy. I needed to be alone to get my thoughts in order. I put some space between us. I needed distance to do this. He was about to mess everything up. "Keith, we aren't together anymore. That was just some dumb high school crush."

"Once upon a time, you promised me you wouldn't lie, Lexi."

"And you promised me you wouldn't leave. So I guess we're both lying again!"

I grabbed my bag and spotted my keys before I jumped out.

"Go home, Keith. I don't *want* to be saved." I slammed the door and squeezed my eyes shut. The last thing I needed was Antonio showing up here looking for me and finding out I wasn't alone.

I felt sick the whole way back to the clubhouse. I couldn't let Keith ruin this. I didn't want him involved and getting hurt. I wasn't stupid enough to think he would let it go either. God, what a mess. Passing the 106 freeway made my skin twitch. What *if* I just left? Would he really do what he said he would? Would he hurt…

Stop. Antonio wouldn't hurt—he would *kill.*

Would anyone even notice I was gone?

Pulling into my spot, I met Will. He smirked at me as he pulled his cell phone from his ear.

"He's waiting for you."

***

Wait.

What?

Ouch.

I slowly sat up. My head pounded and my teeth felt wobbly. Carefully moving to the mirror, I sucked in a sharp breath. My cheek was a deep shade of blue and was three times as big as it should be. Closing my eyes, I let the hurt in and pushed the emotion out. He had never done this before, but it shouldn't have been a surprise.

The door slowly opened, as did my eyes.

Antonio stood, arms at his sides, his feet shoulder width apart, his neck contracting. His eyes held mine as they made his point.

Don't disobey him again. He turned away, stepped outside, and shut the door.

Sliding to the floor, I leaned against the bed and broke down.

CHAPTER TEN

Keith

"Well, fuck me sideways, he *is* alive!" Mark's voice burst through my truck speakers. There were pros and cons to my father updating my truck. "Great to hear your voice, brother. Look, before Cole takes the phone from me, I have to ask. Can you get me those ketchup chips you keep munching on but never share? Your mom was out, and Three wouldn't pass the message along. What is up with that girl? I asked nicely, but—"

"You called my mom?" *Why am I surprised?* Mark knows no boundaries.

"Yes. So where was I? Oh, right, so—"

"Wait, wait, wait!" *What?* "How do you know my mom?"

"Well, she called your cell the night before you left. You were off with Cole, so I answered. I decided it was fine since you made me watch Abby and the Doc make out." I smiled at his dig. "She wanted to know if there was anything you needed

216

for when you got home, and I suggested some new underwear—you're welcome, by the way. Any*who,* we got talking, and we hit it off." I heard a strange noise. "Yes, Savi, just a second. Look, Keith, about those chips."

I rubbed my head at a stoplight, wondering why I didn't see this coming. Mark always won over people. Of course my mother would just eat him up.

"Yeah, fine, I'll bring you some when I see you next."

"Two bags, please. Big ones."

I rolled my eyes.

"Yeah."

"Yes, fine!" Mark huffed. "Here, Savannah wants to speak with you. Cole is waiting *patiently...* not!"

I shook my head as I was handed off to her. I felt like I was calling home after a few weeks of not talking to my family. Everyone wanted their turn.

"Hey, Keith, how are you? Chip anyone yet?"

I smiled at her warmth. I missed her. "No, not yet, though I have someone in mind. I'm okay. You?"

"Oh, you know, a little sleep deprived, but all good. So, you miss the mountain yet?"

My foot pushed down on the pedal, and I crept through the intersection toward the clubhouse. It had been four days since I had last seen Lexi, and I was hoping she had cooled off a bit.

"Yes, I do miss it. How's my little sidekick doing? Causing trouble?"

"Always. Umm..." She cleared her throat. "I want to ask you something, but you have to promise not to kill Abigail."

"Depends."

She muttered something about the fact that she shouldn't, but I knew she was going to ask it anyway.

"Besides Three's wedding, are you home because of a woman?"

"Oh! Step back!" Mark shouted from the background. "Keith has a lady friend? Road trip! Shotgun!"

"Done?" Savannah snickered before she cleared her throat again. "Sorry. Look, Keith, if there's someone back there, please promise you won't come home until you're ready."

I looked at the empty seat next to me, where a few nights ago I had the love of my life wrapped around me. Yes, the sex was amazing, but it wasn't about that with Lexi. She made my life full; she completed me. Jumping out of choppers, scaling mountains, tracking down cartels had nothing on the rush I got simply by being near her.

"I wasn't planning on it," was all I offered, but then I remembered who I was talking to. "I'd really like you to meet her, Savi. She's pretty amazing."

"Anyone you fight for, Keith, has got to be pretty amazing. I...well, I would be honored to meet her, when you're ready, of course. If you need to talk, you know how to get hold of me."

"Miss you, Savi."

"Me too. Now I'm handing you off to Cole, okay?"

"Sure." I eased into a gas station and sat back so I could give Cole my full attention.

"Keith, how are you doing?" Cole's voice was light, but I could tell it was laced with business.

"Hanging in there."

"Good to hear. Okay, I think I found the perfect location for what we've been discussing. I'd really like to have your input on this. At the risk of over-stepping your family vacation, can you get away tomorrow for an overnight trip?"

"Yeah, sure, I can do that." I pulled my laptop out of my bag and turned it on.

"I'm flying into Charlotte, North Carolina tomorrow morning. I'll send you a ticket, and we can meet up there."

"Sounds good. I'll see you then."

Reversing the truck into the open road, I headed to the clubhouse.

I felt the vibe was off as soon as I arrived. Besides checking on Lexi, I wanted to talk with Elliot. I had a line on a possible job for him if he wanted it. I knew at some point he would need it. I was still a little pissed at Lexi for rushing back here. I knew she felt something, although she continued to deny it. But this thing had to be seen through before I would ever have a chance of fixing things with her.

Knocking on Elliot's door, it slowly opened under the pressure of my fist.

"Elliot?"

He was sitting on his bed looking at the wall, his back to me. Something was definitely off.

"Hey, man, what are you doing?" He didn't answer, so I did quick check over my shoulder and slipped into his room.

219

Rounding the bed, my stomach nearly came into my throat. One of his eyes was bleeding, and it looked as though someone had tried to remove it with a butter knife. His skin was pale grey.

"Jesus, fuck, man." I dropped down in front of him, but he remained frozen. "Hey, Elliot, can you hear me?"

Blood dripped down his cheek and trickled off his chin to his chest. His good eye slowly moved over to look at me.

"She...she didn't answer her phone," he whimpered in a voice that sent a chill down my spine. "She didn't answer her phone," he repeated, and I could see he was in shock. He needed a hospital. Now. I pulled my phone out and called Clark. Christ, she had been back for four days. Why would they do this to him now?

"Hey, man, everything—"

"Meet me out back in the alleyway!"

"Copy that." Clark knew better than to ask questions.

Reaching for Elliot's arm, I practically carried him outside, stopping a few times when I heard voices. Thankfully, they were having a meeting in the bar. Once outside, Elliot started to whimper again at the sunlight.

"Why did they do this to you, Elliot? What the hell happened?"

His head flopped around. "They dragged out my punishment. This was the...the..." He found the word. "Finale."

I shook off the anger and pushed on.

"Come on, man, keep moving. We're almost

220

there."

Clark's squad car turned down the alley and stopped in front of us.

"What the hell happened?" Clark grabbed Elliot's side and took his weight off me.

"Punishment. He needs a doctor now. You'll have to take him. I need to see if Lexi is okay."

"I got him. Go."

I gave a quick nod before I raced back inside, where I took a couple of breaths to calm myself. I needed to act normal, not like I just helped Elliot escape from this shit hole.

It took me a moment to spot her in the corner. Her hair was shading her face. The lighting was low, so I couldn't see very well. I was so relieved to see her that my body relaxed slightly. My hand felt sticky. I didn't need to look down to know it was blood. With a drag down my jeans, I wiped my fingers clean of Elliot and took a seat close to the bar. I waited and watched for my opportunity to get her alone.

Antonio was talking to his men, and after he finished his rundown of the hit they were going to do later in the afternoon, he told them all to get back to work.

He snapped his fingers at Lexi, and she stood and headed for the bar.

I decided to stay put until Antonio spotted me. He held up a finger before he leaned down and did a line of blow. With a hop in his step, he clapped his hands together. I couldn't help that my eyes followed Lexi.

"We're going to hit the DR's clubhouse. What

do you think of that, mister soldier man?"

Now, that caught my attention.

"As in, Trigger's crew?"

"Trigger is on the west coast. This is his east coast crew."

"Wasn't killing one of his members enough? Unless you're asking to be nailed to a cross and left to drain out, then I wouldn't agree it was a good idea."

Antonio's grin told me he was excited, and fear was not present at this time. He must have done a lot of coke to be sharing this with me at all.

Shit.

"I think you're nuts." I was honest because all I could see was this backfiring and Lexi being caught in the crossfire. "Trigger will retaliate, and you can kiss all this goodbye."

Antonio rubbed his goatee while he thought.

"Retaliation *will* be suicide." His mouth turned upward, and I could see his obsession with leaving his mark as the most feared crew. It seemed to be all he cared about. "I'll take my chances."

I needed to get Lexi out of there.

I checked the time on my phone and wondered how Elliot was doing.

A sound from out back drew Antonio's attention, and he left to deal with it. I waited for a moment, then headed out back to look for Lexi. I caught a glimpse of her walking like a zombie to the trash cans. I knew she must be really upset about what happened to Elliot, and I wanted to let her know Clark had taken him to the hospital. I hurried outside and found her trying to lift a bag into the trash, and she was struggling with it big time.

Racing up behind her, I grabbed the side of the bag and tossed it in the bin. She didn't say a word and quickly turned away from me and headed back toward the clubhouse.

"Hey!" I grabbed her arm, but she kept her head down, her hair in her face. "What, now you won't look at me?"

She cleared her throat and lifted her head and held my gaze, and then I saw her bruised and swollen cheek.

My hand flew to her face and cupped it gently. She couldn't hide her fear, but she quickly masked it with anger. I spoke first. "I'm going to kill him."

"Don't!" she spat out, stepping back. "Jesus Christ, Keith! What part of 'go away' did you not get?"

"He hit you! He physically hit you across the face, Lexi. And you're okay with this?"

"No!" Her voice caught, but she pressed on. "I'm not someone's punching bag. Shit, Keith sometimes things are not what they seem."

I wanted to yell at her for being so damn naïve, that he was brainwashing her into staying, anything, but for whatever reason, I knew she was trying to tell me something.

"I told you to toss shit at me." I came up to her but kept my hands at my sides. "Knock off your tough as shit attitude, and let me the hell in!"

"That's all I have! All of this is on me! I could handle all this before. I could do it until you came along, and now I'm being pulled in too many directions. I—" Her head snapped back, and I could see she said something she wasn't supposed to.

"What things are you handling?"

"I…" She rubbed her head. "I need to go check on Elliot. I didn't see him this morning, and I'm afraid they might hurt him."

She started to turn but caught the expression on my face.

"What?" Her poor face had fear written all over it. "What did they do to him?"

"They tried to take his eye out." I held up my hands to stop her panic. "He's okay. I got him to Clark, and he took him to the hospital. He was talking, Lex. He was fine."

"Oh my God." Her hand covered her mouth, but sobs bubbled through her fingers.

Not really caring at this point, but with a quick look around, I saw we were hidden from the door. I stepped up and wrapped her in my arms. Surprisingly, she let me, although she didn't hug me back, but with Lexi, it was all small steps. I learned a lot from my life at Shadows, when to push and when not to—well, most of the time, anyway.

"Hey." I gently moved her shoulders so she would look at me. "Elliot will be safe at the hospital. Clark will have a few men watching his every move. You want to come on a trip with me?"

She blinked a few times, and I wasn't sure what was going through her head.

"Is this not enough to prove to you I can't leave again?" She shook her head. I thought she might turn and leave. "Shit, they'll kill Elliot and behead me out front like they wanted to do to that Devil's Reach member."

I lowered my voice. "I'm going to let Clark know their plan."

Her face fell and her eyes widened. "If they ever found out—"

"They won't. They'll hit the clubhouse tonight, and Antonio and the rest will be arrested, and you'll have a few days free." I studied her face harder. "Would you come with me?"

I could see she wanted to be feisty back, but stopped herself. "I don't have much money, Keith. Antonio makes sure I only have enough gas to get around town. I've been skimming off his books, but I need that for later."

"Lexi, stop. I'm asking you to come with me. I don't care about your damn money."

She closed her eyes briefly, and I could see she was interested. She also must realize that once they found out Elliot was missing, she would be the first suspect, and it wouldn't go well for her.

"Will you take me to see Elliot?"

"Of course, as soon as I can."

She shook her hands as if to release her panic. "Yeah, okay, I could the change in scenery." She made an attempt at a smile. That was my brave girl.

After making some calls to Clark and the local Boston Police Department, everything was set in place. They would wait for the strike to happen, then move in and take the guys. I think they were just as excited as I was about this attack. Clark was itching to move on the place.

I told Lexi to keep out of Antonio's way and to pack a bag with enough for two days. We agreed I would be back as soon as I could, and we'd leave together. I only hoped Antonio's plans for the afternoon would keep him too busy to notice Elliot was missing. After all, '*Spit*' was injured, and they would probably expect him to lie low for a while.

I let my bag fall at my feet on the porch where Nan was rocking in her favorite chair. She patted the seat next to her and smiled.

Easing in, I gently squeezed her hand to let her know how much I loved her. I was so thankful for the relationship we had. Not one bad memory stuck out when it came to my childhood. Other than sneaking her booze from Dad's liquor cabinet. I grinned at the thought. I thought I was pretty sneaky.

"How is our Lexi holding up?"

I rubbed my eyes and took a moment before I answered. "I know there's more to her being there than I can say. She doesn't share much, and today she is sporting quite a bruise on her cheek."

"Oh, really? That's terrible. How did that happen? Antonio?"

"Yes. But it was because she was with me. We spent the night together."

She kept her gaze out at the street, but I saw her mouth twitch. "You always were so in love with that woman."

"Yeah." I leaned back and let out a long sigh. "I have dated two women since Lexi, Nan. I tried to get close to them, but there was always something missing. It wasn't them. It was me. Not one of them could ever measure up to her."

She smiled over at me with such twinkle in her eye it made me curious to hear what she had to say.

"You have the Keith curse, sweetheart. We were not made for multiple lovers. Our hearts are made for *the one*. Once we attach and fall in love, that's it. We just hope to heaven we can hang on for the ride. It can be a blessing, but it can also be a curse." Her eyes glazed over, and I knew she was thinking of Poppy. Cancer took him from us when I was ten years old. I knew part of Nan left with him. Now I was just thankful she was still here to remind us of him.

Taking her hand in mine, I kissed the back of it and grabbed my bag.

"Keith," she called out after me. I turned to find her standing at the rail. "Lexi is cursed with the same thing. Help her find her way back home."

I shifted my bag more solidly over my shoulder. "That's the plan, Nan," I said and flashed my mischievous smile.

***

Lexi

I watched as Antonio loaded his handgun and shotgun, and tucked a hunting knife through his belt. God, he could be an ugly-ass man. I never thought he was attractive, but once I figured out his dirty little secret, I decided it was probably not a bad plan to roll with it. He "claimed" me after that, and we never spoke about his problems in the bedroom. His twisted view of sex since he couldn't get it up was our secret. When he was on coke, he scared me. He was capable of enormous strength.

The first friend I made when I came into this gang was a girl named Kara, and when Will was finished with her and handed her off to Hank, she protested. I never saw her again. Elliot said she was beaten and left on a rival's doorstep, but I'm not sure if that was true. At least, I hoped it wasn't. Antonio occasionally liked to grab someone else's girl and make a show of taking his turn with her. I often wondered what he did to them in the bedroom. He probably hit them and blamed them for his inadequacies. I really didn't much care, as it gave me a break.

"You going to sit there, bitch? Or are you going to get me a drink?" Antonio barked, then slapped the ass of a blonde who was leaning over a table. "Lazy-ass piece of shit."

Slipping behind the bar, I poured him a whiskey and slipped a double dose of powdered laxative in just for fun. There was nothing more comical than watching his eyes get big as he hurried off to the bathroom, and with what was being planned for this afternoon, it would be doubly funny. I really shouldn't temp fate, but I couldn't resist.

I sat it in front of him and wished him good luck.

"Where the fuck is Spit?" Will came rushing into the room. "I haven't seen the little bitch all day." He looked hard at me. "Probably in his room licking his wounds like a dog. Little shit doesn't pull his weight around here, anyway. Waste of space."

Umm. "Isn't it Elliot's day to visit the cemetery?" It wasn't, but I was banking he wouldn't remember. I turned to Antonio. "His eye is really hurt, Antonio, and he is my brother. I wish

228

you would go a little easier on him. He may have needed to visit our parents."

He looked over at Will, whose cocky stare honed in on me, and I knew he was about to be a dick. "You know they're dead, right?" He moved closer as I held my ground. I did notice Gordon rise out of his seat, but he stayed put. "Worm food, fertilizer, box of bones."

I couldn't help my reaction as I drew my arm back and punched him hard in the left eye.

Damn! That felt amazing! I fought the will to do it again, but I needn't have worried, as I was brought back to reality with sickening results when Antonio charged at me like a bull. Gordon started toward us but came to a sudden halt.

Suddenly I was turning around like a spinning top, and everything went blurry.

"Antonio! What are you doing?" Keith yelled, keeping me behind him. "You're going to kill her if you punch her in the face again."

I peeked from out behind his arm. This was not good.

Antonio and the rest of the club looked like they were about to pull their guns on Keith.

"Move," Antonio hissed, his nostrils flared. "The bitch hit one of my men and, she needs to be put in her place for that."

"He disrespected her parents." Keith lowered his voice, but it was still laced with authority. "You hit, why can't she?"

"You're out of line, Keith."

"Do I need to remind you I don't run with your crew? I am doing you a favor by babysitting your

229

club while you're out. I'm risking my future for you."

"She doesn't belong to you anymore."

The way Keith's back stiffened made me nervous what was to come next.

"No, she doesn't, but she's beautiful, and it would be a shame to alter that. You made your point before when she broke a rule and left. That's clear. Will is a dick, and you can't deny that. Let it go and focus on the fact you soon get to beat the shit out of a Devil's Reach clubhouse."

Someone whooped from the bar, and the mood instantly changed. Even though Antonio gave me a scary look, he backed off and grabbed his shot of whiskey, downing it. I almost smiled. *Drink up.*

"Let's move!" He turned and stared at me. "You leave, and I'll make sure you look worse than your brother does right now."

"I heard you the other night." I carefully stepped forward and let him kiss me. He held my arm tight for a second, pressing his fingers into my skin to make his point. *Ouch.*

About fifty members rushed out the back door, leaving me with shaky legs and a throbbing right hand. Gordon looked at Keith, and something was exchanged between them. I wanted to ask, but now wasn't the time.

"You have a death wish, sweetheart," Keith muttered at me, referring to Will.

"It was worth it."

He shook his head, but I saw a tiny smile.

"Come on. Let's get out of here."

It wasn't until the freeway that Keith seemed to

relax again. I, on the other hand, was a nervous wreck. I couldn't help but stare out the side mirror to see if anyone was following us.

Keith's hand dropped to my thigh, pulling my focus elsewhere. I moved it back to the gearshift, not wanting to feel that emotion right now.

"I track people for a living, Lexi. I promise you, no one is following us."

I gave him a little nod, but my eyes stayed glued to the mirror.

"You want to know where we're going?"

Ah, yeah, that might be good to know.

"Sure."

"Charlotte, North Carolina."

"Why?" I shifted to look over my shoulder. I was sure that car moved over to our lane at the same time as we did.

"I'm meeting up with my boss and some of my buddies from the safe house where I work."

This caught my attention. I looked up at his face, which was lit up by the car in front of us.

"Oh." I hated it when he mentioned his life with the Army. I went back to watching the car.

"Cole is my boss, and his wife Savannah will also be there." *Oh, that's who Savannah is.* "Mark, another guy from our team, is also coming with his pregnant girlfriend, Mia. I have to do a few things with the guys, and I'll leave you with the girls. Is that okay with you? They are really nice. I'm sure you'll like them."

"Sure." I shrugged, feeling uneasy. *Army wives.* Great. I'd probably get to hear all the bad shit they'd want to share about their lives and hate it

231

even more now.

Keith rolled his head back and let out a long sigh. I knew he was trying, but I was used to freezing out any feelings when it came to him.

I scrambled to de-ice my emotions to try to match his effort. "What kinds of things do you do there at the house?"

"Our objective is to find hostages and get them out, while trying not to get killed in the pro—" He suddenly stopped when he realized how that sounded. "We use the analogy of being like a shadow. You know. We get in and out without being seen. It's not always easy, but it's so worth it when we reunite people with their loved ones."

"Where is the safe house?"

"I can't say."

Oh.

"Who have you saved? Anyone I would know who's famous?"

"I can't answer that either."

Okay.

"Do Savannah and Mia live at the house?"

"Yes and no."

I picked at a piece of thread on my bracelet. "All pretty vague."

"Yeah, it is, but for a good reason."

"If you say so."

The rest of the way to the airport, we stayed quiet while my stomach twisted in endless knots. Keith carried my bag in one hand, while his other kept a tight grip on my hand as we pushed through the sea of people.

I settled into the seat and stared out the window

while mindless chatter buzzed around me. If Antonio got wind of what I was doing, I was dead. I wondered how the attack was going. I prayed everything would go as planned, and the guys would be picked up by the police. What if anything went wrong? This whole trip hinged on the fact that Antonio would get arrested. My palms went cold and goosebumps made me uneasy. Elliot better be okay. I was nervous for him. Nervous that he would arrive home from the hospital before me and start to ask questions. It would draw attention to the fact I was not there.

"Drink?" Keith interrupted my thoughts and handed me a glass of red wine.

"Yeah." I downed the entire thing in a matter of seconds. He replaced my empty with his full glass and ordered another.

My stomach fluttered as the wheels lifted off the ground and we were officially airborne. Once we leveled out and the captain announced we could move about, I handed my empty bottles to the flight attendant as she did a quick sweep of the rows.

I eyed Keith as he opened a magazine. He was so calm it bothered me.

"You hungry?" he asked.

"No."

"You want some water?"

"No." I glanced out the window, watching the puffy clouds breeze by the window. I wondered how far away the other planes were from us. It was all a bit trippy if you thought about how many steel tubes were in the sky at this very moment. How many people were looking in the same direction I

233

was.

Keith tucked the magazine away and removed his hat, running his hands through his hair.

"How about this? I'll answer your questions if you answer mine."

Hmm, that was sort of appealing. "We get two passes."

"Deal."

"Okay, I'll start." I went small first. "Have you ever had any feelings for Savannah?"

He tossed his head back and let out a little laugh. "No, she reminds me of Two too much to ever go down that road. She's pretty, and I love her, but like a sister. Besides, she is married to my best friend, and they have a little girl."

"Had to ask."

"Fair enough." His smile changed. "My turn." *Oh no.* "When I was away for my first tour, did you sleep with Juan?"

"No," I blurted without even thinking.

"Good," he puffed out. "Why not?"

"I waited for you, Keith." I wanted to shut down and close off those feelings, but I fought the urge. "I was hurt, but I would never do that to you. I still hoped you would change your mind and come back to me."

He nodded, and I could imagine I saw some small amount of old stress drop away from him.

"How many girls have you been with since we broke up?"

He held my gaze. "Two."

"Did you love any of them?"

"I wanted to, but no."

234

My chest grew tight.

"Why the gang? You were always so scared of them."

I looked out the window, then down at my hands. I didn't like talking about this—it was hard. "I felt so lost after my parents died. You were gone, and your parents were wonderful, but they had their own family." I cleared my throat. "All I brought to them was sadness. Elliot latched onto a girl who turned out to be a part of the gang, Antonio's cousin. At first they were great to him. Antonio's uncle took to him. One moment he was there, and the next he was gone. I had no one." Pausing to control the anger that began to seep in, I went on. "That's when Juan took pity on me. We started out as friends, and he showed me we could have fun doing things I wouldn't have even dreamt of. Oddly enough, I started to like not caring about the consequences. We had fun." I entwined my fingers. "Then, like every other *Almas Perdidas* member, he did a one-eighty, and one day I got the fist to the stomach."

I suppressed a shudder at the recollection. "I should have expected the same from Antonio, but he was good at making me feel like I was something special. The only thing that kept me going was his secret." I paused, wanting to share this, but it still felt strange.

"The fact he can't get an erection?"

"Yes. I guess he got raped a few times in prison, and now he can't get...you know...an erection. Not that there aren't other ways he gets satisfied, but at least I didn't have to, well, you know. The Garcia

235

brothers have some issues. Lucky me."

I brushed by his discomfort and let that topic drop. I'd said it, and that was all that mattered.

"Poor Clark. I'm sure eventually I'm going to give him a stroke. He bailed me out so many times, more than he should have. "

"Umm, I heard."

"Heard, as in you asked him on this trip home, or did you have Clark watching out for me all this time?"

His guilty expression gave him away. He'd been watching over me this whole time. *Wow. Okay.* I decided to keep going so he understood.

"Antonio and Juan were like oil and water, and when Antonio wanted something, nothing would get in his way. He killed some junkie and pinned it on Juan. The next day, I was ordered to move my stuff in his room and have been there ever since." I flipped my hair out of my face, needing to move. "Not exactly a fairy tale, but it is what it is."

His face scrunched up. "Then why are you there? What do you hope to accomplish?"

"Pass." I rushed the word.

"So you won't tell me why you won't leave?"

"Nope, I can't go there. Sorry."

My heart beat against my chest at a rapid pace. I hated this.

"My turn." I wanted off this subject. "Why did you leave so quickly when you came back four years ago? I heard you were in town. I thought, well, hoped…"

He took a moment and stared toward the front of the plane. Just when I thought he wasn't going to answer, he cleared his throat. "I came back for you. I needed to know if there was even the slightest chance we could be something. I wasn't able to move forward with anyone because all I'd do is compare them to you. It was a horrible feeling pushing away good people. So, I came back, and that morning I ran into Elliot at the cafe."

"You did?" Why didn't he ever tell me this?

"Yes. I told him why I was back, and he told me you had gone through such a rough time, and you were finally happy with Juan. He begged me not to screw it up for you. To let you go and move on."

"What?" He must have misunderstood Elliot. "That was the lowest point for me. Are you sure he said that?"

"It was the hardest thing I've ever done. I didn't want to believe him, but later that night I saw you with Juan outside of Mavis's Place. You reached up and touched his shoulder, and you smiled and said something to him. You...you looked so happy. I knew I had to leave you alone then. I packed my bags and left that night. Barely said goodbye to my family. I was so crushed I needed to be back at the house. I dove into my work and tried to push you out of my head."

"And did you?"

His hand moved to mine and squeezed it tight, then raised it to his mouth and kissed the back. "Never."

I sagged into my seat feeling all kinds of mixed emotions. Why would Elliot do that? Then something hit me.

"If I had decided to be with you four years ago,

how could we be together? You can't tell me much about your life, and there doesn't seem like there's room for me and the Army."

A little smile appeared; it was one I hadn't seen before.

"I would have left my mountain and worked as a civilian. I love my job, Lexi, so much, but I—" He stopped himself. "I wouldn't have gone back."

"Wow," I whispered, not sure what to make of that. I would never ask him to pick me over something that made him so happy. But he went back, and I had moved on.

"Mountain?"

He closed his eyes briefly. I could see he didn't know he had said it. "We like to be up high to see when things are coming."

With a slight smile to let him know I was happy he shared something with me, I went back to looking out the window.

I shifted and let out an unexpected moan. My shoulder was sore.

"What's wrong with your shoulder?"

"Landed on it funny."

I saw him put two and two together, but instead of calling me out, he opened his bag and removed two little white oval pills. "Here." He handed me his water, and I took them, not caring anymore what they were.

Soon after, I felt sleepy and my eyes grew heavy. Keith lifted the arm rest and leaned me against his chest.

"I'm fine," I protested.

"I know." He leaned me down to his huge chest.

"Let the pills ease the pain." He wrapped his jacket around me and kissed my hair. "Just sleep now. I got you."

"Yeah...okay." Too tired to fight, I gave in. Thankful we had the row to ourselves, I kicked my feet up and let my troubles float away for a while.

CHAPTER ELEVEN

Something warm brushed over my face. "Lexi, we're here."

My eyes slowly opened, and I looked up and saw Keith staring down at me with a soft smile.

I jolted up but cringed at my stiff neck.

"You talk in your sleep, you know."

"So I've been told," I muttered, thinking about the time I spoke about Keith when I was asleep. Antonio was less than impressed. "What did I say?"

He didn't reply, just handed me my bag and moved me in front of him as we shuffled out of the plane. We grabbed our stuff and headed to the car rental place.

An hour later, we were on the road heading to Ashville. Charlotte was beautiful. Everything was green and lush. Weaving through the high hills on one-lane highways was incredibly peaceful, and just what I needed to let go of a ton of pent-up stress.

Every once in a while, Keith would take my hand and rest it on the gearshift underneath his. Every time I felt strange and pulled it back to my lap. I was so confused inside right now. I could not let this man inside my head. He brought so much with him. I was too far gone into my new life to handle any more pain and confusion. I actually felt a strange pull for the life I'd been leading with Antonio, and that was hard to get my head around. Wow, I was so fucked up.

"What are you thinking?" He pulled me from my wallowing.

"Things."

"Like?"

I looked over and shrugged. "Things."

"Believe it or not, Lex, you can let your guard down with me."

"I did," was all I said. I knew he'd get the rest.

He let my hand go. I felt a little bad. Here he was taking me on a trip, and I was acting like an ice cube. I was so twisted up I barely knew where I began and where I ended.

"It's just been a long time since I've been on a trip." There, that should be enough.

"Hope you have fun. You could use a little of that."

Yes, that's true.

His phone rang, and someone named Carlos came up on the ID. Glancing at it, Keith turned it over.

Instead of checking into the hotel, we drove straight to the restaurant where we were meeting his friends.

To say I was nervous was an understatement. I almost wished I had declined this offer. I was, after all, "the girl who broke Keith's heart and left him for a gang." Oh my God, I was a fucking wreck!

"Stop overthinking things, babe. They'll love you." Keith took my hand and opened the door. We walked in like we were a couple.

"Well, hot damn!" some guy shouted. I assumed it was Mark. "Cole, you owe me twenty. She is a brunette!"

I had to grin at his outburst.

"Don't ever try to beat Mark. He'll always win."

I nodded. I thought Mark would be pretty entertaining. I recognized Savannah from the picture Keith showed me. She came forward and offered me a hand. Lord, she *was* stunning.

"You must be Lexi. It's lovely to meet you."

I took her hand and returned her kindness with a smile. Mia was next. She stood awkwardly.

"Oh, please, don't." I held up my hands and helped her back down. "It's nice to meet you, Mia, but please sit."

"Thanks." She beamed.

Before I could sit, Mark scooped me into a hug. Keith jumped in and said something in French. I didn't catch it all, but I thought it was along the lines of being careful around my shoulder. Mark stepped away and gave me a small hug and a peck on my good cheek.

"Oh, Lexi, we have so many questions for you."

"No," Keith bit out.

"How old were you when you met?" Mark bypassed Keith's glare.

"Seventeen."

"Huh. Was he always so secretive?"

I shrugged. "Not at first." Fuck, my jabs were

uncontrollable. "No, he was always open with me."

"Really?" He looked confused. "Okay, did he used to sing? Because the man has a voice like an angel."

Savannah laughed out loud and high-fived Mark. I glanced up at Keith, and he shook his head at me.

"He used to sing to Four." I broke through the roar at the table, and they all stopped and looked at me. "Um, his baby sister is thirteen years younger than him and would get him to sing."

"What kind of songs?" Savannah asked.

"This was not the deal." Keith tried to step in, but Savannah and Mark both shushed him.

"Ah, everything from the "Puff the Magic Dragon" to Def Leppard."

Mark shook his head. "What I wouldn't do to have been a fly on the wall back then."

"Cole, I quit," Keith said in a serious voice.

Cole pointed his beer at him. "Don't leave me with them."

Mark touched my hand across the table. "We need to exchange numbers."

"Anytime."

"Lexi." Cole stood and towered over me like Keith did. "It's a real pleasure to meet you. Thank you for joining us here."

I couldn't help but join in the laughter. Cole was pretty funny with his timing.

"Thank you for having me."

I found myself starting to enjoy the warmth these four had to offer. The food was good, and the conversation was better. I actually found myself laughing and carrying on. Was this what life could be like? I loved that Cole always found some reason to touch Savannah, and how Mark kept smiling at Mia every time she spoke. His hand rubbed her tummy, and he lit up whenever she spoke about the pregnancy.

They were each other's family, and I was envious, but at the same time, I was happy Keith had them.

"Ladies." Cole handed Savannah an envelope. "There's a car waiting outside to take you to the local spa for a little girl stuff."

I didn't know how to react. It had been years since I had been to a spa, and I felt a little funny that he paid for us to go, but I followed the other girls as they headed for the door.

"I called ahead and made sure Gus would take really good care of us." Savannah's wicked grin made me glance at Cole, who grabbed her around her waist and kissed her breathless. No one was around, and we were away from the tables, but someone hooted. I thought it might have been Mark.

"Welcome to their relationship." Keith laughed as he caught up to me. "Will you be okay with them?"

"I can handle myself."

"I wish you'd let your guard down a little more with me. I won't hurt you, Lexi."

I had to look away as my eyes went glossy. I was way too confused to think I could just slip into this world, and there was so much more to my life than I could share right now.

"Hey." He turned me so I would look at him while the rest of them headed outside. "You and

244

me, we could figure this out."

"Keith…" I shook my head. This topic had to be closed.

"I won't go home without you, Lex. I'm done seeing you get hurt. You deserve more."

I sighed again. It twisted me up inside.

"Okay, okay, we'll leave it for now. Get lost and have some fun."

He turned and headed for the big SUV the guys had piled into.

Letting out a deep breath, I headed for Savannah where she waited a distance away. She smiled and motioned for me to follow.

***

"Ahhh," Mia cooed as Robert applied pressure to her left forearm. "I think I may have to tell Mark he's been replaced."

Savannah's hair was wet from our steam shower. She agreed and sipped her cucumber water.

We had been at the spa for two hours getting everything you could think of waxed, buffed, and painted. Turned out they did this a lot. I didn't pretend to understand this life; I just took it as I went.

Gus didn't ask questions, but we spoke privately about where he could massage and where not to. My cheek was still tender, so he had me lie on my side so my face didn't have to press into the pillow. He worked wonders on my sore shoulder.

"I think I need to be alone with my thoughts." I laughed as Gus worked the bottom of my feet.

"Well, Gus, you're welcome to join me."

The girls burst out laughing, and it seemed to break down some walls that were building.

After our toes were painted, we sat out on the balcony in puffy blue robes and were given margaritas—virgin for Mia—while they prepped for our haircuts.

Damn, this life felt pretty good at the moment.

"Okay, don't laugh, but Mark bought me this, and I want to use it." Mia pulled out a selfie stick, and Savannah pressed her lips together so as to not laugh.

We leaned in and took a picture of ourselves with our drinks.

"What's your number, Lexi? I'll send it to you."

I closed my eyes and prattled off the number. I'd hide the photo later. This would be one I'd like to keep. It would definitely be a happy memory for me.

"I'm really glad you came." Mia touched my arm with a warm smile.

I was pleased I was wearing sunglasses as I felt my eyes mist over. I really missed having girlfriends.

Savannah set her drink down and turned, tucking her legs up. "Did Keith ever share with you anything about me or my past?"

"No."

"Can I share it with you?"

"Of course."

I spent the next hour listening to their stories. It was exactly what I needed. I wasn't alone, and it gave me hope I might even come out of this okay someday. It turned out even Mia had a story. They respected my privacy and didn't push me for any details of my own life. They just talked.

***

"What do you think?" Felicia beamed at me through the mirror. "You look amazing!"

Wow, my hair looked healthy and shone with tiny light brown peek-a-boos running through it. I'd have to come up with some crazy lie when I saw the guys at the clubhouse. Although Antonio probably wouldn't notice, Will was sure to bring it up. He was such a dick, and I hoped he was someone's bitch at that very moment. I wondered again how everything was going on their end. *No! Don't even go there!*

"Come." Savannah linked arms with me. "We have time to hit the pub across the street. My treat."

Mia came to my other side and smiled. "I *am* really glad you decided to come."

"Me too. What are the guys doing here, exactly?"

Savannah glanced at Mia, then back to me. "You have to ask Keith. The whole *non-disclosure* thing."

"Got ya." I let it go but was still curious.

I should have known the guys were back by the way Savannah sparkled at someone behind me.

"Wow." Keith moved my hair off my shoulder. "You look pretty."

"Thank you."

He helped me out of the chair and gave me a quick spin.

Mark whistled, and Keith shot him a look. I learned quickly that Mark loved to give him shit. Personally, I found it very entertaining.

"Why, thank you, Mark." I smiled up at Keith, who shook his head. I was surprised how I missed his territorial behavior.

"Can we go back to the hotel now?" His hand slid around my waist, pulling me into him. It was the first time I didn't feel the urge to pull away.

"No!" Savannah jumped in before I could. "We have dinner plans."

"Plans," I repeated and took a small step back. Keith matched my movement so he was back to holding me again.

Keith chuckled but looked at Savannah. "I'll remember that."

"No, no, my friend, that was for the code-45 last month."

Huh? Oh, that's right. She told me that meant he carried them around over his shoulder.

"Are we even?"

"For now." She shrugged.

"Mmm." He pulled out his phone and made the same face as before. I noticed it was Carlos again.

Dinner was fun. I hadn't laughed so hard in a long time. I caught Keith's face a few times, and I could tell he knew this was what I needed. As much as I hated to admit it, he was right. I forgot how great normal could be. Reaching for his hand under the table, I gave it a little squeeze.

His attention snapped over to me, but then he went back to his conversation with Cole. His fingers traced over mine.

What was I doing?

The others ordered coffee, but Keith said we were turning in. I reached for my jacket, and he helped me into it.

"Thanks for today, guys. See you in the morning for breakfast." I waved and hugged Savannah, who rose and wrapped me up in pure friendship.

The walk back was chilly. Just what I needed to think. Keith slipped his arm around my waist, and I leaned into him. I hated that I fell into old habits, but it felt so homey.

"What did I say in my sleep?" I had to know.

He chucked as we stopped at a light. "Always have, always will."

Thankful for the darkness, I felt my cheeks flush. "Interesting."

"I thought so too," he said, grabbing my hand and urging me forward.

The hotel was only two blocks away, and we made it inside and up to the beautiful room where a cart greeted us sporting champagne in an ice bucket.

"Really?" I laughed nervously, but it was pretty romantic.

"You can probably thank Savi. That is so her." He opened the patio door and pointed. "This was me."

Peeking around the corner, I saw we had our own fire pit with sticks and stuff to make s'mores.

"You remembered." I suddenly felt tears.

"Summer of '99 we were sitting on Clark's deck, and you said screw romance, you loved a fire pit, s'mores, and—" He opened a cooler. "A six pack of cold beer." He pulled me to him. "This is what our life could be like, Lex. Just let me in."

My walls went up. Of course they did; they always did.

"Don't," he warned.

"Don't what?"

"Put the walls back up the moment I mention a future."

I walked back inside the hotel room and started to remove my earrings. What was I doing here? Was it a mistake? Trying to get myself under control, I removed my dress and hung it neatly in the closet.

"Why won't you tell me what else is going on? It's annoying, you keeping me in the dark." He blocked the path to my bag.

My hands flew to my hips. "You've been gone for ten years, Keith, and a lot has happened. You may order people around for a living, but you can't with me."

"I'm not trying to order you around. I just wish you would share this with me!"

"Share?" I whirled around and grabbed his phone off the dresser. "Then share with me why this Carlos guy keeps calling but you keep avoiding his calls."

His face fell.

"You're going through my phone now?"

Oh, that pissed me the hell off. I never had been, nor would I ever be, that kind of woman. "Thanks for thinking so highly of me. He or she just calls all the time. Hard not to notice you're avoiding answering."

He checked his watch. "I guess we were due for

a fight. It has been twenty-six hours."

I closed my eyes and hated that he was right. I needed to work on that.

"Stop pissing me off, then!"

"Stop being so closed off!"

Holy shit, we got nowhere with these fights.

"Can I get my clothes, please?"

"Why? I rather like you like this."

I rolled my eyes, but a small piece of the old me had surfaced.

"Did I...?" He stopped and narrowed his eyes in on me. "Did I just get a smile?"

"No." I fought to control my mouth.

"You want your clothes?" He gave me a lopsided smile. "Kiss me first."

Letting out a heavy sigh, I pushed down the frustration and stepped up and gave him a little peck on the cheek.

"No, my lips."

"Keith." My hands landed on my hips.

"Lips," he repeated.

Both hands pressed on his shoulders as I leaned up and gently pressed my lips to his. Suddenly, his hands cupped my bare ass and lifted me in the air, gently placing me on the dresser.

"Keith!"

"No more fighting tonight."

He arched my back so my breasts hiked up. One arm hooked under my leg and rested it around his hip, while the other held my lower spine in place.

He dragged his tongue from my jaw to down to my collarbone, making my breath flutter. Swirling it in the dips of my collarbone, he grazed his teeth

251

against my skin and nipped at my shoulder.

It felt so good.

Dropping my head back so he could get better access, I let out an uncontrolled moan. Keith's oral skills had always been my weak spot.

He pulled back, careful not to let me fall, and held me in place with his hips. His sweater dropped to the floor as I clawed at his belt. He stepped out of his pants and kicked them to the side. To my surprise, he was commando.

My gaze dropped down his massive frame. He was just as fit as he was at seventeen; just a hell of a lot more man now. I took in his thick erection, and it twitched at my gawking. I reached out and felt the velvety skin, and heat wafted off the shaft. His chest puffed out at the connection. He closed his eyes and ran a hand through my hair. Just as I went to get on my knees he shook his head.

"Not now." His eyes opened with a different expression. "We're doing this right."

I was confused. I thought when we were in his truck it was amazing.

Moving me to the floor, he removed my bra, taking his time. His hands constantly moved over my skin so he didn't lose the connection. He kneeled on the floor and lifted each foot, tossing my panties on the chair.

Glancing up with dark, liquid eyes, he studied my stomach. His hands moved to either hip, and he touched his lips to my skin.

"How can anyone hurt such a beautiful woman?" he whispered through his kisses.

I became emotional over this tender act. It had

been a long time since anyone had been so intimate with me. I forgot how amazing it was.

"It's okay, Lex," he murmured over the kiss, making it warm again. "I'll protect you." He started to move higher up the side of my breast.

A tear slipped down my cheek, but I managed to control it. *Please don't fall in love again, Lexi! Just enjoy the pleasure and keep your feelings tucked away.*

I needed to tell him—all of it. My heart went off like a wild horse. I couldn't. What if Antonio—

"Hey." He dove down and locked his lips to mine, reminding me where my head should be. He tilted me so his tongue could dance deeper.

Moving me as we stayed in the moment, he carefully eased us down so I was on top.

I was startled by the TV turning on. We must have hit the remote. I smiled into the kiss when I heard Channing Tatum's voice in *Magic Mike*.

"You plan that too?" I joked, pushing my emotions aside.

He grabbed my ass and gave a very sexy agreement from the back of his throat. My toes curled at the sound. His eyebrow raised at my reaction before he smiled. He liked that. With my eyes on his, I dipped low, letting my hair fall around me. He loved the feel of it sliding across his sensitive skin. Smooth like a cat, I backed up until I felt his erection tap my belly.

He took my hands as I got into position. It was like waiting for the rush from a drug that was about to warm your blood to the core. I gave him a little nod to show I was ready, and ever so slowly, he pushed through my opening, stretching me to a size only he could accomplish. Halfway through, his eyes squeezed shut and his grip got tighter. It was so sexy, I couldn't help but slip into old habits.

Once he was completely in, I pulled almost all the way up. His eyes popped open, and I saw he knew what I was doing. I used to fight him for control just to mess with his inner alpha male. It was a fun game and made sex even more exciting.

"Lex," he growled but trailed off as I sank down slowly but at a good pace. "Pony" by Ginuwine circled the room as I took every inch of him. His hand landed on my hip to hold me in place. Instead, I started to flex my back and rode him, and his free hand slid along my belly with a hungry look.

Tuning in to the beat of the music, I set the slow rhythm and watched as he struggled to hold on. Sweat broke across his forehead and his jaw flexed. I knew he wanted it harder.

I grabbed my breasts and palmed the nipples, needing some friction. Tilting back, I dropped my head and let the buildup last for as long as possible. Like climbing the track while on a roller coaster, each click of the rail wound my stomach tighter. I was just rounding the top when I fell the wrong way. Opening my eyes and falling backward from my climax, I saw a wound-up set of eyes challenging me to push back. Brushing my hair out of my face, he hiked one leg up and then the other. Without warning, he slipped inside and let out a sigh.

"I needed this," he said, more to himself. "Ten fucking years."

I went to say something but he started to move, and his arm flexed above me and gripped the headboard. I couldn't stop the rush that appeared. It tipped me over the edge and went roaring south without an end in sight.

Keith didn't stop; he just took my climax and stretched it for as long as possible. Right as I landed, he came with roar. Every muscle locked in place as if he were stone.

I forgot how much I missed his face when he lost control. It almost made me want to try for round three.

My body was spent; I didn't think I'd be able to move.

Flopping to the side, he wrapped his arm around my limp body and buried his nose in my hair.

"Ten fucking years."

We lay together for a while until my dry mouth begged me for water.

***

Brown spread across the crispy crust, changing the shape.

"It's going to burn." Keith shook his head. We had been around the fire pit for an hour, and I saw no end in sight when it came to stopping my midnight snack.

"You dare question my s'mores cooking?"

His hands went up. "I'm just saying I live in the woods, and I know how to cook a marshmallow. You are going to burn it."

I smirked. "The woods, hey?"

His face twisted; he had slipped again.

"I have never slipped up before." He shook his head.

I held up the perfectly brown marshmallow. "Yeah, that doesn't look perfect at all." I inspected it further. "However, yours..."

"Shit," he yelped when it caught on fire.

"Who's the Boy Scout now?"

He laughed and ditched the stick, taking his beer instead. We sat for a while longer staring at the fire in silence. I was always comfortable with him like this. He was just easy.

"What do those numbers mean?" I pointed to his left forearm where it said 10-13-98 in black script.

"Just a date I wanted to remember."

"Ninety-eight." I quickly did the math. "Ninety-eight was the year we met."

"Yup." He nodded and took a swig of beer.

I began to mull over what happened to Keith that year. I wasn't sure why October was so important.

"The first year, I was only in Iraq." His voice was low. "We spent most of September on lockdown. It was maddening. I wanted to be out there, but enemy troops were spotted around our area. I ended up making a good friend named Tikaani. He was from Alaska. His family owned a homemade jewelry shop that specialized in unique diamond cuts." His gaze fluttered up to mine. "He knew I was in the market for a ring." My stomach dropped. "I drew up what I wanted, and it was ready for me by the time I arrived home. It's stunning, actually, and it's exactly what I wanted, even had the engraving 10-13-98 on it. The first day you walked into my life, and the first and only time I ever fell in love."

My nose prickled as my eyes started to water. How could I have been so stupid? I felt like I failed myself. Something did, however, catch my attention.

"It's?" I needed to know why he said this in present tense.

Nodding, he leaned his forearms on his knees and held his beer between his fingers. "After you left, I told myself I had ten years to hold onto it. If in that time we weren't together, I'd sell it, and it would be me letting go."

I felt the sting of his words, and I welcomed the pain. This whole time, I never once put myself in his shoes as to what my break-up did to him. My hope was he'd find someone better suited for him. I had become so dark inside it wasn't something I want to spread to others, especially him.

"Carlos." He broke my spiraling thoughts. "He's my diamond seller. He found me a buyer, but I just can't go through with the sale."

"Keith," I whispered, but my voice broke.

"Please, don't." He leaned back and shook his head. "I didn't mean to hurt you. I just wanted you to know who Carlos is, that's all."

I swallowed the massive lump in my throat and went back to looking at the fire. My emotions had been like a yo-yo since Keith walked back into my life. It was painful, but on the other hand, it had resurfaced so many good memories. Ones that made me remember a time when I felt loved and protected and happy.

Keith set his beer down and headed into the bedroom. When he closed the door, I broke down and let it all out into the pillow. God, it felt great to loosen some of the laces around my chest.

How could life be so complicated one moment, and the next make perfect sense?

Had I changed too much to be the woman he thought I was? Sometimes I wasn't even sure who I was myself.

"Lexi." Keith came to the door in his jeans and a ball hat. "Come to bed with me."

I nodded, wiped my eyes dry, and joined him.

CHAPTER TWELVE

Keith

Lexi seemed to be quiet this morning. I pretended not to notice over breakfast. Mark was in full swing with his jokes and helped to keep the mood light. Savannah, on the other hand, looked like she had a little too much to drink and sported sunglasses and kept shaking her head at Mia, who looked to be in the same shape but for a different reason.

"Rough night, ladies?" I smirked and tapped Savannah's shades.

"Mark had a brilliant idea to play a drinking game, and needless to say, I lost."

"Or did you win?" Mark piped up. "You did win a sexy dance from yours truly."

Cole glanced at me, and I raised my hands. "None of my business what you do behind closed doors."

"Mark lost his traveling rights," Cole hissed, then completely deadpan, said, "But the man can dance."

Savannah started to laugh, hitting the table then her head. "Ohh, I hate you all."

Mark chuckled, then looked at Lexi. "Don't worry, sweetheart, I've saved the best moves for you at the wedding."

She rubbed her arms uncomfortably. "I'm not sure if I can make it."

"You will." I wrapped my arm around the back of her chair.

"I will?"

Leaning in, I kissed her collarbone. "I'll explain later."

On the drive back and on the plane ride, Lexi stared out the window, only talking when I asked her a question. No doubt she was shutting down and preparing for what was to come.

After we made it back to Boston, we stopped for a quick bite to eat. I noticed Lexi barely touched her sandwich. I wanted to her to open up, but now wasn't the time.

My phone beeped, and I asked her to read it.

Clark: 1-10.

"Type back the same numbers."

She did and put it back in the center console.

"Thanks."

"What does that mean?"

I checked my blind spot and eased over. "It means we have a cover story ready for you, on why you were gone."

"What? Really?"

"You went to visit your old family friend. You hired him as the bondsman for Antonio and his crew. They won't be getting out for three more days." I glanced over. "So I want you to come to Three's wedding with me. That is, if you want to."

"I, ah…" She paused, then surprised me when she reached over and took my hand. "I'd love to."

A grin shot across my face, and I kissed her hand.

"Okay, so you hired a bondsman who was a family friend. You left because you needed the help to bail them out, and…"

"No offense, Keith, but they won't buy that."

I pulled my sunglasses down and gave her a look. "Glovebox."

Inside was a file folder with receipts for a hotel, food, car service, and the bonds bill.

Sifting through the papers in disbelief, she looked over at me. "So you bailed them out?"

"Well, I did put them in there."

She shrugged. "Okay, wow. Oh! What about Elliot? When do I get to see him?"

"He arrived back this morning."

"Damn, you thought of everything."

"Not everything," I muttered.

Lexi looked down at her hands, then pulled out her phone and sent a text, and a few seconds later she looked up, smiling.

"Do you mind if you drop me off at my parents'? Elliot wants to meet there. We need to chat about a few things."

"Sure, just call me when you want to be picked up."

"Thanks."

I dropped her off and saw her disappear into the graveyard. I wished I knew how she was feeling.

***

"Pink or yellow?" Three held up a couple of photos of Gerber daisies.

Two was behind her and held up a finger.

"Pink," I said while I desperately fought off a yawn.

"I think so too." She placed it on top of her 'yes' pile.

"Okay, table chart or color chart?"

Two again held up one finger.

"Table chart."

"Ha, that's what I think too." She beamed at me. "See, you need to be home more to help me with these things. A male's touch is always appreciated."

When she turned to the side, Two and I high-fived in the air. She always had my back on the girl stuff.

Nan set a drink in front of me and motioned for me to follow her out front.

"No, Nan, I need him," Three pouted.

"I may not be here ten minutes from now, dear. I veto you."

"Nice, Nan." I chuckled, picking up the much-needed drink, thankful for the out. "Three, I think you got this covered. You know you're going to do an amazing job regardless of what any of us think."

"True." She sighed, then pulled out another binder and called out for One, who dashed upstairs.

Once outside, Nan parked her wheelchair next to the door and moved to her rocking chair. She waited for me to join her.

"You find out who Two has been seeing?" I settled in, and when Nan didn't answer, I looked over and saw her face.

"I did."

"And?"

"And I'm not really sure how you're going to take it."

"Well, that's a great opening."

She sipped her scotch and took a moment. "Normally, I would wait and let her tell you, but I don't think she will. She's too scared, and honestly, I don't blame her."

"I'll be fine as long as it isn't anyone associated with the *Almas Perdidas* gang."

She cleared her throat. "Not exactly."

"Come on, Nan, out with it."

"It's Clark."

Clark! I nodded as I let that sink in. I wanted to be mad that my best friend didn't say a word about seeing my baby sis. On the other hand, I didn't think I could have matched a better pair. Wow, I actually surprised myself at how accepting I was. *What the hell is wrong with me?*

"I really need you to say something right now, because your father has a tranquilizer gun I could use if you're going to attack them."

"No, I'm happy for them."

"You are?" Two shouted from the doorway. I turned to find her wide-eyed at her outburst.

"Oh, so now you're getting Nan to do your dirty

work?"

"I didn't want you going all big brother on me, and Nan and you have this weird bond, so yes, I used her as a shield to soften the blow."

"She's got you there, kid." Nan ditched her empty glass and moved on to her backup flask.

Two moved to lean against the rail diagonally across from me.

"How long?"

She scratched her chin. "Six months."

"Is he good to you?"

"Very." She nodded without a missing a beat.

"Why Clark?" I had to know. He'd been like her big brother since we were kids.

"Why are you best friends with him? Because he's a great person with a huge heart. He makes me happy, and we have a lot of fun together. Not sure if it will last, but I hope it does."

I smiled at Nan. "Where did my pigtailed, snot nose, little shadow go?"

Two tucked her hands in her pockets. "I grew up, but don't think for one second I don't still need you."

"Whoop, work those buns, Patrick!" Nan suddenly yelled out to our new neighbor who had taken up running…though I wasn't sure for how much longer now that he was being verbally harassed by Nan.

Patrick's mouth dropped open as he looked over his shoulder.

"Yeah, I'm talking to you, sweet cheeks."

"Oh. My. God." I covered my mouth in horror while Two just shook her head.

"See what she's turned into? She's flippin' Betty White."

Nan batted her hip to move. "Look at that ass. I could just bite it."

"On that note." I stood and hurried inside.

***

Lexi

The graveyard was empty, like it normally was these days. Elliot was on the bench looking straight forward. I saw the bandage over his eye and I wanted to run to him. My poor brother.

"Hi." I gave a small wave. "Are you okay?"

"No." His tone was flat, but he took my hand and pulled it so I would cuddle with him on the bench. The last time we did this was when I was sobbing in my bedroom right after our parents died. "Lost all use of the eye. Will sure made his point." Before I could get upset, he moved on. "Where have you been?"

"Working on bail bondsmen and stuff." Skipping the part about my weekend, which was obviously better than his had been.

"You're a bad liar." He chuckled darkly. "I'm just glad you're back."

I wasn't.

"El, can I ask you something?"

He shifted so he could see me better. "Yeah."

I really didn't like the feeling that went along with this question.

"Why did you tell Keith four years ago that I was

265

happy and with Juan when you knew I certainly wasn't? Juan and I were becoming friends, but you knew how unhappy and lost I was without Keith." His face fell, but he kept his good eye on me. "You made him leave. Why?"

"Would you have left?"

"Maybe not right away, but yeah, we could have left this hell and had a better life. Who knows where we'd be right now. I'm just confused, El. Why would you do that to me?"

He let out a long sigh and rested a hand on top of mine.

"I thought you wanted to be here at that point, and Juan was around. I thought you liked him."

I sat up straighter. What was he talking about? "That's not true. I never wanted to be here, Elliot. *You* did, not *me*. Why would you tell the one person you knew loved me and wanted me to leave and forget about me?"

"Don't put that on me. You did a stellar job of that years ago, Lexi."

"Ouch," I whispered and wrapped my arms about my mid-section.

"Yeah, that was low. I'm sorry." He stood with a huff and paused for a moment, then his face grew anxious and pale. "Look, Lexi, bottom line was I was afraid of losing you. I know I was being selfish but I didn't want you to leave."

I wanted to be furious with him for his words, but I pushed it aside because I did understand that feeling. "I would never have left you here, El, never. I really wish you hadn't done that, but I guess I get it."

266

I suddenly felt the need to do something I'd been thinking about. I pulled my phone free and started to type. Elliot's gasp when he looked over my shoulder at what I wrote told me he didn't agree, but I didn't care.

Lexi: It's Lexi. Check the south gate, fourth container in. DR member is waiting for you.

Before I tucked it away, I got a response.

Clark: You just made my year. Stay safe. Delete these messages.

If anything happened to me, I needed to know I left this world doing something right. I quickly deleted the texts.

"Come on." I motioned for him to join me closer to our parents. We sat together and lit a joint, passing it between us as we studied their headstones.

Elliot pulled his sleeves down when a gust of wind came by, kicking up leaves and swirling them into mini portals.

"Are you happy Keith is back?"

I nodded and picked a piece of grass free from dirt. "Yeah, I think so, but it's been hard letting those feelings back in again."

"We need to get out of here, Lexi. I can't keep doing this."

"I know." I moved to lean against Mom's stone, pretending she was here with us. "I just need a little more time, then we'll go."

"It's been a year since—"

"I know." I cut him off. It wasn't worth the risk even saying it out loud.

"You sure this is going to work?"

"Christ, I hope so."

Elliot rubbed his head like something was bothering him.

"What is it? Just say it, El."

He covered his mouth and puffed out his cheeks. He was really struggling. Which, in turn, made me nervous.

"I need to tell you something without you freaking out on me."

"That's not the best line to start with."

"Fuck me, I'm going to be sick." His face went pale. What the hell was he keeping from me?

"I know you think Juan was the one who got you into the gang, but it wasn't."

My stomach twisted. *Excuse me?*

"Antonio told me I could skip the initiation if I…" He paused to try to read my expression, but I just stared back at him. "If I brought you into the gang. I had showed Juan your photo, and he…he really wanted you."

What? I stood on shaky legs, my world spinning. I couldn't believe what I was hearing.

"You sold me out, your own sister, so you could get out of killing someone?" Saying it like that wasn't helping my case, but he knew what I meant. "Why in the world did you even want to be with these assholes?"

"The girl…she was what I needed at the time—"

"What, you couldn't get a chick anywhere else?"

268

I could feel my heart break. "So you told Juan he could 'have' me after we lost our parents! I was lost and alone, so you just figured he would, what? Take me off your hands so you could have some girl? You felt guilty leaving me behind, so you made a fucking deal? Oh my God, my own brother, my own *twin!*" I wanted to sob and hit something all at the same time.

He pushed to his feet, but I held up my hands so he wouldn't touch me.

"You are my brother, remember?" I cried. "We come first before anyone else. I can't believe you would do this to me. You are disgusting. Stay away from me!" I held my pounding head as the world moved in the opposite direction.

"Lex."

"No." I stuck my finger in his face. "You never liked me being with Keith, not even in high school. I get it, I found my soul mate early, and that took up a lot of my time, but dammit, Elliot! He made me happy, and you made damn sure the moment he was gone you drove in that wedge nice and deep. If Juan hadn't taken me into the club and in a different direction, maybe I would have been able to wait out Keith's tour. I wouldn't be with Antonio now!" I was all over the map with my scattered emotions.

"Ten years, Elliot! Ten years I have battled inside about not being there when he came home from the war. Instead, I was in that horrible dive of a bar with Juan drinking a beer in the morning. I literally watched as I broke the heart of the only person who ever loved me into a billion pieces! All because I loved you so much that I didn't see the truth!"

"Lexi, please!"

I lowered my voice as disappointment and disbelief drained away my energy. "And look where it got me, Elliot. I hope you're happy. Your twin sister who loved you more than anything, who would have done anything for you, is getting her ass beat every time she does the wrong thing. Stuck with a creep like Antonio who degrades me every day. Thanks a lot. Mom and Dad would be so proud of you."

Elliot's bloodshot eye was wet, but he fought the tears. He just stood there and took everything I had to say.

I went to leave but turned back to remind him once more of who we were. "We're twins. You hurt, I hurt, remember? Where was that promise when you *sold* me off?"

"I'm sorry," he whispered with his head down.

"Me too."

It was only a twenty-minute walk to Keith's house, and I knew it would be the best thing for me right then. I needed time to grapple with everything that had just happened. The pain of what Elliott had done was so raw I was bleeding inside. One step forward, three steps back in the shit department.

Fifteen minutes into the walk, my cell vibrated.

Elliot: I'm sorry, Lexi. I made stupid choices and now we are both stuck in this mess. I never meant to lie to you. I just was so lost. I hate this life and just want Mom and Dad back.

I started to cry. I hated being mad at him. We had been so close our whole lives, and that was what hurt the most.

Lexi: *Just give me a few days.*

Elliot: *Okay.*

As I stood in front of Keith's door, I decided to keep this to myself. I didn't need Keith hating Elliot. He had enough in his life right now, and this certainly wasn't something I wanted to share.

CHAPTER THIRTEEN

Keith

The Next Day

"Looking pretty good, First Sergeant." Nan rolled into my room, double parking next to my bed.

Buttoning up my jacket, I grinned at her in the mirror. "So do you." Her bright orange dress made her face glow.

"Wait until you see Lexi." She grinned, topping off her drink from the belly of my bear. "She could wear a paper dress and it would be on the cover of Vogue the next day."

I chuckled. Nan was right. Lexi was absolutely stunning, especially when she smiled.

Nan locked her chair in place and stood, snatching up my phone.

"You two give me hope that love can still be present even after all these years."

"Poppy never will forget you, Nan."

"I know." She smiled to herself. "We'll just pick up right where we left off." She hit a button on the screen. "That's why I picked out something frisky for my funeral. We'll have a lot of catching up to do."

"Oh, Lord, Nan." I laughed as her eyes closed when the music started.

Artie Shaw, "Begin the Beguine," flowed from the crisp speakers, and she started to move her shoulders, swaying side to side.

"I remember the first time I saw your grandfather. It was the town fair, and people from all around had come out to enjoy the rides. String lights crisscrossed around the ballfield, and the smell of cotton candy was everywhere. I was next to the Ferris wheel with my girlfriends, laughing and watching it go up so high." Her hands went to her chest. *"When this song came on, I felt someone watching me, so I looked over and saw a strapping young man in neatly pressed pants and a wool overcoat smiling at me. He gave a little tip of his hat before he started walking right in my direction. Oh, Lord, my heart beat so fast, and my cheeks burned. The other girls tried to get his attention, but he didn't even waver in his step. He was fixed on me."* She turned the music up a little higher, then pushed off the desk she was leaning on. *"He asked me to dance and offered his hand. Without a thought, I took it and let him lead me to where a few others were spinning and shuffling."* Her hands went up as she swayed. *"At that moment, I knew he was something special. I was sixteen when I met*

273

him. Who was I to know what love was? But that didn't matter, and we never looked back."

I stood in front of Nan and held out my hand. She smiled, taking it. With my hand in hers and my other on her back, I eased her around the room, carefully spinning her just a little. Her chuckle made my heart swell. I lifted my chin and played my part well. There was nothing I wouldn't do for my Nan.

I knew this would be forever etched in my memory, me dancing around my room with one of my most favorite people, her eyes closed and her lips in a smile. I knew she was back there at the fairground dancing with Poppy.

As the song ended, I leaned down and gave a little bow. That's when I caught Lexi watching us from across the hall.

"Go on, sweetheart," Nan whispered. "Just because my love is put on hold right now doesn't mean yours has to be."

"I love you, Nan."

"Of course you do." She sat back down in her chair. "What's not to love?"

"True."

Stepping into the hallway, I watched as Lexi shifted her weight from foot to foot. Her head dipped as she gave me a small smile.

She looked…perfect in a dark purple dress that clung to her curves and hit right above the knee. Her hair had a tiny wave through it and shone under the light.

"That's actually quite sexy." She pointed to my

uniform.

My hand brushed down the side of the jacket, happy she liked it. "Thank you. You look amazing."

She nodded before she picked up her long coat and purse. "We should probably get going. Don't want to upset the bride."

An hour later and I was thankful I was standing in the wedding at an angle. My jaw was locked in place as I watched my baby sister be handed off to someone else. Danny was great, and he was aware of what I did for living, and that made this day a bit easier. Lexi was dabbing at her cheek with a Kleenex. She was just as much a part of this family, whether she believed it or not.

The roaring crowd pulled me from my trance. Three tossed up her hands and cheered with everyone else. She blew me a kiss as they walked back down the aisle.

"One down, three to go." Dad slapped my shoulder. "Who knows, maybe Two will be next." He pointed to Clark, who had taken her hand as they walked out together. I was pleased I had cleared the air with my best friend before the wedding. I wanted Two to let loose and have fun, and in all honesty, I was happy for them. I knew Clark would kick anyone's ass if they ever touched her.

"Maybe."

At the reception, the chairs were pushed aside, and the music "2 Heads" by Coleman Hell swirled around the dancefloor. Mark hadn't stopped shaking it with Savannah, and made good use of the fact the rest of us hadn't had time to get our buzz on yet.

The two of them were jumping around like it was a rave and were shouting the words.

Three couldn't get enough of them and kept joining in their crazy moves.

Mia and Lexi went to get a drink and left me with Cole. He leaned back and tossed a pair of keys at me across the table.

"What are these?" I picked them up and checked out the keychain that read **'*Dusk*.'**

"Keys."

I shot him a look and watched his mouth curve upward. "You need to be closer to your family, and…" He flicked his head in Lexi's direction. "I want you to run the new safe house."

"What? Really?" I almost needed him to repeat it.

"Yes, under two conditions. You'll need to come back and visit Shadows every month or two, and you remain with Blackstone. I will not lose any more members."

Holy shit. I leaned forward and offered my hand. "Thank you."

"There's no one who could do the job better. Savannah wasn't overly pleased, but she'll get over it." Cole's face lit up as he looked over my shoulder. "W-o-w."

"Beware the Dog" by Be Impressive made its way to my ears as I turned to see Lexi breaking it down with Mark, who was shaking his chest like he was at a cabana.

"Is it wrong that I'm jealous of his moves?" Mia sank into the chair next to me.

"I'm not sure if you should be," Cole muttered,

but he gave her a wink.

I laughed before I stood, downed my drink, and made my way over to the three of them. I grabbed Three and spun her into the group. Mark lowered himself to the ground and back up again, yelling the chorus. Lexi was laughing so hard she had to hold onto Savannah for support.

Three held up her camera and started to snap some pictures. I twirled Lexi around, took her head in my hands, and kissed her, hoping Three would get the shot. When I let go, I waited for her hesitation, but she just gave me a shy smile. I took her hands and started to dance with her while Mark *tossed coconuts* in the air around us. Where did he get these moves?

Nan, in her chair, shoulders swinging, joined the craziness. Mark came up behind her and grabbed the handles and started to do the train, but instead Nan reached behind him and grabbed his ass.

"Oh, Nan, I wasn't ready!" Mark stepped in front of her. "Okay, do it again! I'm flexing now."

I shook my head at Dad, who just covered his eyes. Those two were dangerous together.

While Mark taught Nan the Cabbage Patch move, I soaked up every moment I could touch Lexi. It was great to see her let loose and have some fun.

I caught Three as she raced by and mouthed. "Slow song."

She gave me a thumbs up and pretended to wipe a tear at how happy she was for us.

A moment later, the DJ came on. "Time to slow this down a little."

Cole was suddenly at my side reaching for Savannah, who had caught the eye of Danny's brother.

Lexi moved her arms around my waist and rested her head on my chest as Adele's powerful voice sang "Someone Like You."

Placing my chin on her head, I let out a long sigh, loving that she wanted me at this moment, not the other way around.

Our bodies formed one as we swayed in a circle.

Savannah mouthed, "Her eyes are closed," then she smiled with such happiness I could have shed a tear. I wanted this so badly it physically made me ache. I knew we had a lot to get through before we could be us again, but dammit, I'd sell my soul to keep this woman. She was mine.

"Keith?" She looked up at me with glossy eyes.

"Yes."

Her eyes flickered back and forth as if she were carefully trying to choose the right words.

"Never mind."

"What is it?" I urged her to tell me.

"Thank you for this."

I smiled and dipped down to catch her lips. She let me, and I lost myself, not caring that we weren't alone. It wasn't a passionate kiss. It was slow and meaningful and held so much promise.

***

Lexi

My thumb brushed back and forth over the

handle of my mug without care in the world as I watched the steam float away. It made me envious, and I wished I could lift myself up and join it where it was going. These past three days had been nice—relaxing, even. Been a while since I felt like I was seen for more than just a body.

A strong breeze blew my hair around, occasionally interrupting my view of the quiet street. I was resting on the wide railing of the front porch. One foot straight out in front of me, the other bent so I could rest my chin on it, I needed a moment to gather myself. I knew I had to go back to the clubhouse, and I was strangely torn up about it. My emotions were a mess. I knew I didn't love Antonio—hell, I didn't even like the bastard—but I had spent a lot of time in his life, and it held a certain comfort level I had become used to. I knew I had a job to do, and it was time this came to an end.

"Hey." Keith came out holding his keys. He leaned down and kissed my head. "Are you sure you're ready?"

"I'm sure. Let's go."

My phone vibrated in my pocket, and I quickly pulled it free, thinking it was Elliot.

Yellow: Should we meet?

Keith gave me a strange look.
"Who's that?"

Lexi: No.

"No one."

My stomach was in a nasty twist that grew tighter as we drew closer to the clubhouse. Every stoplight, I fought the urge to hop out and run. Keith kept his hand on mine, giving it a squeeze here and there. Occasionally, he would ask if I wanted to change my mind. I knew he would spin this car around on a dime if I even hesitated. I had convinced myself I couldn't allow myself to fall under Keith's spell again. Some wounds were still too deep to get past completely. Although I had begun to think that over time some might heal, I would not go there right now, not with what I had to do.

Sweat broke out between my shoulder blades as I reached for the handle and opened the heavy metal door. Keith had dropped me off a block away, waiting to be sure it didn't look like we arrived together. The smell hit me with a wave of nausea, and I was weak in the knees, but I raised my chin and stepped into the room.

"Where the fuck have you been?" Will grunted as I pushed by him, hoping to find Elliot. "Hey!" He grabbed my arm. "I'm talking to you."

"Get off me!" I hissed, not in the mood for his shit today, and using him as a catalyst to get my anger flowing.

Spinning around quickly, I managed to break his hold and headed for the bar where Antonio charged at me like a bull.

Shit.

"I'm not sure if I should beat you into a grave or fuck you into tomorrow!" I braced for the blow but was surprised with the rough kiss I got instead.

"Hey, boys! Let's hear it for my girl who broke us out of that shit hole!" The bar erupted, and I managed to produce a strained smile as they drained their drinks.

"Okay, boys, get the fuck out of here and do what I asked." He waited for them to leave, then he shoved a drink in my hand and gave me a funny look, but one I knew all too well. This drink was laced. "Drink up," he ordered.

I set it on the bar top. "I want to see Elliot first."

His stance straightened and his eyes burned into mine. "What?"

"Antonio, you have no idea what I had to go through to get you guys out. Give me a few minutes to let my brother know I'm back safely."

He shoved the drink in my hand again, his expression ugly, and that's when I heard it.

The sound that would haunt me for as long as I was on this earth.

Pop! Pop!

Antonio shoved me away from him and ducked behind the bar like the coward he was.

A woman started to scream from the other room. My gut instinct told me to move, and I raced toward the screams and flung open the door.

I became weightless. My skin prickled as the blood dropped to my toes, and my lungs froze in position. The world simultaneously stopped spinning and spun out of control at the sight of my brother, my twin, lying on the floor with his blood pumping from a massive hole in the side of his head. "No!" I screamed and dropped to my knees as my head grew light. My hands shook as I tried

281

desperately to put things back the way they were supposed to be. Brain matter dripped from my hands. "What did you do? What did you do?" I screamed in his face. "You can't leave me here! You can't!" Painful sobs ripped from my chest and rattled in my throat. "Elliot, wake up!" This was a joke! A fucked up prank by Will. Will! He was hunched oddly in a chair, and blood had soaked through his shirt and pooled onto the floor below him. More blood dripped from his lips, and I realized there had been two gunshots. That realization was oddly soothing.

As the room came into focus, I saw pictures strewn all over the floor. On shaky knees, I grabbed the closest one and tried to absorb what I was looking at. Even in my stunned state, the ugly truth got through.

"Holy shit!" Antonio nearly laughed behind me. "What a fucking mess."

I couldn't handle it. Dropping my head back, I let out a nasty, horrific scream.

My mouth tasted like tin as I sobbed, holding the picture. Everything hurt. It was as though someone held a match to my skin and the fire crawled up to scorch my heart.

"Get up, Lexi!" Antonio ordered, frustrated with my mourning.

"Fuck you," I hissed, not caring. Nothing mattered anymore. My brother, who had been nothing but their punching bag, had been driven to kill himself because of this picture. The gun by his hand made the tiniest impact. He shot Will.

"What'd you say?" He reached out to grab me,

but I coiled back out of his reach, and I felt something hard hit my foot.

"I said fuck you, Antonio." My voice was low and oddly steady. Reaching down for the broken chair leg, I swung it at his head, smashing his temple with good force.

His hand covered the side of his head for a second and his eyes bugged out in pure anger.

"Yeah, that's right, asshole! I know Will killed my parents!"

He must have been on coke or something, because he stood without registering any pain and cracked his neck like I hadn't just smacked his skull with a heavy piece of wood. He was bleeding, but he didn't seem to care.

My heart pumped rapidly, and things were becoming blurry. My emotions wanted to take over, and I fought to keep them back. My brother was dead. My brother was dead. Holy shit, I couldn't stop the loop that went round and round my head.

"Were we just a game to you? Did you know me before you killed them?" I wasn't even sure I wanted to know at this point.

"Fine, you want to do this?" he yelled, causing my breathing to catch. "Fine! Your mom was so scared." He smirked at my flinch. He was there? Of course he was. Hunters traveled in packs. "Your foolish dad thought he could save her. He begged for Will to spare her miserable life, but that's not the rules, is it, Lexi?" His head tilted to the side as he spoke. "Your dad went first. One shot to the head took him down. Your mother's scream was just the icing on the cake before—"

"Ahhh!" I lunged with all my strength, but he was waiting for it and grabbed me and slammed me to the floor. Just as he hauled back his foot to kick my stomach, Keith came flying into the room. He grabbed Antonio and tossed his bloody body into the wall.

I turned away from the sounds of Keith beating him. It would only be seconds before the rest of the crew joined in.

"Elliot," I cried out and rushed to his lifeless body. I shook as my hand found his. It was limp, and I wanted so badly to feel him squeeze back.

"Why couldn't you have waited?" How could he do this? "Oh God, I should have told you about our parents, but I needed more time. I'm so sorry!"

"Lexi." Keith broke through my sobs. "We have to go now!"

"He's gone!"

"Now, Lexi!" He hauled me to my feet and rushed me down the hallway. My legs were lead; I wasn't even sure how my knees bent.

One of the men stopped in our path, looking confused but pointing his gun at us.

Suddenly, Gordon wrapped his arm around the man's neck, knocking the gun to the ground and pulling him out of the way.

What the hell?

I could barely keep up as Keith dragged me along.

Everything happened so fast. I was shoved into his truck, and we sped down the alley to the main road and gained even more speed. *We're going to get a ticket,* I thought. My nails dug into the door handle and my feet pressed hard into the floor. I needed to ground myself to stay calm, but for some reason I wanted to giggle. This was the first time I had witnessed Keith turn on his Army instincts. He said nothing as he watched the road and his mirrors, speeding through red lights and switching lanes without any warning. I was too far lost inside to care what happened. Silly thoughts came to the surface, like if we crashed, I wondered if my brain matter might splatter out like El's.

Oh shit, I was losing it.

He made a hard right and turned down to the parking lot of the lake. I saw Clark standing by his squad car with its engine running.

Keith slammed the truck in park and rushed around to my door, yanking it open. He scooped me out and placed me on my feet and took my head in his hands.

"Go with Clark. He'll keep you safe until I get back."

The reality of the situation hit me. "Keith, what are you doing?"

"I need to check on my family, make sure someone is there to watch them in case Antonio retaliates. Please go with Clark. I'll call you on my way back."

"I don't like this, Keith." I wanted to panic, but now wasn't the time.

"I know." He kissed me quickly and handed me off to Clark, who sat me in the back of the car.

"Elliot's dead, Clark. Shot. Lexi's in shock. I'll explain it all later. Keep her safe!"

"You know I will." Clark's face was full of

questions, but he gave a nod, and Keith sped off toward the highway.

***

The sun was going down, and I was stuck pacing the floor of this shitty motel. Clark wanted us hidden and chose this place. I had officially broken down seven times. Seven times I told myself Elliot was in a better place. Seven times I cursed his name and let the hurt consume me until there was nothing left to do but pace the ugly pea green shag carpet. I wasn't sure how I would grieve once Keith came back, but right now I only knew this situation was more fucked up than they could possibly know, and I couldn't do anything about it.

I peeked out the filthy brown curtains and saw Clark was on the phone. Sliding the window open a little, I listened.

"Yeah, she's here, man, don't worry." He paused and removed his cap, scrubbing his fingers through his hair. "Not good. She seems to be going through it in waves. Won't touch a thing to eat, but that's expected." His hand swiped over his mouth. "Gordon should be there in about ten minutes. He got caught up in the chaos."

What? Was Gordon working with the police? I shook off the fog and tried to remember. He was always around, never said much, mainly just watched. Wait, was that why he stood up when Antonio was going to hit me that time?

I leaned closer to the window.

"Look, man, if you're going to do this, you better

be prepared for if you get caught. Doesn't matter what coast you're on. Trigger's gang won't blink an eye before snapping your neck. They'll personally deliver your body to your parents."

No! Feeling my head go light, I sat on the mattress and tried to put the pieces together. That conversation just blew what little bit of fog was left from my head straight out. Then I felt the burn. It started in my fingertips and raced up my arms. It filled my heart and fueled my anger.

No one was going to kill Antonio but me.

Fingering the phone out of my pocket, I quickly Googled the closest place and ordered six large pizzas and three bottles of soda on Clark's Visa. How was he a cop? Who left his wallet on the table, anyway?

After that, I went through his bag. Thankfully, he was at the bottom of the stairs, and I would hear him come up. Yes! I felt the spare gun tucked in his case. I loved Clark, but he was so predictable. Twisting the numbers on the lock, I put in his street number, the same one he used on his phone, and tried a couple of pin numbers. Ha! It was his hockey numbers from high school. 1119.

Predictable.

Then I waited.

A little Honda showed up with Tony's Pizza on the top, and out jumped a kid looking real excited for a tip. Clark walked over, holding up his hands, telling the kid to go back.

Grabbing my bag, happy Keith had thought to snatch it from the chair when we exited the club, I headed out the door. Keeping low, I raced across the balcony, down the stairs, and out across the back street. Seeing a bus, I ran ahead to the bus stop.

Digging for the change in my pocket, I scrambled on before the driver closed the doors.

"Thanks," I huffed. I knew my face said it all; I was emotionally drained. Dropping the change, I took a seat and glanced over my shoulder at the disappearing hotel. There was no sign of Clark. *Good. Keep talking.*

***

Keith

I was staring at someone else, someone who would haunt me for the rest of my life if I wasn't careful.

Blackstone wasn't with me. I didn't have my men. I didn't have backup. One wrong move and I could be staring down the barrel of a gun with no way out.

I made sure my sweater was pulled well down on my arms to hide the fact I didn't have the snake around my forearm. I twisted and knotted the red bandana around my wrist and checked over my clothes. Red oversized sweater, baggy jeans, and Vans. Looked about right.

"Ready?" Gordon checked his watch. "They'll be arriving in twenty."

"Yeah." I checked my gun clip and followed him out to a blue 1975 Mustang.

Gordon started the car, and we pulled out and

headed to where the old crossroads met just outside of town. We picked this place for a reason.

Parking in the shadow by the fence, we waited.

"So, special forces?" Gordon asked. I guessed the silence bothered him.

I checked my phone once more to make sure everything was good. Nothing new from Clark.

"Yeah."

"A little more to it than working a beat."

"It has its moments." Twin lights came in to view. "Here they come."

Dim headlights pulled into the clearing. Once they parked, they both rushed to the woods to take a leak.

"Works for me." Gordon chuckled. "Wasn't looking forward to knocking a few heads out tonight anyway. Let's move." I barely heard him; I just wanted this shit over with.

We rushed over, again running along the edge of the shadows to the side window of the truck.

Gordon was the lookout. "Go," he whispered.

Using a crowbar, I wedged it into the back door and gently tapped the window. Between the pressure and the force, the window cracked and broke inward quietly. We hurried to gather the bricks of cocaine, stuffing them into a duffle bag.

"Good?" I asked as we both looked off toward the woods.

"Oh shit! No." Gordon pulled his gun free. We pressed against the side of the truck.

"Come on, dude, I'm hungry, and they don't pick up for another thirty. Let's grab something," one guy complained.

Snapping my knuckles, I mentally prepared for a fight.

"Now go." Gordon dipped low and started racing back to the Mustang.

Now it was my turn to play my part. I raced behind him and dropped the bag, stepping boldly out of the shadows. Acting like I had hurt my knee, I was sure to show my red bandana for them to see.

"Hey!" one of the men called out and took a shot in my direction. Dropping lower, I waited until the tires of the Mustang were next to me for cover.

I dropped the bag with the drugs on the floorboard and dived inside, and we peeled out of the open lot. More shots hit the car, and one took out my side mirror.

"How many bricks?" My words were rushed as we were pressed for time.

"Six, I think." Gordon swung into traffic, making the car next to us swerve. They blasted their horn at us.

"Go!" I slammed down on the dashboard.

Just as we blew through two major intersections, a semi-truck came out of nowhere, and we had to make a right turn, cutting off a whole lane. Everything in the car went flying, including my phone. It disappeared in the back somewhere.

"Shit!" Trying to spot it was pointless. It was too dark, and I had to hang on.

"Hold on!" Gordon shouted as he pulled a U-ey and dove down an alley so narrow I thought we might not fit.

Crack! The other side mirror ripped off the door, leaving us with just the rearview.

My heart pounded. Normally, I loved the rush but this was different. This was too personal for me to get my usual thrill.

"Sure fucking glad this is Antonio's car!" Gordon hissed as we came to a really tight spot.

"You won't make it!" I yelled.

"Yeah, I know!" He slammed on the brakes, but we were going so fast we wedged between a trash bin and the wall. I flung forward, hitting my head on the dashboard.

"Grab it," I yelled as I kicked the windshield out with my boot and crawled through.

"Here!" He tossed the bag to me and climbed out. We were only one block from Antonio's clubhouse.

"Go, and then get out," I ordered.

Gordon flung the bag on his back and ran toward the clubhouse. He needed to plant the drugs and get out before the Devil's Reach got there.

Pressing my hands against the dented hood, I took a moment, hating not knowing how it was going with Clark. I liked the constant communication I had with my own team at times like this. It was hard working blind with someone I didn't know.

Scrambling through the broken glass, I fished around for my phone, and under the seat in the debris I found it, but damn, it was smashed to shit. With a curse I tucked it away.

Fuck!

I shed the clothing I had worn to my own underneath. I pulled a ball hat on and walked back to the main street, then to the diner just down from the clubhouse.

I opened the door, and the hostess squinted at my head.

"You need some ice?"

"I need to use your phone, please."

She nodded and pointed to a phone on the wall.

"Thanks."

It rang and rang.

"This is Clark. Leave a message."

I rubbed my head and tried to clean up the blood as best I could. "Clark. It's done. We are in place, phone broke, at a diner across the street." I slammed the phone down in frustration. This better fucking work.

Taking the booth in the back so I could get a good view of the club, I let out a long sigh.

I ordered some coffee and waited.

Twenty minutes later, just as I thought I might go mad, I heard the deep, haunting rumble of the engine. Not one, not two, but the entire crew raced by and stopped in front of the clubhouse.

I jumped to my feet. "Get down!" I yelled to the staff. Loud cries and screams faded as the staff rushed out back to safety.

The lights flickered off, and I was left staring out the window at one of the most epic battles this town would ever witness.

It was hypnotizing to watch as the Devil's Reach got into formation and raised their weapons in unison. I'd hand it to Trigger; the man ran a tight crew.

Bracing myself for it, I ducked and watched as a quick nod from their president brought a spray of thousands of bullets at the front of the *Almas Perdidas* clubhouse.

It was like a million fireworks going off at once. Wood flew at least fifty feet, and the vibrations blew out the windows around me.

"Keith!" someone shouted over the madness. "Keith!"

I turned and found Clark screaming at me from across the restaurant.

He mouthed something, but I had to duck, so I could barely read his lips.

The bullets stopped as quickly as they had begun, and the roar of the engines as they raced by was deafening.

Once they passed, I stood and looked back at what was left of the clubhouse. A giant dust cloud encased the building, and the screams of nearby people brought home the reality to me.

"Lexi!" Clark grabbed my shoulders and shook me. "She left!"

I shook my head as I absorbed his words.

"Lexi left a while ago. I tried to call you, but you didn't—"

Swinging the door open, I ran as fast as I could across the street to the clubhouse that was now on fire.

I forced my brain into training mode. It was the only way I could stay calm. Still, a cold, slow niggle of doubt slipped through the cracks, making my blood run cold.

The place was like the aftermath of a cartel battle in Mexico. Bloody dead bodies were flopped over everything. Arms and legs were mangled in twisted positions. I started to sift through the mess, but I didn't know where to start. I forced myself to think.

I heard a strangled laugh. I turned around and saw Lexi rocking back and forth slowly on her heels. She held a gun at a smirking Antonio. He was propped up against the leg of the pool table. One arm had blood pouring out, and his other hand tried to stop the bleeding.

"You think I'm scared of you, bit—"

Bang! Bang!

As I ran to Lexi, she turned, her face pale. Then I saw her left side soaked in blood. She brushed by my fingertips as she collapsed to floor.

Lexi!

***

Lexi

I opened my eyes and squinted at a bright light. People were rushing around me.

"She's lost a lot of blood."

"How old?"

"Thirty-one." Keith's voice. I couldn't see him.

"Okay, sir, I need you and your family to give us some room."

"Let's go, guys." Clark's voice was low.

"Lexi, we love you!" Keith's mother?

Am I crying?

"Can I stay with her?" Keith asked, and the doctor looked at me. I slowly shook my head. "Lexi!" Keith called out, confused.

"Sir, please, you'll only hold up the process."

The doctor hovered over me, looking worried. "Ahh, Miss Kline, we have a problem."
Oh shit, now what?

***

"Good morning." Nurse Robin opened my blinds to let in the morning light. "Are you going to eat for me today?"

Pushing the button on my bed, I rose to a sitting position. I was on day two in the hospital and was feeling a little better than yesterday. Thankfully, the bullet went straight in and out my left shoulder. Nothing major was damaged. The only thing it did was give me a giant wakeup call.

"Yeah, I'll try." I cleared my throat. "Could you please pass me my phone?"

"Sure. It was ringing a lot yesterday." She handed it to me and said she'd be back with my breakfast.

Five missed calls from Yellow. Shit. Swiping it open, I called him back.

"What the hell happened?" I wished he was a little nicer.

"I'm done."

There was a small pause. "Lexi, we had a deal. If you want your brother's murder charges cleared, you need to stick it out another four months."

"Elliot is dead." My throat stung as I forced the words out. "I held up my end of the deal. I gave you all the information I could on the *Almas Perdidas,* and now in return I want nothing but to be left alone. Your Guns and Gangs will just have to do without me now." I hung up.

"Is that—?"

I turned my head sharply to see a pale-looking Keith standing in the doorway.

"You were working with Guns and Gangs?"

Flopping my head back to the pillow, I closed my eyes and let some tears fall.

"Jesus, Lexi, that was an incredibly dangerous deal to make."

"I did it for Elliot." Drying my cheeks, I flinched at the pain in my shoulder. "Elliot got jumped one night and defended himself with a golf club. Ended up killing a girl, thinking it was someone else. He was going to get life until I struck a deal with a DEA agent."

"Yellow?" Keith suddenly realized who Yellow was.

"Whenever I had some information for them, I would put a yellow rose in with the red ones on my parents' grave. He knew what day I went to visit, so he'd wait for the signal."

Keith sank into the chair next to me. "How long have you been doing this?"

"Eight months."

"Why didn't you tell me? I would have understood."

I nearly smiled, and I knew he caught it. "Keith, you came walking back into my life like the force of a hundred men."

"I guess, but still…Lexi."

I turned to face him. "Where is the safe house located?"

He closed his eyes, getting my point.

"We all have secrets, Keith. Some we can share, and some we can't."

Keith tossed his ball hat on the bed and rubbed his head.

"Look, we can go through all of this after we get you home."

Home...

My mouth was dry and I needed water. How was I going to explain?

"Um, I think I'm going to take a breather for a bit. All of this has been a bit too much."

His expression became worried. "Breather?"

"I need some time to think. My brother, who was my best friend, just killed himself. Will, someone I've known and lived with under the same roof, killed my parents. I need some time to process that before I can look ahead to the future."

He stood, looking pissed. "I know, and we can do that together."

I shook my head slowly. "I need some time alone, Keith.

"Time?" I could see that word stung him. "Was ten years not enough?"

I bit down on my cheek, trying not to lash out. "Don't put that decade all on me! You left me, remember?"

"Fuck, Lexi, we wasted half of our lives chasing each other. Here we are with a chance to be us again, and you want to take another break." His hands covered his face. "Here we go again. History repeating itself. Well, now I know how Cole felt."

Huh?

"This—" I paused, seeing everything so damn

297

clearly now, "—is why we don't work."

I'm not sure how much time passed as we stared in opposite directions. We were so different; that was evident now. One of us just had to pull the trigger.

"Sell the ring."

His head snapped up.

"Sell the ring." My eyes softened so he knew I wasn't trying to fight anymore. I was so tired of fighting. "I'm not good for you." My words tore from me, and acid filled the open wounds. Why was this so hard? Because I was truly saying goodbye, but in the right way this time. No hurtful digs, just "I love you so much, and that's why I'm letting you go." It could never work.

"We have so much baggage it will just sink us. You need to be loved, Keith, in a way I never can."

He leaned forward and grabbed my hand. "You don't get to make that call, Lexi."

"Yes, I do." I kissed his fingers.

"No, Lexi, don't." His eyes filled and spilled over. I had never seen Keith cry like that, and it just about killed me.

"I love you, Keith. Always have, always will. But sometimes that's not enough."

"Lexi, you just need some time to heal."

"Hey." I pulled him closer and kissed his cheek as a goodbye. "You don't get it. I don't *want* to be saved."

He suddenly stood like he finally got it, and then turned away. I couldn't watch, so I closed my eyes before I heard the door shut behind him.

"Goodbye, Keith."

There. I did it. I did it for him.

My good arm flew across my face as I cried myself out.

I heard he came by every day, but I made sure he couldn't see me. I even left a day early so he couldn't intercept me. It was harsh, but Keith had to see I meant what I said or he would never give up.

CHAPTER FOURTEEN

Eight Months Later

Lexi

Pushing the cart through the aisle was a lot easier before. I really took it for granted. My cart was overflowing with junk food, but I didn't care. Dipping my plain chip in the peanut butter made my eyes roll back in my head. I was so hungry.

My phone lit up, and I answered.

"Hi, Emma, where are you?"

"Just at the pharmacy. I'll be at least another twenty. You still at the market?"

Dropping a package of gummy worms into the cart, I sighed. "Yes, buying way too much, but whatever."

"Who cares?" She laughed. "Lucky bitch. I'll meet up when I'm done."

"'Kay."

Stopping at the candy department, my eyes stung when I spotted the Hubba Bubba tape. I really missed all his friends, especially Mark. I wondered what Keith was up to, but really, that wasn't any of my business anymore. My life was here now.

I took the little money I had squirrelled away from Antonio's club and drove to Nova Scotia where my cousin Emma had offered me a place to stay. She had made the same offer after my parents died, but at that time I couldn't bring myself to leave Boston. It was where my parents were. I realized I had missed Canada, and it helped me reunite with my roots. I did hear Father Kai went to jail. I didn't care to know why. I was just happy at the news and hoped he was now someone's bitch.

Clark tried to reach out. I answered once and heard the Devil's Reach never got charged with the killings of the *Almas Perdidas* members. Something about one of them testifying it was another crew from North Carolina. Of course the police department kept quiet. They were just happy to get their city back. He did mention one of Trigger's crew came in and spoke to him and wanted to say they were sorry I got hurt, and they were in my debt. Clark said he had told them it was me who gave them the location of where their member's body was. He told me their motto was "Never Forget." I asked Clark what that meant, and he said I should ask Keith. I didn't say anything to that. What was there to say? Afterward, I changed my number and left.

I needed to start over.

***

Keith

"Hey, Keith?" Mike poked his head in the door. "Frank called, and Officer Caden just sent his paperwork through. He is officially part of the house."

Removing my glasses, I leaned back in the leather chair Savannah gave me as a move-in gift. I let out a deep breath. "That's a relief."

Mike nodded, coming into my office as I pulled out two crystal snifters and a bottle of brandy. Pouring us each a double, I placed his in front of him as he sank into the chair, looking as tired as I was.

Raising it in the air, I leaned forward to tap his. "Dusk is finally fully staffed."

I closed my eyes and let the warm amber slide down my throat. This had been a maddening experience. I had so much more respect for the Logans. Filling a houseful of people you needed to be able to trust was incredibly hard.

"Oh," I leaned back and pointed to the table off to the side, "a package came for you today."

Mike quickly glanced over. "Thanks."

"Look, I have to know, what is in those boxes?"

His eyes closed before he started to open the box. "I was always the big kid, tall, thick, scary looking. I didn't have friends, and the ones I did only used me as their shield. One day my mother came home with one of these." He held up an odd looking troll doll with blue hair. "Ugliest things I've ever seen, but they became my friends. They never made fun of me, never hurt me, never looked at me

302

funny. They were just always there." He smiled, placing it back in the box. "My mom sends them to me every month. I tried to tell her I don't want them anymore, but truth is they carry some kind of comfort." He started to laugh. "Now you know why I never shared it with you guys."

"Yeah, Mark would have a field day."

"Yeah."

"Secret is safe with me."

"I know it is."

I left it at that; no need to go on.

Mike would be my right hand man at the Dusk house. Cole, of course, had the same rules for him. He must visit Shadows, and he must remain on Blackstone.

I wasn't overly surprised when Mike asked to be transferred here. We had always gotten along, and our personalities matched well.

"I think I may have recruited Davie." Mike grinned, sliding the glass over to me and resting his ankle over his knee. "Savannah nearly removed my balls when she heard me speaking with Dell."

It was the running joke right now for us to piss off Savannah with stealing their staff.

"You better watch your back." I laughed. "She's getting better with her paybacks. I found one of Liv's diapers jammed in my suitcase. Thankfully, Mark sniffed it out before I left."

"Thanks for the heads up." He stood. "All right, boss, I need to go see how Abby is dealing with the kitchen staff. Thank God she offered to help out."

"Yeah, sounds good."

Once he left, I grabbed some paperwork and

headed out onto my patio. It wasn't long before I passed out.

***

"Yes, I got the memo, thanks." I balanced the phone between my shoulder and ear as I tied my sneakers. "Oh, Cole, I hired that young guy you wanted. Um, Officer Caden. He officially moves in this Friday."

"Wow, that's great. So you're fully staffed?"

"I am." I glanced at the time and saw I was late. "Shit, Cole, I have to go. Can I call you later?"

"Sure thing."

Hurrying down the stairs and into my car, I sped through the three checkpoints and onto the open Ashville road.

Things were different now. I was the primary operator of the new safe house in North Carolina. Still a member of Team Blackstone, I went there a lot. I did miss Montana, but I was there so much it was like I never left. Besides, Mark's twin boys were a handful and liked to bite.

I loved being so close to my family and getting to spend a lot more time with them. Three loved being married, and Two's relationship with Clark was moving along pretty fast. Nan was particularly happy to have me around to keep the bar stocked.

As for Lexi, she had decided to drop off the radar. We both spent a lifetime chasing something that just wasn't there. It hurt like hell, and I would always be in love with her. I did meet someone. She worked at the bike shop in town. She was nice. She just had a lot of energy I found I couldn't really to connect with, but I was sure in time it would get easier.

You shouldn't have to try to like someone's personality. You either click or you don't. I tried to push Savannah's words out of my head.

"Hi." Amelia's eyes lit up as I came forward and kissed her lips.

"Hey, how are you?"

"Better now." She smiled and held my hand as I looked over the menu. "Oh, so..." She pulled out a catalog. "What do you think about Barbados?"

My stomach twisted. She wanted to do a trip with her sister and knew I'd done a lot of traveling. So she was picking my brain. However, I didn't want to think about Barbados...

"How about Cuba?" I offered instead.

"Ohh..." She flipped through the pages and pointed to the white beach. "Yes, I could vacation there, no problem."

My phone vibrated twice in my pocket. I pulled it free and saw it was an unknown text. *That's odd.* I quickly Googled the area code. Canada?

Opening the message, it took a moment for the picture to download.

Unknown Number: Thought you should know...234 Ocean View Rd, Queensland NS Canada.

The picture popped up, and I nearly choked on my water.

"Are you okay, hun?

"No."

The End...

Come on, like I'd end it like that!
Keep Reading...

EPILOGUE

Halifax International Airport was small enough that I found the car rental place easily.

"Seriously." I shook my head at the girl behind the counter.

"Sorry, sir, but that's all we have right now."

"Right." I grabbed my bag and made my way toward the Prius.

After a Tim Horton's coffee run, I opened my phone and typed in the address from the text message.

Her picture stared at me. I had printed it off. It was beautiful. She was on a patio, in a long yellow dress, staring off toward the ocean, holding her very pregnant belly and looking so happy.

Pulling onto the highway, I headed toward Queensland Beach. I wished I hadn't had the coffee, as the twisty roads made my bladder ache. Thankfully, there a little diner called Trellis that was kind enough to let me use their restroom. I decided to eat something since I wasn't sure how this visit was going to go.

Sitting at a table in the corner, I texted Cole to check in, and then called Mike to see how things were going at the house.

"What can I get for you?" the lady asked, holding up a note pad.

"Ah, fish and chips, please."

"Water?" She eyed my empty glass.

"Please." She went to leave, and I stopped her. "Can I ask you a question?" She turned and looked interested. I leaned down and removed her picture from my bag. "Do you know her?"

She took the photo and chuckled before she handed it back to me. "Lexi? Yeah, she actually works here."

Seriously?

Her head tilted, and she looked me over hard. "Oh my God," she whispered before she broke into a smile. "You're Keith, aren't you?"

I tried not to get excited about the fact that Lexi had spoken about me.

"You know about me?"

She looked over her shoulder before she rested the coffee pot on the table.

"She carries your picture around. She told us that you were in Iraq on tour." She shrugged. "I always thought she was making you up so people knew she was off the market." I couldn't help but smile. That was Lexi for you.

"Debbie?" The manager called her name.

She held up a finger. "Look, she's working tomorrow morning. I'm sure she'll be excited to see you. She's convinced your son is going to have your eyes."

Son?

I felt as though I was punched in the gut, not sure if I might laugh or cry or maybe both at the same time.

I didn't end up eating my dinner. I just started at her photo, and the word *son* bounced around in my head.

That's my boy in there. My hand covered my smile, and my heart leaped with excitement. A boy.

Finally, after Debbie packaged up my food, she helped me get a room at the Sea Breeze Inn for the night.

My room was small but had a bed, a shower, and a fridge, so I was happy. Opening the patio doors, I leaned my weight on the rail and watched the whitecaps flicker in the moonlight.

The coastline here was spectacular. The ocean wasn't blue, but a light gray, the beach a soft brown, but it was the smell of the seaweed I really enjoyed. It reminded me so much of home. I loved the Atlantic.

I held the phone to my ear as it rang.

"Hello?" Mark whispered.

"Hey." I wondered why I wasn't calling Savannah, but for whatever reason, Mark seemed to be the right fit for this. "Got a minute?"

"Yeah, hang on." I heard him whisper something to Mia, who hummed in agreement, then a door being shut. He yawned, then cleared his throat. "What can I do for you?"

"Well, I found out where she's working, and that she's pregnant with my son."

"Shut the hell up! A boy! Oh, dude, this is

amazing." I could hear his excitement. The boys would be ruling Shadows again. Well, maybe…

"Thanks, man. I, ah, I heard she was talking about me. One girl even knew who I was. Guess she's saying I'm away on tour right now. I'm led to believe it was her cousin who send the text, and that is who she is living with."

"Really? Huh."

I leaned forward and rubbed my head and sighed heavily. "I don't know what I'm doing here, Mark. I mean, I'm so pissed that she didn't tell me, but on the other hand, I think she's happy here. I-I don't know what to do."

"Honestly, Keith, I can't answer that, but what I will say is you've been chasing this girl for the past decade. You're like magnets. There's always something that happens so the two of you collide again. Maybe this is a sign. I think you need to tell her once and for all what you're really feeling. Bottom line is she's having your baby, so you will forever be connected."

"Yeah, that's true."

I kicked my feet up and changed the subject. He was right. I just need to be honest and see where it went. Regardless, I would still have a piece of Lexi, not even just a piece of her, but a piece of us both. *Our son.*

"How's the boys?"

"Dude, they bite!" His voice went high and made me laugh. Right there, that was why I called Mark. "I think they get it from Mia."

"Clearly."

"Hopefully, they'll have their father's dance

moves. That would be such a waste of a talent to have it stop with me."

"If you can teach Nan to *Cabbage Patch*, there's no doubt your boys will be able to move."

"Mmm, true." We both went silent, and I closed my eyes, seeing Lexi's smile. "You good?"

"Yeah, I am. Thanks, Mark."

"Thank me when you get her back."

The next morning, I packed my bag in the car in case a quick exit was needed.

Stepping into the diner, I nodded at Debbie, whose face glowed when she saw me. She nodded toward an empty table I was guessing was in Lexi's section.

Then I saw her balancing a tray on her hand and shoulder, moving awkwardly through the people.

Lowering the tray, she started to pass out the plates to a family of four. She smiled and laughed when they pointed to her stomach. She must have felt me, because she suddenly looked over, and her face dropped and her hands flew to her belly.

Thankfully, the place wasn't busy yet, because this was going to happen right now. I hurried over and blocked her path in case she went into flight mode.

"I can't believe you didn't tell me," rushed out of my mouth a little sharper then I meant to.

She started to say something, but instead she shook her head, trying to control her emotions.

"How? I mean, you had a…" I gestured vaguely in the direction of her belly, thinking of the IUD she'd gotten while living at the clubhouse.

She shrugged. "Must've lost it. There were a lot

of…blurry days in my life back then."

"A boy, huh?" She nodded. "You name him yet?" She nodded again.

"Brandon," she whispered. My first name, and it was my ticket to move forward.

I reached in my pocket and pulled the box open, setting it on the empty table next to her.

Her eyes went from the engagement ring to me. She started to cry.

"I'll say this one last time." I leaned down and showed her I was finished with this game. "Toss any shit you have at me, Lexi, and I'll keep taking it because that's what people do when they love someone."

"Keith," her chin quivered, "I…"

I took her hand and stepped closer, breathing her in. My tears got the best of me, but I didn't care. I went with the truth.

"You think all these years I was trying to save you, but really, you were the one saving me."

She slowly leaned over and picked up the box and removed the ring, placing it in my hand. I was waiting for the icy walls to shoot up.

A sob followed by a laugh broke the silence. She brushed her flushed cheek. "You held onto this for eleven years. How can I say no to someone who has loved me for that long?"

She held up her hand, and I slipped the ring onto the finger of my first and only love's left hand.

The place broke into cheers, and I kissed her breathless.

"I don't care where we live, here or there. No more time apart. Promise?"

"Promise." She looked up at me like she was seventeen again. "Take me home?"

"Which home?"

"Your home."

I buried my head in her neck, and I broke.

My hand found her tummy and I rubbed a first hello to my son. "I love you, Lexi."

"I love you too, Keith. Always have, always will."

ACKNOWLEDGMENTS

Ana Armstrong
Ariana McWilliams
Mary Drake
Gordon Drake
Erin Smith
Corporal George Myatt
Paul Mick

ABOUT THE AUTHOR

J. L. Drake was born and raised in Nova Scotia, Canada, later moving to Southern California where she now lives with her husband and two children.

When she is not writing she loves to spend time with her family, travelling or just enjoying a night at home. One thing you might notice in her books is her love of the four seasons. Growing up on the east coast of Canada the change in the seasons is in her blood and is often mentioned in her writing.

An avid reader of James Patterson, J.L. Drake has often found herself inspired by his many stories of mystery and intrigue. She hopes you will enjoy her books as much as she has enjoyed writing them.

Facebook:
https://www.facebook.com/JLDrakeauthor

Twitter:
https://twitter.com/jodildrake_j

Website:
http://www.authorjldrake.com/

Goodreads:
http://www.goodreads.com/author/show/830031
3.J_L_Drake

Made in the USA
Lexington, KY
30 October 2017